Sons of Sigurd

Driven by revenge, redeemed by love

When Sigurd, King of Maerr on Norway's west coast, was assassinated and his lands stolen, his five sons, Alarr, Rurik, Sandulf, Danr and Brandt, were forced to flee for their lives.

The brothers swore to avenge their father's death, and now the time has come to fulfill their oath. They will endure battles, uncover secrets and find unexpected love in their quest to reclaim their lands and restore their family's honor!

Join the brothers on their quest in

Stolen by the Viking by Michelle Willingham
Falling for Her Viking Captive by Harper St. George
Conveniently Wed to the Viking by Michelle Styles

And the story continues with

Redeeming Her Viking Warrior by Jenni Fletcher
Tempted by Her Viking Enemy by Terri Brisbin

Coming soon!

Author Note

This story is the third installment of the Sons of Sigurd series. This is the first time I have been involved in a collaboration of this nature. It was a real privilege and honor to work with four other authors whose work I greatly admire. All the authors are very excited about what we have achieved. While this book can be read on its own, there is an overarching story that plays out across all five books that I hope you will enjoy.

While doing background research, I stumbled across the murder of King Aed, the king of Strathclyde after Constantine I, and how his young sons were spirited away to be raised in Ireland in approximately 878. No one knows precisely where the assassination took place, who did the deed or the actual date, so I have used some license. The use of the word *vicus* in various chronicles points to Nrurim being connected to a religious house, but scholars have yet to pinpoint its precise location.

I do hope you enjoy Ceanna and Sandulf's story as much as I did writing it.

I love getting comments from readers and can be reached at michelle@michellestyles.co.uk or through my publisher or Facebook or Twitter, @michellelstyles.

MICHELLE STYLES

—

Conveniently Wed to the Viking

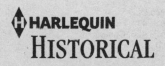

HARLEQUIN
HISTORICAL

Recycling programs
for this product may
not exist in your area.

ISBN-13: 978-1-335-50559-0

Conveniently Wed to the Viking

This edition published by arrangement with Harlequin Books S.A.

For questions and comments about the quality of this book, please contact us at CustomerService@Harlequin.com.

Harlequin Enterprises ULC
22 Adelaide St. West, 40th Floor
Toronto, Ontario M5H 4E3, Canada
www.Harlequin.com

Printed in U.S.A.

Born and raised near San Francisco, California, **Michelle Styles** currently lives near Hadrian's Wall with her husband and a menagerie of pets in an Edwardian bungalow with a large and somewhat overgrown garden. An avid reader, she became hooked on historical romances after discovering Georgette Heyer, Anya Seton and Victoria Holt. Her website is michellestyles.co.uk and she's on Twitter and Facebook.

Books by Michelle Styles

Harlequin Historical

Return of the Viking Warrior
Saved by the Viking Warrior
Taming His Viking Woman
Summer of the Viking
Sold to the Viking Warrior
The Warrior's Viking Bride
Sent as the Viking's Bride
A Deal with Her Rebel Viking

Sons of Sigurd

Conveniently Wed to the Viking

Visit the Author Profile page
at Harlequin.com for more titles.

For Elena F.

Prologue

*Autumn 874—the Kingdom of Maerr,
on the west coast of modern-day Norway*

How were you supposed to tell your brother, your oldest and most revered brother, that you were the one responsible for his beloved wife's death?

Sandulf Sigurdsson sat cradling his injured sword arm and watching the path from the north for his brother's imminent return. He was no closer to answering that question than he had been when his father's helmsman had pulled him from the smouldering wreckage of the longhouse.

The last thing his eldest brother had said to him before he left was, '*I'm counting on you, Sandulf, to watch over my beloved and keep her safe.*'

Sandulf had tried. As the youngest, Sandulf had spent his entire life trying to keep up with his four older brothers, trying to get them to see a grown man worthy of their respect with four warring seasons under his belt instead of the small boy toddling around behind them waving his wooden sword. He thought he'd put those doubts to rest this last summer when the action he had taken had turned the tide of the battle. Certainly, his father had approved and welcomed him officially to the strategic discussions they had had after the victory, but his brothers, particularly Brandt, had been dismissive and continued to tease him.

Inside the longhouse, he'd found the perfect spot for Ingrid to sit after she'd confessed to feeling unsteady before the ceremony started. It was a spot near one of the doors so she could get outside easily if the air became too close in her advanced state of pregnancy. He'd even found her a cushion so that her back could be eased and a dish of her favourite honeyed plums before she had the chance to complain. She'd laughed, offered him a plum and commented what a good husband he'd make some lucky woman when his time came.

Then the chaos had erupted.

From sweetened plums and laughter to a charnel killing house filled with blood and smoke in the space of five breaths.

In less than the time it took for a spark to fly up from the fire and die, his father, the great and fearsome King of Maerr, protector of the family, had had his reign cut short in the most brutal fashion. His middle brother's fiancée and her father's throats had been slit as they entered the supposed sanctuary of the longhouse. Flaming torches were tossed on to the rush-covered floor before anyone realised the doors had been bolted.

Despite the choking smoke swirling about the longhouse, Sandulf had attempted to fulfil his promise and get his charge to safety before giving in to his natural inclinations and attacking the murderers. But with her large pregnant belly, Ingrid's movements had been slow and awkward. After discovering the bolted door next to them, he had ushered her towards the concealed door behind the high table, the one his father had insisted only the family should know about.

Half-hidden in the growing smoke, an assassin with a silver scar like a shooting star emblazoned across his cheek had blocked their way, his sword wet with blood. His grin had increased when he saw Ingrid's distressed loveliness. He tore her from Sandulf's protective grip, slicing through Sandulf's forearm, declaring she'd be his prize. She'd screamed and beat at him with her fists. Sandulf had drawn his sword and attempted to free her, tearing an arm ring from the attacker, but another assassin had struck him from behind, forcing him to his knees. Sandulf had rolled and struck back. They'd tussled for a while, grunting and slashing at each other until he'd finally managed to disarm the female assassin, cutting her on her back. He made sure she was down before pivoting to confront Scarface and coming face to face with a sight more horrifying than any he could have imagined.

In the last rays of the sun, Sandulf shuddered and knew the image of the man standing over his brother's dying and defiled wife would linger in his mind for the rest of his life.

When the woman assassin had cried out, Scarface had abandoned his prey, and they'd both vanished into the smoke. Sandulf had stood guard over Ingrid, powerless to do anything more than bear witness as the life seeped from her womb. Her chest had wheezed and rattled as she gasped out her final words. He had not abandoned her to chase after the woman, Scarface and their two companions. He'd stayed by her side until the flames had licked them both and his father's helmsman had arrived, insisting he move or die.

A shout went up and the party led by his eldest brother returned, not to the resplendent wedding feast they must have been expecting, but to a ruined shell of a longhouse, all of the boats hulled below the waterline, and the dead and the dying laid out in rows exposed to the autumn sun.

Sandulf raced towards his eldest brother, reaching him before anyone else. 'Brandt, there's something you must know,' he whispered, starting to say the piece he'd rehearsed in his mind—delivering his brother's wife's final message—but Brandt pushed past him with hard impatient hands and turned towards their mother who gestured towards where the bodies lay.

An unearthly howl emerged from his brother's throat when he discovered his wife's mutilated body.

Sandulf started towards where Brandt crouched.

'Leave him,' his half-brother Rurik said with a curl of his lip. His gaze seemed to take in Sandulf's injured arm and the gash on his head. Small injuries. Injuries which would heal in weeks, unlike the ones his middle brother had endured, the ones which would take years to heal. 'What happened?'

'They went into the longhouse... I tried to...' Sandulf's throat closed and he knew no words could do justice to the carnage. 'Father is dead, Rurik.'

The others started speaking, drowning out his words. Sandulf waited until they had stopped and Rurik turned to go. He grabbed his arm. The look Rurik gave him spoke of his contempt at Sandulf's failure.

'I tried to stop this. I injured one of them, on the back,'

Sandulf began his speech again, intending to tell him everything about his fight to save Brandt's wife, show him the arm ring he'd wrestled from Scarface and explain about the female assassin, but Rurik stopped him with an impatient gesture.

'Only marked? Were you not able to kill even one of them? You with the fabled sword skills you always boast of?'

Sandulf gulped and closed his hand about the arm ring. 'No.'

His half-brother stalked off in search of his twin, without waiting to hear more.

'Sandulf,' his mother called, reminding him of his duty towards Brandt.

Sandulf gulped and obediently went over to Brandt to try again. 'Brother.'

His brother's eyes, which had been so full of life and love for his wife when they parted, were bleaker than Maerr in January. His face had settled into unfamiliar harsh planes which reminded Sandulf of their father when he was in one of his fearsome moods. 'Yes?'

Sandulf straightened his spine. The time had come. He knew what he had to say. 'I stayed with her until the end. She didn't die alone.'

Brandt's gloved fingers closed about Sandulf's neck, cutting off his air, and as they tightened they made the world go dark at the edges. Sandulf struggled against the force, but his struggles made his brother grip tighter. 'You should have given your life for her.'

His mother's screams for Brandt to stop echoed in Sandulf's ears. 'Please, please.'

'Enough. If we fight among ourselves, our enemies

win.' The hard arms of his father's helmsman forced them apart. Sandulf gulped a lungful of life-giving air.

'I will kill him, Joarr. I swear it.' Brandt wiped a hand across his mouth. 'One job I gave him, one job, and my dolt of a baby brother couldn't even do that. Just like he made a hash of the last battle and we were stuck on that promontory.'

'I...' Sandulf's throat worked up and down. He fingered the arm ring in his pocket. If he showed it now, Brandt might not realise its potential. 'I tried. You weren't there. It happened so fast. The doors were bolted.'

'You froze, Sandulf. You froze last summer and the summer before that. You always freeze and expect others to come to your aid,' Brandt said, his face turning a deeper shade, the same shade their father had always turned before he exploded in temper. Brandt drew his sword. 'You are a disgrace to the family's name. Father isn't here to protect you any more...'

'Enough killing, I said!' Joarr's voice resounded around the yard.

Even Brandt in full temper had enough sense to obey Joarr, the man who had taught them all navigation skills and was considered one of their father's best fighters. Brandt collapsed full length beside his wife's corpse, his body racked with sobs and cries of anguish about how it should have been him.

'You need to get Sandulf out of here,' his Aunt Kolga said moving from her seat where she'd been holding her only son close—a thin weak lad several months younger than Sandulf. 'Brandt is like his father. In that sort of temper, anything can happen. He may be sorry afterwards, but sorrow cannot bring the dead back to life. You and I both know that.'

Standing beside Joarr, Sandulf's mother, Hilda, became white-lipped. There was no need for his aunt to explain further. Everyone knew who his aunt blamed for her husband's death and why.

'I know,' his mother said in a barely audible voice. 'I am the one person you don't need to remind of what Sigurd was capable, Sister. I can see much of him in Brandt.'

'I can help in the search,' Sandulf shouted before his mother agreed to send him away to somewhere boring with his cousin where he'd be safe. And he didn't believe his aunt—Brandt knew where the lines were drawn. He knew how to control his temper. 'I can help hunt them down. I am more than capable of wielding a sword. Every man will be needed to revenge this…this insult.'

'Leave that to me and your brothers,' Joarr said. 'There is truth in what your aunt speaks. Brandt in this temper will kill first and suffer remorse after. You have been trying everyone's temper sorely, Sandulf, since this summer's final battle. Luck was with you in that victory, but it won't always be.'

Sandulf regarded his brother who slowly rose to his full height. His ravaged features showed how deeply he felt this blow. 'Give me another chance. I saw the assassins. I know things. You will see. I have value to you and my brothers.'

Brandt's lip curled. 'How many times have I heard that claim fall from your lips, only to have it proved wrong? Like our last-but-one battle where you failed to protect the flank, seeking your own glory instead!'

Brandt never hesitated to bring up Sandulf's faults, claiming he needed to learn lessons. Their father had believed his explanation that he'd seen the enemy creeping about and had gone out to engage them, even if the others refused to. Sandulf rapidly examined the ground. His throat tightened. His father would never again speak in his defence.

'One of my new husband's ships leaves for the Rus with a view to trade down to Constantinople on the next tide,' his aunt said, putting a hand on his mother's sleeve. 'A place can be found for Sandulf. I am certain of it. By the time he returns, Brandt will have forgiven him.'

Hilda covered her face with her hands. 'Not that. Many who go never return. Isn't there another way?'

His aunt resembled Hyrrokkin, the most fearsome of the frost giantesses. 'Give him a chance of living, Sister. The winds of change have finally arrived. You know this as well as I.'

His mother examined the corpses rather than confronting her older sister. 'I lost a husband today. I've no wish to lose my youngest son. In time Brandt will forgive.'

'Why should I forgive him when the assassins who did this to my wife still have life in their bodies?' Brandt drew his sword and pointed. 'Go to Constantinople, Sandulf, and let your big brothers clean up the mess you helped to create. I'm done with you. We have all finished with you and your excuses. You are not worthy to be called my brother.'

Rurik and his twin came to stand shoulder to shoulder with Brandt. With a sickening thud, Sandulf realised the sole reason why his middle brother Alarr was not there standing beside them, too, was because he was injured so badly he was incapable of standing. His brothers, the great sons of Sigurd, his boyhood heroes, were united against him. They were banishing him without listening to his story or understanding the truth.

Sandulf gripped the arm ring and glared back at them. Brandt had no right to command him, but he'd do it anyway. He'd find the assassins who'd murdered Brandt's wife and he alone would destroy them. Then all his brothers would see that he, too, was worthy of being called a son of Sigurd. Worthy of being their brother in arms rather than the nuisance whose presence was merely tolerated for the sake of blood ties.

'I accept your offer, Aunt, with pleasure.'

Chapter One

*June 877—near Dun Ollaigh,
Kingdom of Strathclyde, Oban, Scotland*

Once, Ceanna of Dun Ollaigh in Cenél Loairn had believed in handsome heroes who would ride in on a white horse and rescue her in her hour of need. She'd loved the stories her old nurse had told her and had wanted to believe they were true. She'd listened with eager ears and wasted time looking out of the narrow window of the old tower, waiting for her destined hero to appear, when she should have been concentrating on her needlework.

Now a grown woman, Ceanna knew they were simply stories to soothe a restless child to sleep.

Heroes on white horses coming to save maidens from all manner of disagreeable tasks did not exist, but evil men, monsters with human faces, did. She could control her destiny, if she took action.

She refused to be married off to a leering monster simply to aid her stepmother's quest for power, while the dawn of each new day saw her father grow weaker and weaker until he had become incapable of standing or stringing together a coherent sentence.

Her father had barely recognised her when she whispered goodbye that morning. She feared he'd be dead before the month was out. Then everyone in Dun Ollaigh would be without their protector and the entire fortress, as well as the village which nestled at its base, would be at the mercy of Feradach, her father's captain of the guards, the man her stepmother had picked to be Ceanna's husband. And he was far worse in her opinion than the heathen horde who had nearly overrun Alba last summer.

She'd laid her escape plans to perfection, pretending to go along with the proposed marriage until they stopped watching her. At this moment, her stepmother and Feradach would be at the church, waiting in vain for the promised sacrificial bride. Instead, the bride was on her way east to her aunt's double monastery—or she would be once she had discovered where the guide she'd hired had disappeared off to.

Ceanna wrapped her cloak tighter about her body, wishing she'd changed out of her wedding finery with its gold-embroidered form-fitting red gown and the intricate hairstyle, but every little delay risked an unceremonious march to the altar.

Unfortunately, her guide had failed to wait where they'd agreed and she'd been forced to go into the tavern which she knew he often frequented. At Ceanna's signal, her solitary form of protection—her wolfhound—slunk into the shadows and settled her head on her paws.

'Where is Urist ab Urist?' she said to the tavern owner who glanced up from filling a tankard. 'He travels to Nrurim today. I've a message for him.'

The man stopped what he was doing, his eyes widening slightly when he recognised her. 'You do us great honour, my lady.'

Ceanna frowned. So far she had kept her departure quiet, but now she was desperate. She had to hope some loyalty to her father and respect for the family remained.

She kept her chin up and ignored the curious glances she was receiving from the customers.

At the tavern keeper's studied blank look, she tried again. 'Urist ab Urist. He drinks here regularly so don't go pretending you have never heard his name before.'

'He departed. Won't be back for weeks. After Nrurim, he intends to go to St Andrews, my lady. There is more to it than delivering messages to members of the late King's court, if you ask me.' The tavern keeper gave a deliberate wink. 'He is hoping that by the time he returns his troubles will have vanished. He should've known better than to try to manage several women at the same time. Perhaps his visits to St Fillans and St Andrews will teach him the error of his ways.'

The entire tavern burst out in knowing laughter. Ceanna rapidly examined the dirty rushes which littered the inn's floor.

It was obvious that her erstwhile guide had a complicated private life of which she'd been ignorant. A dishonest man who juggled several women. Not the ideal person to guide her to her aunt and her new occupation as a holy maid, but he'd been the only person willing to undertake the journey...

A great pit opened in her stomach. In all of her many calculations, she'd never anticipated that he would leave without her. Urist had taken her gold and vanished, leaving her vulnerable to her stepmother's band of murderous thieves and ne'er-do-wells. She should have known him for a rogue and a scoundrel.

Ceanna firmed her jaw. She had not come this far simply to submit. In theory, she knew the way. She'd visited her aunt three times before; she was the abbess at St Fillans, which was located on the outskirts of the royal vicus of Nrurim. But a woman travelling that distance on her own was unthinkable and Ceanna refused to take any risks that she didn't have to. When she was younger, her father had often praised her caution and her conduct as being proper for a Pictish lady.

'Departed? Where? When?'

'At first light today, apparently,' came a voice from the shadows. The accent was foreign but there was a certain ease to the way he spoke, as if the speaker possessed an intimate familiarity with Gaelic. 'Waiting for stragglers and any who have paid for his services in gold appears to have been beyond him. I wish you better luck than I have had in discovering his precise whereabouts or indeed his direction of travel.'

Ceanna narrowed her gaze. The speaker's tone had a smooth honey-like quality to it, as if he wanted to lull her into doing whatever he desired. There was something untamed in the way the man moved out of the shadows. He wore travelling clothes, finer than she had seen before except on the late King. The faint light made his hair shine a brownish gold. He was taller than the average Pict, or even a Gael.

She blinked and belatedly realised that she was staring.

'Are you one of those stragglers?' she asked, hastily smoothing the folds in her gown and concentrating on the dirty rushes. Staring at someone like him could get you killed. Everyone had heard the stories about the Northmen and their murderous ways.

A thin smile played on his lips. 'Let us say I have urgent business in Nrurim which I've no intention of delaying.'

Urgent business? The double monastery which her aunt ruled over dominated the town. St Fillans of Nrurim was one of the few establishments which still catered to both men and women under one head, a privilege reserved for women of royal lineage since the time of her aunt's namesake, St Abbe, two centuries before. Her aunt never allowed anyone to forget her heritage.

Ceanna doubted one such as this man could have business there. Men from the North were not Christians; they were heathens who entered monasteries to sack and burn. But maybe they were just stories. And hadn't she had enough of those? She needed to fear her actual enemies, not random men she encountered in taverns.

Her mouth went dry. Had he been sent to follow her and ensure her return to Dun Ollaigh? Was this why her escape had been straightforward so far?

'What sort of business?' she asked, ensuring the cloak was wrapped tightly about her. 'Why would one such as you need to travel there?'

He shrugged. His fine wool cloak moved, revealing a broad sword with an intricately carved handle. She'd be willing to wager that this man had secreted several other weapons on his person. He was dangerous, beyond a shadow of a doubt.

'My own business and no less urgent for being personal.' He raised his brow and his look appeared to take in every detail of her wedding finery. 'And you? I assume you've business there as well if you wish to send a message with Urist.'

She lifted her chin and tried to pretend a confidence she did not have while the knots in her stomach grew painful. 'My own business, too.'

'So were you also intending to travel there? On your own, without companions? Dressed in that manner?'

His gaze travelled down her form again. She was painfully aware of her deficiencies, as her stepmother had called them—from her short stature to her overly generous figure. She wished she had bound her breasts and dressed as a beardless youth or put on something loose and tatty. The man appeared to see her for what she was—an unattractive, expensively dressed woman massively out of her depth for the task she was about to undertake.

'Urist has my trunk which contains my travelling clothes.' She gulped, belatedly remembering that no one was supposed to know her business. 'My trunk is what my message is about. It goes to my aunt.'

He lifted a brow. 'Indeed. I rarely enquire into a lady's dress requirements.'

Ceanna's cheeks burnt. No one need know more than was absolutely necessary. No stranger required her life's history. She made a mental note to redouble her efforts to live up to the promises she made in her prayers which she recited each night before she went to bed—ways in which she could improve.

She cleared her throat and attempted an icy stare. 'I'd assumed he'd wait until I arrived...with my final message...before heading out. Obviously not.'

'Are people normally required to wait for *your* messages? The real world is rarely that accommodating, even for delicate ladies.'

His tone implied that he considered she wouldn't go five steps before breaking down in tears or worse. Ceanna gritted her teeth. She'd wept her last tears at her mother and younger brother's gravesides. She was finished with being the meek and mild daughter who obeyed her father's wishes—or what her stepmother claimed were his wishes. Her father in his right mind would never wish her married to a coarse brute like Feradach with his wandering fingers and vulgar jokes.

She firmed her mouth. 'Delicacy is a matter of opinion. The fact remains—my plans must alter if I'm to… to complete my business. Most vexing.'

His smile grew broader and transformed the chiselled planes of his face to something which caused her throat to hitch. She rapidly examined the ground and attempted to keep her heart steady. 'I'd use a harsher word than vexing, but I agree with you. Urist's early departure has caused my plans to alter as well, but I maintain my resolve.'

Ceanna belatedly remembered that she had decided to meet people's eyes instead of looking away. She forced her gaze upwards. 'I didn't ask for your agreement or your approval.'

'Understood.' A distinct twinkle lit up his deep blue eyes. 'Any particular reason for choosing our missing guide?'

She cleared her throat and began the speech she'd run through a hundred times in her head. 'His reputation for reliability is held in high regard among people I trust.'

Other points sprang into her mind: Urist had been the only one planning to travel and the only one whom she'd considered would remain silent about her intentions. He had every reason to love her father, no reason to be loyal to her stepmother—or indeed Ceanna's intended—and a tendency not to ask penetrating questions. Also, gossip had it that Urist and her erstwhile bridegroom had nearly come to blows earlier in the year over some matter involving mouldy grain. She'd felt like the stars had finally aligned for her when she had learnt of his proposed departure.

She might be able to make it to her aunt on her own, but she wasn't foolish enough to think it would be an easy task.

She'd been there before, but danger always lurked, particularly now that the countryside was so unsettled with King Aed having been recently killed. It was one of the reasons her stepmother gave for marrying her off so quickly—to safeguard the estate. But these were points of which she felt both her aunt and the stranger in front of her should remain in ignorance.

'Very reliable,' she repeated in a louder tone in case he'd failed to hear her. Several of the regulars glanced up from their beer.

'I fear you were misled.' He shrugged. 'We both were.'

'He will have had his reasons. He may have left word.' Ceanna forced her lips to turn upwards. 'I intend to enquire. I suggest you do as well.'

'You do that. I suspect you will get the same answer I did. No one knows anything. A conspiracy of silence.'

'I'm not you.'

'True enough.' He saluted her with his tankard. 'I wish you better fortune than I had.'

Ceanna gritted her teeth. By now someone would have noticed her disappearance. They would comb the hall first, then the woods, then finally the town and this tavern. She had to be well away from here before that happened.

'People are wary of strangers who ask other people's business while keeping their own a secret.' She glanced about the tavern. Except for the old gentlemen at the back who were playing a game of dice, everyone was studiously examining their ale, pretending not to have spotted her.

He shrugged. 'How difficult is it to get to the fabled Nrurim—that is the question.'

'Surely, everyone knows how to get there,' she said, wrapping the cloak tighter about her.

A shadowy dimple played in the corner of his mouth. 'It is to the north-east in Strathallan, but beyond that I require a guide. Are you also in need of guidance?' He stroked his chin. 'My guess is that you are. Therefore, I'm afraid I can't be of assistance.'

She ignored him and turned towards the tavern owner. 'How long since Urist ab Urist departed?'

'Before first light. They were going to go slowly up to the ford.' He lowered his voice and turned away from the stranger, ensuring the other villagers also couldn't hear him. 'I was to tell any lady who asked, but no one else, particularly no warrior. Urist was nine kinds of jumpy last night. He kept talking about unexpected developments and the need for secrecy. He paid his bills in full, something he rarely does.'

Ceanna nodded. He was going slowly to give time for the stragglers—most likely her—to catch up if they knew where to head. Or at least she hoped she'd interpreted the cryptic message correctly. Urist did not head towards the ford, but away from it towards the loch.

'I thank you kindly, then. I'll find another to…to deliver my message.' She briefly nodded and started to back towards the door. Catching up would be possible if she hurried.

'Not so fast.' The stranger's hard fingers gripped her arm. 'We have not finished our discussion.'

'Yes, we have. You have your business to attend to and I've mine.' She glared at him. 'Our short acquaintance has ended. Release me.'

'I've no wish to alarm you, but my need to get to Nrurim as soon as possible drives me.' He slowly released his fingers, but continued to stand far too close. Ceanna retreated a step and put a hand over the place where his fingers had been. 'If you know where he is, take pity on me, I beseech you.'

At the end of his speech he fell to his knees like a supplicant. She stared at him for a long breath without speaking. With a sigh, he rose. 'I'm in no mood for tricks which Pictish guides play on unwary travellers.'

'I've as much idea as you where Urist could be,' she said, secretly crossing her fingers. A small stretching of the truth, but did a man from the North deserve the full truth, considering what he and his countrymen had put her land through? Considering how he had grabbed her arm and demanded she tell him what she knew? Urist clearly didn't trust him. Why should she?

He put his face closer to hers. 'I paid gold in advance. Do you think it right to cheat a man?'

She twisted the folds of her gown over and over between her fingers. 'You will have to take the matter up with Urist. I cannot help you in that.'

'You must!'

The entire tavern went still at his raised voice.

The tavern owner jerked his head towards the door. 'Out, Northman scum. You've finished your drink. We don't need your sort nosing around here, bothering people. Go now.'

The remainder of the tavern stamped their feet and thumped their fists on the tables in agreement.

The stranger seemed to sense the mood of the drinkers had altered and departed without a backward glance or another word.

Ceanna forced the air into her lungs. She was safe here. The tavern owner was a sworn liegeman of her father's. She had little doubt that he'd counsel her to remain here and wait for the next guide, that he'd tell her there was always another guide. But if she did that, she'd be discovered and dragged back to the unwelcome marriage while the people here were punished. It was better that they knew nothing about her plans.

'My lady…'

She gave what she hoped was an imperious nod, but greatly suspected that the effect was ruined by the way one of her braids suddenly developed a life of its own and fell over her forehead. 'I will bid you good day as well. You delivered your message as Urist hoped you would.'

'That one. The Northman. He has killed many times before. I am certain of it. It is in the deadness of the eyes.' The tavern owner shook his head. 'I should have refused him food and drink. Return to Dun Ollaigh and send word to your aunt instead. Stop this foolishness about finding Urist. I wouldn't trust him further than I could toss him.'

Return to Dun Olliagh only to die from an unfortunate but well-timed accident? She knew what she'd overheard two nights ago and the plans her stepmother had. Ceanna swallowed the rising indignation in her throat.

'It's no crime to drink or eat peacefully. I presume he paid you in advance,' she said when she trusted her voice.

'Aye, he did. Handsomely. Far better than this lot.' The tavern keeper laughed, but then sobered. 'Will you be safe, my lady? I can provide an escort back to Dun Ollaigh and your father.'

'Your offer is kind, but I make my own way.' She measured the distance to the door. Running would simply alert people to the fact that she wanted her freedom. She would advance slowly and then run.

'Whatever trouble ails you, my lady, you'll be safe here under my roof.'

Ceanna covered his rough hand with hers. Safe under his roof, but for how long? A true counterweight to her stepmother in the long term had to be the church as she was fresh out of heroes riding to her rescue. 'I know how my father values you and your service to him.'

His cheeks went pink and he ran his hand through his hair. 'I don't know what the world is coming to. Your father gravely ill and that woman—'

'Neither do I, but I have to keep on.' She took a deep breath and attempted to remember the speech she'd practised, the one in case anyone misguidedly tried to halt her progress. 'I've been blessed with a profound vision: that my future lies in Nrurim with my aunt. Ignoring such a vision would be against God's will since it came to me when I knelt at evening prayer.'

The words sounded hollow to her ears, but the tavern keeper looked at her with a kind of awe. Inwardly Ceanna smiled. Maybe her idea of posing as some sort of holy maid had merit. If she tried hard enough, one day it might become true.

'May the angels guard your footsteps, my lady.' He clapped his hands together. 'You must see my lady wife, Bertana. Get food for your journey. An empty belly never did anyone any good.'

Ceanna's stomach grumbled obligingly.

'There, it is all settled. Eat before you faint. I remember your mother's funeral, my lady.'

Ceanna ground her teeth. She had collapsed at her mother and brother's funeral, but it had been from the grief which had locked her knees and the knowledge that her father intended to remarry far too quickly.

The last time she'd eaten was yesterday evening and goodness knew how long it would be before she could eat again. She had to be practical. A few words to Bertana who had always been kind would not hinder her journey. 'Briefly.'

The tavern owner tapped his finger against his nose. 'I know, my lady, I know.'

No one made a fool of Sandulf Sigurdsson, particularly not a diminutive woman with a haughty tilt to her nose who was dressed more for a day at court eating sweetmeats, exchanging gossip and playing the lyre than tramping through the dust, and who would undoubtedly make unreasonable demands on everyone once the journey began. *If* the journey to Nrurim ever began. He'd witnessed the look which had passed between her and the tavern owner and he knew that Urist had left instructions for her on where to find him.

Sandulf gritted his teeth. For all her obvious failings, that preciously dressed woman was his best hope of fulfilling his quest and finding the murderous butcher who had slain his sister-in-law. He knew his eldest brother had lost their father's kingdom and that the new ruler was his aunt's husband. He also knew nothing he could do would bring the dead back to life, but he could ensure those who had killed Ingrid were punished.

Sandulf struggled to hang on to his temper now that he was out of the tavern. He contented himself with kicking a stick hard and sending it skittering down the road.

A large wolfhound lumbered out of the shadows and returned the stick to his feet with an earnest expression on its face. Sandulf picked up the stick and threw it again, harder this time. The dog chased after it and returned it swiftly, dropping it at his feet. Sigurd smiled wryly. One creature in this benighted place liked him.

'What do you think, dog? Does she know where my guide is?'

The dog sat on its haunches and pointedly stared at the stick until he threw it again.

'I will avenge Ingrid's death. I will fulfil my vow. I will return to my family,' Sandulf muttered when the dog returned for a third time. In the years since he had left Maerr, he had learned the hard way what to do when his problem required a different approach. He had ceased to be the headstrong warrior who had rushed down the slope to engage the enemy without a thought towards strategy. He knew the value of watching and waiting until the time was right.

A wet nose nudged his hand. Sandulf automatically reached into a pocket and gave the grey wolfhound a morsel of dried meat and hard cheese. The dog gave a soft woof in thanks.

'At last, a creature who understands I mean no harm here.'

The dog tilted its head to one side and gave another bark, this time pointing her nose towards the tavern and wagging her tail. Sandulf noticed the fine iron collar which was about her neck. There was only one person in that tavern who could own such a creature.

'Is your lady in some sort of trouble?' he asked the dog. 'Is that why she appears to be fleeing Dun Ollaigh?'

The dog tilted its head even more to one side and barked again.

Sandulf laughed. 'As if you'd know. You see, this is what comes from being on my own—I start speaking to animals as if they'd answer back. My brothers used to say I was touched in the head but they always found a reason to belittle me. The one thing I haven't missed is their continual ragging.'

He fingered the arm ring he'd wrenched off the scarfaced assassin that fateful day.

Since his arrival on these shores, one of his brothers, Rurik, had forgiven him and Sandulf had begun to feel hope that one day they would believe he was worthy of being their brother and their equal. After some persuasion, Rurik's new bride, Lady Annis of Glannoventa, had provided him with the name and location of the man who had brutally murdered Ingrid and her unborn child. He was called Lugh and was hiding in a monastery near the town of Nrurim. Sandulf had accepted Rurik's word that he and Lady Annis had put the past behind them and both wanted to savour their future together.

Regaining one brother's trust was a start, but it was only the first step on his road to redemption. He still avoided his reflection in ponds or in burnished glass. The prospect of seeing his father's eyes peering out at him, rebuking him for his many failures, was far too great.

Sandulf shook his head, went further into the shadows and concentrated on the tavern, willing the woman to emerge.

The door opened and an urchin ran out, banging straight into Sandulf. Sandulf allowed the boy to bounce off him while the dog gave a low rumble in the back of her throat.

'Ugh, what did you have to do that for?' The lad rubbed the back of his head. 'Why don't you watch where you are going?'

'Maybe you should watch where you're going,' Sandulf said menacingly, putting his hand on his sword.

The colour drained from the lad's face. 'The Northman.'

'You are in a hurry to get somewhere.'

'To Dun Ollaigh. To tell them…to tell them that…' The boy's face creased. 'You ain't going to harm me, are you? I know what your kind are like.'

'You're going to tell them that the woman they are no doubt searching for has been safely found and is at the tavern.' Sandulf inclined his head and permitted a humourless smile to cross his lips. 'Safe for a hefty price, I'd imagine. I, too, have encountered men like that tavern keeper before.'

The boy's eyes bulged. 'My Lady Ceanna shouldn't be wandering around on her own, getting lost and into mischief. My master decided…given that…the Northman warrior…that is to say…'

His voice trailed away again, but Sandulf knew he was being used as a scapegoat.

'I'm a good guesser.' Sandulf struggled to contain the

surge of excitement. Provided he kept feather-brained Lady Ceanna alive and progressing on her journey, he stood a chance of arriving in Nrurim before Lugh learned of him. She knew where the guide was and no one, particularly not the tavern owner and his lad, would keep him from achieving his goal. Lady Ceanna would be going to Nrurim if he had to carry her every step of the way. 'Your task will have to wait.'

The lad closed one eye and peered at him. 'To wait? Why?'

Sandulf reached for a length of rope. 'Your lady has business elsewhere.'

Chapter Two

No one lurked outside the tavern in the late afternoon sunshine. Even the handsome stranger with the hard eyes had vanished. Ceanna shut the door with a quiet click. Her luck had held, but she wondered about unseen eyes watching her, waiting for her to make a mistake. She quickly shook her head. Far too late to worry about them.

She snapped her fingers. Vanora, her wolfhound, trotted out from the shadows. The dog gave a sharp bark and licked her hand. There was something in the way Vanora held her head that made her seem overly pleased with herself. Ceanna dismissed the notion as fanciful. She needed to break her habit of making Vanora seem more than she was. Another saying for her list: dogs were dogs, not people.

'Some guard you are.' Ceanna crouched down and gave her dog's ears a stroke. 'It looks like you've been busy searching for food. We need to go now before they start looking for me in earnest. Bertana could talk the hind legs off a donkey. I was certain she was stalling for some reason, but she ran out of excuses and I escaped.'

Vanora looked longingly back towards the shadows. Ceanna peered into the darkness, but nothing moved.

'I mean it, Vanora, now. I've wasted enough time. Our luck holds.' Ceanna held out a meat pie. 'Bertana sent this for today's journey. You need it more than I do.'

Vanora downed the pie in three gulps. She then sat on her haunches and looked hopefully for more.

'We go now. No looking back. Or hoping for more. That's all I have until we reach Urist. And he will be waiting. I know it.'

Vanora nodded as if she understood.

Ceanna quickened her footsteps away from the tavern, putting distance between her and the building, turning this way and that as she went towards the river and then doubled back to the track which led towards Taigh an Uillt and the Pass of Brander towards Ben Cruachan.

Once she was in the woods properly, she paused to take a lungful of fresh air and tuck her gown higher. The narrow skirt made walking normally nearly impossible and she dreaded to think about the state of the slippers she wore. Stout boots and a roomy wool gown were safely tucked away in the trunk Urist had appropriated. When she found him, he'd wish he had chosen a different course of action.

Vanora did her usual circling about her. She noticed that the dog kept going behind her, but every time she glanced around, nothing was there and Vanora did not appear to be unduly worried. Ceanna pushed the concern away. Her stepmother's lover wasn't that subtle. Nerves—that's all it was. She would stop jumping at shadows starting now. Face forward.

On the bend before the river, a twig snapped in the stillness. She quickly turned and saw the Northman from the tavern following her. When he spotted that she had seen him, he gave a little wave.

'Why didn't you tell me that he was following?' she asked Vanora. The traitorous dog smacked her lips, sat down and refused to move.

'Is that your dog?' he called.

Ceanna wrapped her arms about her waist. Out here, he loomed larger than he had in the tavern.

'I should warn you that she can be quite fierce if provoked.' Her voice sounded unnaturally thin and high. She pushed an errant plait behind her ear.

'Saves her fierceness for your enemies, I assume. We became friends earlier.' He crouched down and beckoned to Vanora who obediently trotted over. He handed the hound a morsel of dried meat.

The traitorous dog licked his hand and looked up at him in mute adoration. Ceanna ground her teeth. Normally, Vanora was wary of strangers and particularly men. However, she appeared to have made an exception with this man from the North.

'I refuse to think it is mere coincidence.' She stomped her slipper hard against the dirt.

'Coincidence can be a wonderful thing.' He made a bow, the sort which was more suited to the King's court than a muddy track in the middle of nowhere. 'Under such pleasant circumstances. I suspected this delightful creature belonged to you, Lady Ceanna.'

He stroked Vanora under the chin. The dog flopped down beside his boots and revealed her tummy. Ceanna wished she would display a little more dignity. And somehow, this man had discovered her name.

Ceanna tugged Vanora's collar and the dog gave her a

hurt look. 'She can be quite ferocious. Truly. One word from me and...'

'She senses I mean you no harm. We both want the same thing—to travel to Nrurim untroubled.'

No harm.

Ceanna knew what men from the North were like and how they raided. She took several steps backwards when her feet caught in the gown and she went tumbling. A very unladylike oath emerged from her throat.

'I saved your life earlier, Lady Ceanna, if that makes any difference to your attitude.' He held out his hand. It was long fingered and well made. There was a little scar at the base of his thumb.

Ceanna ignored his hand and scrambled to standing. Her gown tore under her arm and she tightened her fists.

'Saved my life? What nonsense are you spouting?' She gave vent to her utter frustration. 'Out with it, man. What have I ever done to you? Why are you plaguing me? What right do you have?'

'That man who runs the tavern sent a runner towards Dun Ollaigh. That runner failed to reach his destination.'

'I never asked you to kill for me.' Ceanna put her hand over her mouth.

'He became entangled in some ropes. He'll be found in due course—safe and well.' His eyes sent a chill through her. 'I kill when necessary. It wasn't necessary.'

'Good to know.'

The Northman nodded towards Vanora who was now wagging her tail. 'Your dog provided invaluable assistance.'

'Why did you do it? I've nothing you want.'

'You're going to get me to Nrurim, even if I have to

carry you the whole way. I, Sandulf Sigurdsson, give you my oath on this.'

Ceanna stared at him for a long time, her throat working up and down, but no sound emerged.

Vanora gave a sharp bark and the noise seemed to release her voice.

'You could have approached me when I left the tavern. Why follow me in such a way?'

'Because I didn't want to alert anyone.'

'I see. You were looking out for my welfare rather than afraid to take the risk.'

Sandulf stared at Lady Ceanna with her tangled mess of plaits and bedraggled gown. Giving his oath was supposed to make her accept him with open arms, not question his motives further. She should be grateful that he was willing to risk his sword arm for her, rather than berating him.

'Because—' he said, ready to lecture her, but stopped.

A fleeting uncertainty and vulnerability flashed in her eyes which she quickly masked with a frown. A long-forgotten memory of how hard he'd tried to be brave when he changed ships and the enormity of what he'd done washed over him. He, too, had had to learn to be grateful of a stranger's help.

He rubbed the back of his neck. She was right. He had not wanted to take the risk. Getting to Nrurim meant far too much to destroy this chance for reasons of pride or gallant behaviour.

How to explain without giving the full story, but enough to give her reason to trust him? Trust was a far more precious commodity than he'd realised when he was a boy. And he needed her trust or it would be harder to fulfil his quest, except his mind was a blank as to why she should trust him.

'Because…' he said again, hoping the right words would magically appear in his mouth.

'Because is not an acceptable answer, not even the second time you try it.' She cut him off with a sharp wave of her hand. 'I've switched my course often enough to know you must have been deliberately following my footsteps. The truth, if you please. Do you intend to slit my throat or harm any of my relations?'

Sandulf regarded her for a long time. Despite her overly primped appearance, this woman possessed a backbone—or perhaps it was simply foolhardy naivety. Few women would speak to a warrior in that tone. His mother or Aunt Kolga maybe.

He forced his voice to be low and slow with more than a hint of honey. 'If I'd confronted you outside the tavern, all it would have done was alert our trussed-up friend and his pals. I reckoned you wanted to keep your departure quiet. I considered it was time to make my presence known as I am now sure we are not being followed. You can cease being frightened.'

She wrapped her arms about her waist. 'I'm not frightened.'

'Startled, then.'

Her features relaxed, reminding him of a blackbird he'd tried to tame as a boy. He had taken the time to feed it crumbs and it had eventually trusted him. Alarr had laughed at him, saying he was wasting his time, but the bird had eventually ridden on his shoulder. Until his father had decided that his son needed to concentrate on his sword skills and the bird disappeared.

'That was the reason you showed yourself now? The

knowledge that I had managed to lose all my pursuers except for you?'

Sandulf reached down and gave the dog a bit of cheese. 'Your dog wanted more to eat.'

She rolled her eyes. 'Vanora's hunger. Is that the best you can do?'

'Vanora is an unusual name for a dog.'

'Stop trying to change the subject.'

He slowly rose and held out his hands, palms upwards. 'I apologise if I frightened you. My sole intention is to travel to Nrurim and attend to my business there. Take me to our guide.'

Her teeth worried her bottom lip. 'How do you know I am going to meet Urist?'

Sandulf exhaled. Finally. She was listening.

He ticked off the points on his fingers. 'Earlier, the tavern keeper was insistent that he had no idea of Urist's travel plans. You show up and he mutters some words to you in Gaelic which seemed to indicate that Urist was making for the ford. He immediately insisted I leave. I assumed Urist left another message for you. The ford makes little sense for someone travelling across country to Nrurim.'

Her blue-grey gaze widened. 'You worked that one out quickly.'

'I went through the ford on my way here. Why go back that way? I followed my hunch. Waited and watched. Made friends with your dog. Dealt with the potential threat to your escape. You need me, Lady Ceanna, as much as I need you.' Sandulf held out his hand to the dog who gave it an obliging lick. 'Why is she called Vanora?'

'After Arthur's Queen. You know Arthur—the one

who saved the Picts and the Celts from Saxons and who will return in our hour of greatest peril.'

Sandulf rubbed the back of his neck. Lady Ceanna's accent was very different from his Northumbrian sister-in-law's and the other Gaelic women he'd met on his travels, but nevertheless pleasing to the ear. 'I have heard the story, but I thought the Queen had a different name. Gwenevere or something like that.'

'In Pict land, or what used to be the country of the Picts, it is Vanora.' The woman arched her chin higher. 'Like most in this kingdom, my dog has good reason to be wary of men from the North.'

At her mistress's words, Vanora came over to her, gave a lengthy sigh, bared her teeth at Sandulf in a half-hearted manner before settling at Lady Ceanna's feet— as if to say that even though she considered her mistress to be making a mistake, she sided with her. Sandulf respected the dog's loyalty.

'Vanora let me know that lad was not to be trusted,' Sandulf said, keeping his voice gentle. 'She has chosen me as your protector.'

Ceanna knelt and buried her head in the dog's fur. 'She is a good dog. The best. She appears to trust you.'

'You should, too.' Sandulf willed her to accept his words. 'With me at your side, you won't need to go three times around a copse unless it is common practice among the people in these parts.'

'Was it three times or are you guessing?'

'I counted after the first circuit. It helped to pass the time. You repeated the action with three other copses. Repeating manoeuvres does little to shake off pursuers.'

'And your former guide refused to take you further for what reason?' Ceanna forced a smile. She refused to explain that the copse manoeuvre had come from one of her favourite tales when she was small. Another reason, if she needed it, not to believe in anything but her own ingenuity. But he had a point about the repetition. Another thing to add to her list.

'Personal.' His eyes sparkled like summer sunshine on the bay below Dun Ollaigh. 'I'm certain you will understand, since we are not yet *intimate* companions, personal remains personal.'

Ceanna mentally shook herself. Intimate companions indeed. Her destiny was to be a holy maid, a nun, not a warrior's woman. He expected his charm to carry him through as if she was one of those women who fell into a fluttering heap at the slightest hint of promised affection. She knew the limited extent of her charms, even without her stepmother's long recital of her flaws this morning.

If he wanted her help in getting to Nrurim quickly, he was going to have to answer questions rather that spout innuendo and suggestion. He was going to discover that she was serious, not all sighs and soft words as she suspected most women were with him.

'How did you threaten your guide?' she enquired with a honey-laced voice. When he merely looked at her, she continued in a sterner voice. 'I must warn you that men from the North are not well liked around here. We know what the Northmen from the Black Pool did on our shores last summer and how hard we had to fight. My father still bears the wounds he received in the defence of Dun Ollaigh.'

Wounds which refused to heal and which made him irritable. The truth was that her father had not been the same since her mother and young brother had died. And he'd changed even more after he married her stepmother.

This last illness combined with the wounds had seen him acquiescing to his wife's demands that Ceanna marry while he could still give his blessing to the match.

The Northman brought his fingers together. 'We had a slight disagreement on the way forward. He has returned to Northumbria without shame.'

Slight disagreement or was he put in fear for his life? She suspected the Northman rather understated the situation. She somehow doubted that the stranger was entirely innocent in the matter. But she was prepared to play along with his ruse. 'What doesn't he like about Dun Ollaigh that he left you stranded?'

'He saw someone he wished to avoid.' Sandulf Sigurdsson lowered his voice. 'He has a complex relationship with the various women in his life. I'm sure you understand the predicament.'

'A trait shared with many guides, it seems.'

He gave a snort of amusement. 'He didn't leave until I had made arrangements with our missing guide.'

'Who left without you. Did he fear you?' She tugged at the cuffs of her gown and heard another tear from the shoulder region. The gown was more sausage casing than a garment suited for any sort of strenuous activity. She swore softly.

'We're both inconvenienced, my lady.' He gave a decided nod. 'Urist ab Urist ought to have known I wouldn't give up, particularly not when I have parted with gold. My previous guide warned him what I'd do if anyone attempted to cheat me. He rather embroidered the tale of me on the voyage and how I declined a pirate's offer to go to Éireann.'

Ceanna tugged Vanora closer. The traitorous dog merely made eyes at the stranger and licked her chops as if he were her new favourite person. Honestly, that dog. 'Impressive company you keep.'

'I make no claim about the faithfulness of guides. Some can be cowards. Some can be cheats. Some can be honest men who have another agenda.' He tilted his head. 'Did he demand payment from you in advance? Or did he expect to be paid at the end of the journey?'

'I paid him half in advance and the rest was hidden in my trunk—the one he appears to have taken with him,' Ceanna admitted, inwardly wincing and trying not to think about the trunk she'd deposited with Urist and everything it contained. She'd been naive in the extreme. 'I know the route he must have taken.'

'I guessed correctly in following you, even more so in making myself known. You no longer have to be afraid.'

His smile transformed his face, making him seem more approachable. With its high cheekbones, full lips and aquiline nose, it was the sort of face to haunt a woman's dreams. Ceanna made an irritated noise in the back of her throat. If she intended to convince her aunt that she had had a sudden vocation to become a holy maid, she had to stop noticing the shape of a man's face or the breadth of his shoulders. Holy maids spent their waking hours in contemplation and uttering cryptic remarks about the future. Ceanna wondered if their knees ached as badly as hers did after any service or if holy maids kept their minds on more spiritual matters.

'What is your name?' she asked in order to stop thinking about such things.

'Sandulf Sigurdsson, at your service until we find our guide, my Lady Ceanna.'

Ceanna kept her hands at her sides. 'How do you know my name?'

'The lad who was sent to go to Dun Ollaigh told me.'

'Voluntarily?'

Sandulf Sigurdsson's face settled down into far harsher planes. All warmth fled from his eyes. 'I take no pleasure from torture. The lad lost nothing but his dignity from me. You have my solemn oath I'll keep you safe.'

'And you are a man who makes a lot of oaths. Do you keep them?'

'Without honour, I am worthless.'

'I will bear that in mind.' Ceanna turned and started walking briskly along the track, ignoring the way her gown curled about her legs like a rope bent on tripping her.

'Here, where are you going?'

'The sooner I get to Urist, the sooner I can rid myself of you, Oathkeeper.'

Keep this woman safe.

The words pinged around Sandulf's brain as he slowly made his way along the increasingly muddy and narrow track at Ceanna's side. The late afternoon sun gave way to a gloaming twilight which caused the shadows to lengthen while wisps of mist began to rise from the loch, making the going that much more treacherous. He knew what had happened the last time he'd tried to keep a woman safe: he'd failed. He tore his mind away from the image of Ingrid's body and the events in Maerr on that terrible day.

Once they'd discovered the whereabouts of their guide, his responsibility towards the Lady Ceanna would end. Sandulf regarded her from under hooded eyes. She was the sort of person a man might overlook the first time, but his gaze kept straying back and finding new things to focus on—the curve of her neck, the length of her fingers, the precise shape of her mouth.

Her clothing, with its heavy gold-brocade trim and tight sleeves, was not the sort one travelled in and had rapidly become mud-splattered. The deep crimson red might be fashionable, but it did little for her complexion. And her slippers were made for dancing rather than tramping through the sticky mud on the track. However, no complaints passed her dawn-kissed lips. She simply stepped around the next puddle.

His mother and aunt's complaints would have blistered his ears if they had been caught in the same predicament. He'd heard the nasal whines about one injustice or another throughout his entire childhood. His father had assured him all women complained about every inconvenience. All women, it would appear, except Lady Ceanna.

She stumbled over a root and put out a hand to break her fall, but Sandulf caught her elbow and managed to keep her upright. Up close he saw the dark bruised shadows under her eyes and the pinched whiteness of her mouth. Their breath interlaced for a long heartbeat.

Her sigh hissed out through gritted teeth. 'I am perfectly capable of standing on my own two feet.'

'The polite thing to say when rescued is thank you.'

'Thank you for breaking my fall. I did not see the root. Will you please release me? I stand on my own feet quite easily. I've done so since I was small.'

Sandulf glanced up at the darkening sky. He tightened his grip on her elbow. 'We are stopping.'

She pulled away from his fingers. 'We need to keep going, towards Urist. I can walk all night if needs be.'

It wouldn't have taken much more for Sandulf to have left the imperious woman standing there, more than half-dead from exhaustion. He'd had his fill of overbearing ladies in Constantinople, the ones who were certain that the world needed to be remade for them, but getting to Nrurim before Lugh learned of his pursuit and vanished into the night again was the only thing that mattered.

'You might be prepared to walk through the gloaming, but I'm not.' Sandulf clicked his fingers and Vanora sat in the dirt next to him, giving small whimpers. 'Neither is your dog. She senses what I do—we need to halt for the night.'

Her face became mutinous when, despite her gesture to go on, the dog yawned and settled down next to him. 'The bend in the river is not far from here and we have to catch up with Urist.'

'But the mist rises and I can see moorland beyond those trees,' Sandulf explained slowly, using the deadly quiet voice which had made people run from him in Constantinople. 'My half-brother's wife warned me about the treachery of Alba's moorlands before I left her hall to go on this journey. The mist has led many strangers astray. I intend to heed her advice.'

Lady Ceanna pointed towards the greying horizon. 'The track is very well defined up to the pass. I doubt the mist will be that heavy. It is summertime after all. I have lived here all my life and—'

'You guess about the mist's strength. It clouds the sun and it has become much cooler.' He held out his hand. 'It begins to rain, my very stubborn lady. Soon it will pelt down and destroy what remains of your hairstyle. I assume you are proud of the plaits. It must have taken an inordinate amount of time to achieve.'

'It did.'

'Are you going to remain stubborn?'

'I could say the same of you. I've never met some-one more stubborn than you.' She crossed her arms and raised a brow. 'How do you know the mist will be heavy?'

'I prefer not to take the risk.' He stroked his chin. 'You appear three-quarters of the way towards being dead on your feet.'

'I'm not.' She stumbled over a rock this time. Sandulf instantly put out a hand and caught her elbow, steady-ing her, ignoring the pulse of warmth which travelled up his arm.

Up close, her lashes made a dark forest against the alabaster of her skin. But he could also see the tired red-ness which threatened to overwhelm her storm-tossed eyes. Lady Ceanna was close to collapse, but he sus-pected she'd deny it until she fell to her knees in exhaus-tion. The irresistible force had met an immovable object. 'When was the last time you slept?'

'Over two nights ago,' she admitted, tucking her head into her chest. 'I had things to do. Plans whirled about my head, rendering sleep impossible. My feet are clumsy be-cause of these stupid slippers and this impossible gown. Why I ever agreed to it, I've no idea.'

'A good night's sleep won't do you any harm.'

She made to move off, even as the mist began rising and swirling about them. 'Urist will be getting further ahead. I've no wish to inconvenience you any longer than necessary.'

'We'll move more quickly than he does, particularly if we are both rested.' Sandulf laughed to himself. He remembered a time when he was the one who had stubhornly refused to give in, who kept going, despite the cost to everyone else. It had been a hard lesson to learn. He never considered a woman might have a similar drive

'How do you know?'

'Experience with travelling.' As her sceptical look increased, he added, 'Urist will have at least one cart in his group. He is taking your trunk and unlikely to carry it on his back.'

She looked up as a large raindrop fell on her nose. She wrinkled it in a delightful fashion. 'And you have travelled far.'

'From Maerr in the north to the Rus in the east and down the great rivers to Constantinople. And then across the seas to Strathclyde.' He kept his gaze on the increasing rain. The journey had been far harder than he'd ever imagined. When he'd left Maerr, he'd considered himself equal to anything. He hadn't realised how privileged he'd been, how much he'd had to grow up and how quickly.

Her eyes widened 'Further than I've ever dreamed of travelling.'

'If we keep on, your feet will be torn to ribbons.'

'The sooner we reach Urist, the sooner I retrieve my stout boots. There, you see I'm not totally impractical and feather-brained.'

He watched her intently. He'd been mistaken earlier, outside the tavern, in his assessment of her. Lady Ceanna was not one of those fluttering females he'd encountered elsewhere. Lady Ceanna was another sort of woman entirely. 'If you were truly feather-brained, we would not be having this conversation.'

'Getting to Urist is the point of this.'

'You presume he goes to Nrurim the way you think he will, that the tavern keeper did not seek to mislead you.'

She opened and closed her mouth several times. 'I hadn't considered that.'

'Which do you want more?' he asked as if he were coaxing that blackbird he'd tamed as a child. 'Nrurim or Urist? Give in, Lady Ceanna. If I carry you, our progress will crawl.'

'Nrurim.' She sighed. 'Very well. I give in. We stop. My feet ache and you're plainly exhausted. For your sake, then.'

'It is not a competition to see who can keep up, my lady, but who finishes. My father's helmsman, Joarr, once told me that when I tried to outrun my brothers who were carrying heavier packs. He was right, even if I didn't see it at the time. It is about ensuring everyone in a group makes it. A harder task than you might imagine.'

Her cheeks flushed. 'Is there anything I can do about my feet? Please?'

'Unfortunately, I'm not carrying a spare set of boots, but I do have some ointment which might assist.' He reached into his pouch and produced a small jar.

'I'd like that.' Her spine stiffened. 'I can put it on my feet myself without your help.'

'Did I say otherwise? You are capable of many things, my lady, including applying ointment to your feet.'

Lady Ceanna possessed a certain luminous quality to her smile which he'd failed to fully appreciate earlier. 'I'm pleased you understand that I am not one of those ladies who cling like a vine. I take pride in my accomplishments even if it is merely looking after my bruised feet.'

What had happened to her to make her this way? Women like her should expect to be pampered. Sandulf shook his head. It was none of his concern. His mission was ensuring Lugh received the justice due him for

Ingrid's murder. Once he accomplished that, then he could begin living again. He was not going to prove Brandt, or the others, correct by losing his focus and allowing his best chance to slip through his fingers.

'Are there any huts around here? Places where we could rest?' Sandulf asked.

She shrugged. 'I haven't seen any. I'd like to keep close to this track. If we wander off in the mists, looking for something which doesn't exist, we might lose our way entirely.'

Her lips turned up as she threw his excuse back at him. Sandulf muttered a curse which made the smile grow.

'You doubt your ability to rediscover it.'

'I know the general direction Urist is going in. I can navigate by the track, the hills and the lochs we encounter. It is just...' She plucked at a loose thread on her gown. 'You and I...we barely know each other.'

'You fear spending a night alone with a strange man, I understand. I gave my word that I'd protect you.' He willed her to understand. 'That includes protecting your honour, my lady. I will ensure nothing happens to you.'

She covered her eyes with her hands which made her suddenly appear very small and alone. Something unfamiliar turned over inside him. And he knew his oath was more than words earlier; he wanted to protect her, mainly because she was trying so hard not to need any protection. 'Am I that obvious?'

'Most brides don't need to run away in their wedding clothes.'

'I left before I married.' Her teeth worried her bottom lip. 'I... I am going to become a holy maid. I had a vision.'

Sandulf tilted his head to one side. He knew little about fashion in this kingdom, but he doubted nuns wore gowns as revealing as the one Lady Ceanna wore or answered back in quite such a bold fashion.

'Came on you suddenly, did it?'

The corner of her mouth twitched. 'Crystal clear. Better to know before the marriage.'

Sandulf pointed towards where a large oak stood at the side of the track. The tree had become gnarled and windswept with age, but its leafy canopy would offer some semblance of shelter. Even now, Lady Ceanna's eyes drooped with exhaustion. 'There is a hollow in that tree. It should serve our purpose. Unless you would like to chance the rain.'

As if on cue, the rain began to lash down, pelleting them with hard wet drops.

Lady Ceanna crossed her arms. 'Where will you shelter?'

'Beside you. We should keep dry enough.' He kept a carefully neutral face. 'I promise I don't bite unless you wish me to.'

Her back went straight and her eyes flashed fury. 'A holy maid is a noble calling. If a holy maid says something should be protected, it is done without question, as she speaks directly to God. No one wishes to risk eternal damnation.'

Sandulf rubbed a hand against the back of his neck. 'I've never forced myself on an unwilling woman and have no intention of starting with you.'

She ducked her head, hiding her expression, but he saw the redness in her cheeks. 'Another oath, Northman?'

'I'm more at home with warriors than holy maids.'

'Then we will pray our acquaintance will be of short duration.'

She stalked over to the tree and sat while Sandulf collected an armful of bracken fronds which he laced over their heads for a roof.

'It will keep the worst of the wet out,' he said.

Ceanna eyed the makeshift structure. Already she could hear the rain starting to hammer on the fronds, but they were dry underneath. 'I shall pray that it works.'

Vanora immediately curled up at her feet. The dog wagged her tail furiously when she realised Sandulf meant to sit next to her mistress. Sandulf sat, trying to make himself as small as possible, but their arms brushed. She moved as if he had burnt her.

She eased off her slippers. Her stockings were torn to shreds and several blisters had formed. Her gown tore even more as she leant forward to examine her foot. He frowned, but handed her the ointment he'd acquired in Constantinople.

'A little goes far.'

'It smells pleasant.'

'Frankincense. Shall I assist?'

'I can do it.' She rapidly put some on her feet and sighed as the ointment worked its magic. 'Thank you. They feel better already.'

He was about to ask her if she wanted any of his hard cheese when he heard a gentle snore.

Sandulf broke off a bit and gave some to the dog. 'I'll keep the first watch.'

Chapter Three

Ceanna woke with a start and a head swirling with confused images about broad-shouldered warriors who were willing to fight for her and protect her; who had gentle touches and cherished her. Nonsense dreams which had no business in her practical waking life.

Her hand encountered fine wool, warm and soft. Ceanna snatched it back. She froze. Her head was nestled against the crook of Sandulf's arm. At some time in the night, rather than sleeping propped up against the oak tree as she'd planned, she had turned into his chest and now was snuggled up to him in the most intimate way possible. She started to move, but his arm tightened, pinning her against him. If she lifted her mouth even the slightest bit, her lips would brush his. The thought made her go warm all over. Her mouth tingled as if he had indeed placed his against hers. She ran her tongue over it.

His eyes flared slightly as he looked down at her, but Vanora snuffled, breaking the spell.

Ceanna rapidly scrambled away, nearly tripping over Vanora as she did so. So much for her proud declaration that she had a vocation to be a holy maid. She'd practically offered herself to him. Uninvited.

He stretched his arms above his head. In the early morning light, his muscles rippled, making her more aware than ever of their close proximity. 'You're awake. Excellent.'

Ceanna swallowed hard, unable to rid herself of the knowledge that he knew where and how she'd been sleeping and that it amused him. *Amused him.* The thought was like a bucket of cold water poured over her head. He wasn't interested in her, not in that way. Men never were. They were interested in the dowry she could bring to their marriage, rather than her limited charms. 'I slept soundly.'

'You snored.' At her look, a dimple creased his cheek. 'A solitary snuffle and very soft at that.'

'I forgot to do my beatitudes.' She screwed up her eyes and rapidly recited the various sayings she'd sworn to remember. 'There, that is all. Oh, and remember to put ointment on my feet.'

She belatedly crossed herself and gave thanks. Holy maids were supposed to speak to God, rather than making lists.

'What are you doing?'

'Going over yesterday so that I can make today better.' She rolled her neck and arms, trying to remove the pins and needles from how she'd spent the night. 'I normally say them at night while I plan how my next day will go. I like the certainty of knowing what to expect.'

'Sometimes it is best to adapt and let things evolve.'

'My feet are not as sore as they were last night. It is amazing how restorative a night's sleep can be.' She rapidly put on her slippers before he had a chance to inspect them.

'Let me see.'

'They're fine. I promise.'

'I will judge the state of your feet, Lady Ceanna, before we continue.' His tone did not allow for any refusal. 'You may have plans, but I have responsibilities.'

He reached over and captured her ankle with gentle fingers. Tiny pulses of warmth radiated outwards from them. Ceanna forgot how her lungs worked. She held herself completely still.

He eased off the slipper and ran his hand slowly and methodically over the length of her sole. He set the foot down and lifted her other foot.

She concentrated on a spot above his head and tried to remember why she was not attracted to this man. His touch was strictly impersonal even if her heart whispered *what if*. Men, as her aunt had pointed out on her last visit, were often enticed by considerations other than the physical, which was fortunate for Ceanna and her prospects of a good match.

'Are you satisfied?' she asked into the silence. 'Will they do? We don't have time to waste. We need to catch up with Urist today. Once we are there, I can ride in his fabled cart.'

He let go abruptly and stepped away from her. 'The mist is lifting.'

'I will take that for a yes.' She hated the small bubble of disappointment which sprung up in her breast. He wasn't going to try to steal a kiss. 'I will keep up.'

'You have so far.'

Ceanna wished she could see his expression, but the grey light before dawn hid it very well. It bothered her that she wanted him to think well of her. She rapidly fiddled with her hair, releasing the last of the plaits and then redoing the hairstyle into something far more simple. 'You make it seem like some great heroic act.'

'You'd be surprised. Most ladies I've met would be weeping. I regret I took you for one of those feather-brained females when we first met.'

'I make no comment about the others, but I rarely cry or bemoan my lot. I try to plan my way out.'

He turned and gave her a searching look. 'I'll keep that in mind.'

'We need to go if we are to have any hope of catching Urist today. I am hoping our time alone together will be as short as possible.'

'Are you sure this is the correct way?' Sandulf asked after they had rounded another bend and the empty track stretched out before them across another piece of open moorland. The sun was far higher in the sky than it had been when they had set off, but they'd made good progress.

He was glad to put the distance between him and the place where they had rested. Waking up with her warm body in his arms had been a pleasant surprise. He hadn't expected his body to respond in the way it did to her nearness. He'd almost stolen a kiss and the only thing which had stopped him was the dog's bark. He'd made a mistake in touching her feet and slender ankles, feeling her flesh respond to his touch. It had taken all of his self-control not to pull her into his arms.

He stared up at the sky with its gathering clouds.

Lady Ceanna had been quite clear last evening that she wished to become a holy maid. From what he knew of such women from his time in Constantinople, they kept themselves pure in the service of their God. And she was a lady, not a woman who frequented taverns. Right now, he would concentrate on getting this holy maid to the guide and the whole party to Nrurim. Then he could focus on his duty again. Once completed, he'd find soft arms and even softer thighs between which to forget himself.

'Are you sure this is even the right track? I would have thought—'

She pointed. 'It is how the path to Nrurim goes. Over this rise and towards a wood which has a river running through it, from what I can remember, before climbing to the first pass.' She gave him one of her sideways glances which him made inhale sharply at the way her eyes sparkled. 'Are you suggesting we should stop and rest? Again? My feet are fine.'

He concentrated on the track.

'I'm happy to continue on, if you believe you are capable of it.'

'I'm a stout packhorse, even if I am dressed like some outlandish maiden at court.' She stepped and caught the hem of her gown. She let out a muffled oath, but put her hand over her mouth. 'A bad habit. One which my aunt is sure to correct.'

Sandulf tilted his head to one side and watched her. 'Is that the sort of thing holy maids say?'

'When they tear their gown for the seventh time in quick succession, yes.' She wrinkled her nose at him in a way that he found utterly charming. 'You mock me. You think my vocation lacks sincerity, but I did have a vision. And I knew I had to follow my destiny.'

'Even holy maids are permitted to get exasperated.

Or did I miss something?' He paused, trying to discern what she was not saying. She had mentioned this vision of hers several times, but he'd never met anyone less likely to have such a thing. 'Are they supposed to be calm and serene at all times? Waiting for the next glimpse into heaven?'

Her eyes became a vivid blue. 'One of the first things I'm going to do when we discover Urist is change into my travelling clothes. You've no idea how difficult it is to move in this.'

'Freedom to move means something to you. Most women—'

'I'm not like my stepmother. I like to get things accomplished rather than passing on work to other people. Allegedly I bustle, instead of gliding like I should do, which is why I'm always tripping on the hems of my good gowns.'

'Sometimes people should mind their own business.'

Her laughter rang out. 'My stepmother has strong views about how ladies should behave.'

He smiled back at her, relieved to get their relationship back to more familiar ground after the shaky start to the morning. 'Then I hope we find him soon for the sake of that gown. It is far too pretty to become rags.'

'It deserved a better owner.'

'It suits your colouring.'

She fiddled with the tie on her cloak, wrapping it round and round her little finger. 'You must have something wrong with your eyes. Red makes my nose glow.'

'I see perfectly well, my lady. More lies from your stepmother?'

A low sound made the laugh die on his lips. He listened for several heartbeats, waiting for it to repeat, but the sound of silence crushed the soul.

'Is there a problem?'

Sandulf attempted to ignore the prickling in the back of his neck, the one he always got before a battle. 'I would have thought we'd have caught up with Urist by now.'

'You've heard something.'

'Are we lost?'

A tiny frown appeared between her arched brows and her pointed chin took on a stubborn cast. 'I know how to get there. That wasn't why I needed a guide precisely, it was more for protection. Urist can be vexing, but I find it difficult to believe that he truly left me stranded. There will be a logical explanation as to why it has taken longer than I thought it would.'

'You wanted safety because the road can be hazardous.' He nodded. 'You were being cautious. A lone woman travelling and all that. But you changed direction several times yesterday when you were tired.'

She glanced behind them again. Her face relaxed when she realised that they remained alone on the track except for Vanora, who was sniffing a butterfly. 'I would not be foolish enough to start off without knowing how to arrive at my destination.'

She was running away, he was sure of it now. It was why she'd set out dressed in that fashion. Sandulf gritted his teeth. The good thing was that she did not fear what lay before them—she feared what lay behind. Behind he could handle. In front? He thought about the assassin who was hiding in the monastery at Nrurim. Lady Ceanna was not a target, despite his dream in the grey light of dawn.

'Why are you going to Nrurim?' he asked, trying another way. 'The truth this time.'

She started marching down the road, her gown swinging to reveal the slenderness of her ankles. 'I am going to become a nun, a holy maid. I told you last night before we went to sleep. A great desire—a vision, if I may be so bold as to call it that—came over me. I have to go and consult my aunt. Urist understood.'

He frowned. Lady Ceanna remained wary. She might be many things, but he doubted she had been precipitously overcome with religious fervour. 'Suddenly? Without delay?'

She looked up at him through a forest of long lashes. 'Isn't that the best way, when you know a course of action is the correct one?'

Sandulf kept his face carefully blank. Lady Ceanna bore no resemblance to any nun he'd ever encountered. Not that there had been many, but the ones he'd seen appeared to be overcome with a great desire to serve God and they wore sober clothing, not dark crimson gowns which were designed to show off every curve. Neither would they feel soft in his arms as she had done last night.

He frowned. Noticing Ceanna's curves showed that he had been without a woman for a long time, since before he left Constantinople. However, while he was happy to notice the curve of her mouth, the last thing he would be doing was sampling it. He would respect her right to her claimed vocation. Women went willingly into his arms or not at all.

He refused to think about earlier and how he'd barely restrained himself from kissing her lips.

'Because of this desire to be a holy maid, you had

to leave your home immediately? Leave your family? Dressed like that? A dress suited more for a wedding or a betrothal?' he asked, trying to piece together the truth of what she refused to tell him.

She abruptly stopped. Her brows drew together, making her resemble a kitten which had encountered water for the first time. 'What do you mean? Are you questioning my vocation? Don't I have the right to travel without people questioning me?'

She stalked off with her backside swaying. Sandulf forced his gaze to lift higher and attempted to ignore the hardening in his groin.

'I wondered if you were running away from someone, rather than running towards something,' he called after her.

She glanced back. A spark of mischief shone in her eyes. 'We'd agreed our business was our own. The subject of my vocation is a private matter for me, as I had understood such things should be. I beg you will refrain from speaking about it again.'

'It makes a change from speaking about the weather or where Urist could be. I've never encountered a holy maid to speak with in any great depth.' He shrugged and concentrated on the track. Her reaction confirmed what he'd already guessed. While she might hope their time together would be short, he hoped it was even shorter. The last thing he needed in his life was dealing with some wilful woman who refused to do the bidding of her family.

She coughed. 'Very well. Yes, my wish to become a holy maid was not something I foresaw happening the last time I visited my aunt. The vision came upon me suddenly. But she needs to believe in it as well as I.'

'Your aunt? What does she have to do with anything?' He willed her to confide. Ceanna was keeping secrets and those secrets could get them both killed, especially if half the countryside was even now in pursuit of her.

She ducked her head so that all he could see was the top of her *couvre-chef.* 'My aunt is the abbess. I will need her permission to join the church and devote my life to God.'

'The abbess is your aunt?' He thought about what knowledge he'd gleaned about the monastery. He knew it was a double monastery and ruled by a woman, rather than a man. He also knew that the current abbess was a powerful figure in her own right and had ties to the Alpin family who ruled Strathclyde. Lady Ceanna was exactly what he sought: the key to his entering the monastery without the assassin detecting him and escaping. Finally, the fates had embraced him.

She kicked a stone and sent it skittering down the track. 'My mother's sister, but...'

'I'll take that as a yes.' He examined her from under hooded eyes. 'Unless you persuade her that this is a true and holy vocation, you think she'll refuse you entry?'

Her hand went to her hip. 'Are you always this inquisitive? It is private business.'

'Holy maids are few and far between where I am from and I am merely taking advantage of the opportunity.' He gave a half-shrug, but his body tensed. He silently willed her to confide in him. 'You should be at court, somewhere where that dress could be admired rather than tramping through the mud with me. It leads me to conclude your departure from home was hasty and carried out with something akin to desperation.'

'I look forward to reaching Urist, who will have my

trunk and my proper clothes.' She tilted her nose up-wards and resembled a strutting blackbird. 'When we arrive, we can pretend we hardly spoke for the duration of the journey.'

'Never spent the night together. Never woke up in each other's arms.'

Her cheeks coloured a delightful pink. 'Nothing untoward happened.'

'We survived the night. Survival is important.'

Her brow lowered, but her eyes started to twinkle, turning from dull grey to brilliant silver. 'You are teasing me. You enjoy teasing me.'

He bowed low. 'Guilty, my lady. I'll do my utmost to ensure your reputation remains untarnished.'

She rubbed the back of her neck. 'I have turned it over and over in my mind. Urist was odd, but I don't think he intended to cheat me. He is loyal to my father. He made a point of telling me that. It was a point of pride for him. Something made him leave early and now I'm wondering if perhaps he was wary of you.'

'Of me?' Sandulf shook his head. 'He should never have taken my gold, if he was wary. It would have saved us both trouble.'

She wrinkled her nose. 'I trust that he waits for me at the bend in the river where there is a good place to camp at night. It is simply further than I remembered, or, as you said, I took a wrong turn earlier. When we last spoke, he mentioned it several times. And I do recognise one or two of the landmarks.'

'Consider the subject changed.'

She rolled her eyes and skittered around a muddy puddle. Sandulf smiled at the indignant twitch of her backside. Somehow that great aching place in his centre, the one which had gnawed at him since the massacre of his family in Maerr, had eased a bit this morning.

Vanora stopped abruptly, whimpered and slunk back against Ceanna. Ceanna bent down and instantly tried to reassure the dog that all was well.

The sound of an owl hooting drifted across the moorland, defying the time of day. Sandulf froze, reached out and grabbed her arm, shoving her behind him.

'What are you doing?'

He unsheathed his sword. 'Stay here with your dog. There is a noise I want to check. You will be safe with her.'

Sandulf tried to bury the sudden unsettled suffocating feeling deep down within him. That specific sensation had taken to arriving at increasingly awkward times since his brother's aborted wedding, but he'd suffered from it ever since he was a little boy. It seldom meant, as his mother had once claimed, that something bad would happen, but this time he ignored it at his peril.

'I am certain the meeting place is close. I saw the forked tree back there. Urist mentioned that in his message.' She pointed in front of them, towards where the owl had hooted.

'Even so, you remain here until I return.' He crouched down so Vanora could see his face. 'Look after your mistress.'

'What is going on? Why are you both so jumpy?' Ceanna started forward. 'I demand to know.'

'Do you, your ladyship? Do you really want to know? I am trying to protect you, as I promised.'

'I am not some child to be fed pap. What is up there and why should I be concerned?'

'I am not certain. It is better to be safe.' Sandulf

pointed with his sword. His nerves steadied with the blade in his hand. He could handle whatever lay ahead. He could keep his promise to her.

Ceanna's eyes widened. 'You expect trouble?'

'I am prepared for it. There is a difference.'

Her mouth became a thin white line. 'I can look after myself.'

'But can you keep quiet? In order to protect you, I need you to be silent. If I tell you to run, you do that.'

Her eyes blazed with barely suppressed fury. 'You go ahead. I can wait.'

Sandulf cautiously crept around the bend and cursed loudly when he saw what was ahead. The scene with its wholesale slaughter was far worse than he'd feared. The last time he'd seen anything close to it was back in Maerr.

He stood looking at the scene for what felt like a long time. Nothing moved. One of the bodies looked to be that of their erstwhile guide, but he was unnerved by the stillness. He methodically checked the ash from the fire—warm but not hot. There was something odd about this which did not sit right. But he saw no reason to keep Lady Ceanna away from this place. Whoever had done this was long gone. But equally it would be a great shock to her to experience it. He knew what women could be like.

What if...? He turned and ran back towards where Lady Ceanna waited with her dog. She sat on a rock, but rose the instant she saw him.

Her brow knitted. 'What is it? Overly active imagination?'

Sandulf pointed towards the scene of carnage he'd

left behind. 'Someone else knew our guide was coming here and they made plans.'

'Plans?'

'They were attacked. Bodies are strewn everywhere. No one lives. We will have to find another way.'

He waited for her to meekly agree or dissolve into horrified sobs, but instead she stood straighter. There was an innate elegance in the way she moved.

'No, I have to see it. I assume the attackers have gone as you've returned safely.'

He stared at her. 'Why?'

'Because the dead need to be honoured. Whoever they are.'

Chapter Four

Ceanna stuffed her hand into her mouth and willed the scream which was welling up inside her to be gone. She refused to disgrace herself. She kept her head erect and walked up to each body, looking at it while the ache inside her grew.

Screaming would make matters worse. Though how this could be worse she wasn't sure. But the destruction which lay before her sent violent shivers down her spine. She should have been here. She should have been one of the dead. Sandulf's insistence they stop for the night had saved her life. Just as his detaining the lad from the tavern had allowed her to escape. She owed him a life debt.

Could the dead hear when you screamed?

Beside her, Vanora gave a soft whimper and clung to her side. Ceanna grasped a handful of her fur and nodded towards Sandulf, who raised his sword in a salute. The simple act restored a small measure of calm and the urge to scream evaporated like the summer mist under the sun.

'Dead, all dead,' she whispered and then cleared her throat. 'Urist's travelling group. Urist lies over there. It was supposed to be a large group travelling. He worried about bandits.'

Her voice sounded amazingly calm and forthright to her ears, revealing none of the awful churning which occupied her gut.

'You confirmed what I thought. Thank you.' He inclined his head before putting a hand on her elbow. It took all of her strength not to lean against him. He gave a little squeeze and then moved away. 'You're doing well.'

'Well for a lady? You expected me to faint, or worse?'

'Well for someone who has not encountered these things before. I was violently ill my first time after a battle. My brothers never allowed me to forget it. Always joking and teasing. It is not easy.'

'Your brothers are less than kind.'

'They'd die for me. And I for them. It is part of the training—they want to make sure I know where I come from, that I stay humble as the youngest son.'

'They should be better.'

He gave a harsh laugh. 'When I see them, I'll inform them that Lady Ceanna, the new holy maid of St Fillans at Nrurim, has decreed they must treat me with respect.'

'It might do the trick.' She stared again at the carnage which was spread out in front of her, trying to be dispassionate. Urist's body lay next to a woman whom she did not recognise, but who appeared to be wearing Ceanna's best cloak, the one she'd carefully packed in her trunk.

A swift anger went through her. Ceanna clenched her fists and tried to hang on to her temper. Proof if she needed it that Urist had actually intended to rob her. He had already sold her clothes to another. 'That was my cloak, the one the woman is wearing. She could have been me.' A sudden realisation sent shock racing through her body. 'Maybe they thought she was me, if they attacked in the night.'

Sandulf tilted his head to one side. 'Could she be mistaken for you?'

Ceanna started to shake. If everything had gone as planned, she would have been the one lying there, the dead body instead of the breathing woman looking at the scene. 'I don't know. She could have been, or she could have been too afraid to run. She didn't stand a chance.'

A great lump developed in her throat. That woman might have stolen her clothes, but she had been a person with a family. It was not right how she died.

Ceanna wanted to be more than a tool to be used by everyone else who sought power or riches. She wanted to matter in her own right. She firmed her mouth and pushed the unworthy thought away. Crying over something was not going to change it and she certainly was not about to show the Northman that Urist's betrayal bothered her.

The carthorses had been brutally slaughtered and a sickly-sweet stench hung in the air. Rifled belongings lay on the ground. Ceanna spotted two more of her cloaks and one of her gowns festooned a branch.

Sandulf motioned to her to remain still. Ceanna nodded and tightened her grip on Vanora. Standing upright was about all she could manage.

Sandulf silently patrolled the perimeter, moving with a stealthy swiftness which reminded Ceanna of a sleek tomcat getting ready to pounce on his prey.

'They could return. We need to put some distance between us and this,' he said, returning to her side and speaking in a hushed tone. He watched her with wary eyes, as if he still expected her to panic. 'We don't know how big the travelling party was, but hopefully most escaped.'

Ceanna wrapped her arms about her middle and stuffed the scream back down her throat. 'Is that supposed to be comforting?'

Sandulf's mouth twitched downwards. 'Honesty saves time.'

'Thank you for your brutal honesty, then.' Ceanna concentrated on where the woman lay, face down. The cloak was now heavy with rain. She hated to think that someone had confused that woman for her. 'Do you think it was a gang of thieves who prey on travellers? Urist was supposed to be an experienced guide. He was supposed to travel with guards. Men with good sword arms, or so he promised.'

'He also promised to wait,' Sandulf reminded her.

'True.'

'I think this was far from a random attack; they were searching for something or someone.'

'How can you tell? It looks like confusion to me.'

Sandulf's face became grim. 'Experience.'

Ceanna swallowed hard. 'You've seen this sort of thing before?'

'Once or twice. It never gets any easier. It's worse than a battlefield. I worked the trade routes with the Rus after I first left Maerr. There was a bandit problem.' His mouth twisted. 'Most who go there to make their fortune end up bleached bones beside some foreign river. It made me determined to make more of my life. That means learning how to stay alive when I encounter something like this, listening to my gut when something doesn't feel right.'

'I feel sick,' she confessed, wrapping her arms about

her middle. 'I keep thinking it could have been me. Perhaps it should have been.'

'A natural enough emotion.'

She put a hand on her stomach and was pleased she hadn't eaten. Her stomach roiled again. 'I won't be sick, though.'

'No, you are not the sort.' He put a hand on her shoulder and instantly her nerves calmed. He believed in her. 'Gather what you need, and we will go.'

'L-Lady Ceanna, is that you? At last.'

Ceanna froze. 'Urist?' she whispered, uncertain if she was hearing things. 'Are you alive?'

Urist groaned from where he lay. He tried to raise himself up on one elbow. 'My lady. You've arrived.'

'Why didn't you call out earlier? Sandulf and I have been standing here for a little while.'

The guide put a hand to his head. 'I… I think I drifted off again. Don't right know how long I have been here.'

Ceanna hurried over to him. She wanted to hug him and shake him at one and the same time. 'I thought…'

He struggled to sit up, but his colour was paler than freshly fallen snow and his right eye was a bloodied mess. 'You don't stay alive for long if you don't know how to play dead and they roughed me up good this time. My head hurts something fierce.'

Ceanna motioned that he should stay seated, rather than rising. 'What happened? Was it a random attack?'

'They were waiting for us, my lady. Waiting for us while we waited for you. They struck in the dark, towards morning, I reckon. My lad was on watch, but he scarpered. That little lad means more to me than anything.'

'Waiting for you? Why didn't you take precautions against bandits?'

'We did.' Urist collapsed back down. 'Or at least I thought I had, my lady. The Northman and his friends… you're in danger from him. I can feel it in here.' Urist struck his chest.

'Listen to me, *Lady* Ceanna,' Sandulf said, shaking his head and interrupting the guide's self-serving explanation. 'This attack may have been planned, but there was little intention of robbery in the mind of the attackers.'

'How can you tell?' Ceanna decided to ignore the sarcastic use of lady.

'They left the trunks. They left the clothes and jewellery. These things have value to thieves and Northmen.'

Ceanna went cold. 'You think they were after something else?'

Sandulf stopped patrolling the site. 'I think it was fortunate you were elsewhere.'

She went over to the corpse who wore her cloak and turned her over. Vacant eyes stared up at her. To Ceanna's surprise, the corpse was stiff, as if the woman had been dead for several days. But it also appeared as if she'd been grossly violated, stabbed through the abdomen.

Ceanna's stomach roiled. She placed her hands on her knees and tried to regain her composure.

'Who?' she whispered.

'Died the day before yesterday,' Urist said in Pictish. He told her the woman's name, and it was someone from the village Ceanna knew only by sight. 'I suspected there would be trouble, my lady, and brought the corpse, propped up in the wagon. It were one of the reasons I left sudden like, my lady.'

'You did what?'

'She died in childbirth, my lady, the night before we left. My woman friend in the village had the idea after she heard about the Northman nosing about. If we ran into trouble, we would have a decoy. She is a bright lass, unlike my wife who shouts.'

'Where is your woman friend?'

'I can't rightly say, my lady. She declined to come on the journey.'

Ceanna's sense of unease grew. Urist had confided in at least one person about her intention to escape, despite his promise to keep silent. 'Keep to the tale.'

'Right. Some of your gold went to purchase the corpse. It takes more than good wishes to put food in bairns' bellies.' Urist pursed his lips. 'I gave my word she would receive a Christian burial. My lad's gone for another cart. He'll be back soon and we can go back to Dun Ollaigh and safety. There is bad folk out there, waiting for you.'

Ceanna winced uncomfortably. That poor woman's body had been mutilated like that because of the deception? She shuddered to think about suffering that sort of fate. But someone had come looking for her. Would they look elsewhere? At the convent? She rejected the idea. Her stepmother would concentrate the search around here. 'It will be seen to, I can promise you that. But why have you done this? Why not warn me about the threat before you left?'

'There weren't time, like.' He gave a sideways glance towards where Sandulf Sigurdsson stood, glowering. Ceanna noted that he avoided answering her question and her sense of unease grew. 'I was worried about that there Northman. He was asking questions. I told the wife there might be an ambush and she said to leave straight away. You never know. He might have—'

That made at least two other people who knew her plans. Bile rose in Ceanna's throat. Urist was stalling and she didn't know why.

'Sandulf Sigurdsson is with me. He did not attack you, nor does he appear to have travelling companions. Your lady friend was mistaken about the attackers.'

Urist's mouth dropped open. 'Even still, you'd do well to lose that man. They did run away quickly once they thought everyone was dead, like. The corpse were the first thing they went for. Not very bright, but Northmen are like that.'

Ceanna rolled her eyes. Like many other Picts, Urist always proclaimed his distrust of Northmen. But in this instance he was wrong. Sandulf was innocent. Urist's loose tongue had probably had something to do with the attack.

Her eyes flickered to where Sandulf stood. His face had its hard-chiselled look back, the one he'd worn at the inn. Vanora had started pacing like she always did when she was upset.

Urist—friend or foe? Danger surrounded her.

Ceanna swallowed her rising sense of panic and forced her voice to remain calm. 'Your caution may have saved my life and I thank you for it.'

Urist collapsed back down. His face twisted into an expression of obsequious subservience which Ceanna instantly distrusted. 'You're too kind, my lady. I knew you would see sense. My lad—'

'Sandulf,' Ceanna said in a low voice. 'We need to speak.'

'What is going on?' Sandulf loomed over them with his drawn sword. Vanora instantly went to him and whimpered.

Ceanna breathed a sigh of relief. His appearance showed him to be the epitome of a warrior. The cowards who had attacked Urist and his party would think twice about attacking a man like Sandulf. But the far better thing was not to have to fight at all.

Ceanna steadied her breathing. Urist had to think she trusted him. 'Rest, Urist. We'll speak more soon.'

She led Sandulf away from the guide. 'Our guide played a trick on the attackers, a trick which appeared to have worked. But something about his story rings false. My stepmother loves making elaborate tableaux as an entertainment for a feast. This feels like one of them.'

Sandulf's mouth became harder set. 'I can't understand what he is saying.' He pointed towards where the woman lay. 'Why is that long-dead woman there?'

'Urist didn't trust you so he took precautions.' Ceanna nodded towards Urist, who was examining his mangled leg.

'I see. He didn't trust me, but he was quite content to cheat me out of gold.' Sandulf rummaged through one of the sacks on the ground and withdrew a gold arm ring which he slipped on.

'What are you doing?'

'Retrieving my property. The guide I hired will not be fulfilling his end of the bargain.' His eyes flashed fire as he called out to Urist, 'No one cheats a son of Sigurd. Be grateful I've allowed you to live, Pict.'

Urist began bleating loudly about the unfairness of it.

Ceanna pinched the bridge of her nose. She had thought escaping from Dun Ollaigh was going to be the most difficult part of her journey. She'd been naive. She should've considered the possibility that her stepmother would play with her like a cat plays with a mouse before it goes in for the kill.

'Those precautions may have saved both our lives,' she said when she trusted her voice. 'He spoke Pictish because he distrusts Northmen, particularly you. He swears your countrymen did this.'

Sandulf made a cutting motion with his arm. 'Northmen played no part.'

'Why not?' Urist called. 'Northmen are all scum, my lady.'

'No Northman would have left gold.' Sandulf plucked a gown from the branch of a tree. 'Or indeed silk of this quality which can be worth more than its weight in gold in the right market. They'd have kidnapped any woman to sell her rather than murdering her in cold blood as she slept. No, it was not my fellow countrymen, but some other form of murderous scum who did this. Probably homegrown.' His smile did not reach his eyes. 'They're hoping that the attack will be blamed on the Northmen. Easier for them to escape justice.'

Urist winced. 'Maybe.'

Ceanna's mouth went dry. Sandulf had voiced her fear—whoever had done this wanted her dead. They'd known where Urist was going, where he'd stop for the night. They might even know they'd killed the wrong woman.

The sound of an owl hooting resounded in the clearing. Urist replied with a trilling noise. Sandulf instantly drew his sword.

'Why did you do that?'

'My lad's returning,' Urist said. 'Like he said he would. He's gone for the healer, my lady. Honest.'

'I thought you said a cart.'

'A cart and a healer.'

'Do that again,' Sandulf said.

Urist blinked rapidly. 'Do what again?'

'It was a different noise from earlier. You trilled twice before stopping.'

'Of course it is. My lady is here now. The lad needs to know that.'

'He needs to know that Lady Ceanna is here,' Sandulf said in a flat voice. 'You traitorous fool! You have used this scene as bait to keep us here while your lad went to bring more men.'

A chill went down Ceanna's spine. This attack had been staged in some part, but for whose benefit? Hers? Urist could be feigning, waiting to draw her in. He could have taken her stepmother's money. She could trust no one.

'To know I am here?' she whispered. 'How could you, Urist? I thought you were loyal to my father.'

'I am looking out for you, my lady. Someone has to. Your father is not himself and you should not be running from your family. My woman friend—'

'All is not necessarily how it seems with this one,' Sandulf said in an undertone. 'We should go, before this lad of his and whoever he has gone to fetch return.'

Ceanna's mouth went dry.

'My stout shoes are in the trunk,' she replied. 'I will watch him, so he doesn't alert whoever is coming until we are ready to run.'

Sandulf gave a brief nod and made his way over to the trunk.

'Did you say something, my lady?' Urist called. 'I am feeling weak again. It is best you stay right beside me. Right beside me.'

'You hit your head, Urist,' Ceanna said, keeping her voice light. 'You won't be able to take me to Nrurim. You know that. You'll need to spend time with a healer.'

'You can go to the healer with me. Wait until my head is better. There will be time.' His mouth twisted. 'Yes, plenty of time. You could send word to your aunt and tell her you have delayed your journey.'

Wait to be recaptured. Wait to die or take a chance on Sandulf being able to protect her. She glanced towards where the Pass of Brander glowered and mentally recited the landmarks they should pass. Her neck relaxed. She remembered all nine marking the way that her nurse had described to her all those years ago.

'I don't have time to waste, Urist,' she said. 'Some day I'll return to Dun Ollaigh and claim my rightful inheritance. I'll make it right to everyone who was loyal to my father. I'll ensure my aunt protects those who were loyal to me and God will punish those who made false promises and betrayed their oaths.'

Urist grabbed at her ankle, but she deftly avoided his fingers.

'Do not seek to detain me, Urist ab Urist,' she warned.

'My lady, do you know what you are doing? Do you even know how you are going to find your way to Nrurim?' Tears trickled down Urist's face. 'I meant no harm. I wanted to save your life. I will keep you safe. If you go with him, you'll die. I know it.'

Keep her safe and most likely inadvertently deliver

her back to her stepmother and her machinations. 'Were you truly attacked?'

Urist stopped his crawling. 'My lady, that you even have to ask that question!'

'Tell me.'

'We were attacked... I mean, you can see this here place and I took quite a blow.'

Not the ringing denial she'd expected. Urist had another scheme, but it had not gone entirely as he had planned.

'Did you ever intend to take me to Nrurim?'

'My lady!' Urist clawed his hand towards her. 'You must believe me. Stay here. Wait. My lad... Your father! He'll worry!'

Ceanna looked towards where Sandulf stood with Vanora and the clothes that he'd picked up from her trunk. His sword gleamed at his side and he moved with great authority and firm intention. He jerked his head towards the road and made a circular motion with his hand.

Ceanna picked up her skirt and prepared to run. She could do this. 'I know who to trust and it is not you, Urist. We were never here. I am but an illusion from the blow you took to your head. We go, Sandulf Sigurdsson. Now.'

Chapter Five

'Remaining anywhere in earshot is a bad idea.' Sandulf forced his voice to stay steady when Ceanna abruptly halted a few hundred yards from the clearing. Vanora sat down and refused to go further. 'Keep moving. We can return once the danger has passed if you require it, if you need more from your trunk, but I'd counsel against it.'

Sandulf's nerves tingled in anticipation. A fight was coming. How much time did he have before they were overrun? How many were there? They were coming, without a doubt. Dispatching Urist in cold blood was unnecessary. Lady Ceanna was correct—the guide's head wound meant the attackers might consider him confused and doubt his tale.

'Something we agree on.' Ceanna's mouth was pinched and her chest heaved with shallow pants. 'Let me catch my breath. Please.'

'Can you run further? Or do I have to carry you?'

She lifted her head and glared at him. 'I can run for as long you need me to. What I need to know is will you protect me? Can I hire you to provide protection to Nrurim, until I get to my aunt? I… I fear I will need it.'

Her voice trembled on the final word, telling Sandulf she was a heartbeat from total panic. Instead of answering her question, he handed her the boots he'd discovered in her trunk.

'Jam your feet into those, Skadi.' He lowered his voice. 'Unless you are determined to have my arms about you.'

Her lips twitched upwards and her cheeks flamed. 'Who is this Skadi?'

'Skadi was a woman who donned her father's armour in order to demand justice from the gods. Her beauty and determination impressed the gods and she became one of them.'

'I'll take the nickname, but your eyes need adjusting if you think I am beautiful.'

He gave a short huff. Her shock was clearly under control if she could joke. And women always liked compliments—his mother had demanded a steady diet of them. She was always examining herself in the bronze mirror his father had brought home as a gift, searching for any flaw.

He dreaded to think what a mess his mother or Ingrid would be in this situation. His back stiffened. Ingrid. He could almost hear her whispering her final words— words which he had not shared with Brandt. He swallowed hard as the guilt washed over him again. After he'd obtained justice for Ingrid, then he would seek out his brother.

'They're on,' she said, bringing him back to the present. 'I'm ready to go. Will you accept the bargain? Will you make another oath?'

'Give me your old shoes.'

She handed them to him with a puzzled expression. 'Why?'

He threw them far into the scrub. The action made him feel better. 'Because you don't need to carry them and our pursuers might be thrown off track.'

'You accept my offer?' She started to fumble with her arm purse.

'Payment on results.' Sandulf grabbed her and started to run again, crashing through the undergrowth, trying to get away from anyone who might arrive and from the memory of his failures.

'Where are you going? The road to Nrurim is this way,' Ceanna said between puffs of breath when Sandulf started off down a faint track.

Sandulf glanced back towards the way they had come. They were probably safe here or a little further on. 'Do you know the way, or must we follow the road to get Nrurim?'

'What are you carrying?' Ceanna asked, deliberately not answering his question. She held out her hand. 'In addition to the boots, did you think to grab a more practical gown?'

'Time was of the essence, but I reckon this should hold you in better stead than your current attire.' He glanced at her. Their run had caused several more rips to appear in her gown, particularly around the shoulders, revealing the cream of her skin.

'My current attire?' Her cheeks coloured delightfully as she rapidly started examining her gown for yet more tears.

She tried to pull up her sleeve and ended up causing the rip to get worse. 'Far worse than I imagined.'

'I didn't have much time to sort out linen, but...'

He roughly shoved a tightly wrapped bundle at her and waited for the complaints that he'd acted wrongly.

Ceanna hugged it to her chest. Her face became wreathed in smiles. 'Thank you. I'd feared all you took was my boots. Not even a sewing kit.'

'Do you need to change right away?'

He winced at her astonished look. Instantly he realised what he'd implied and then thought of the way she'd felt in his arms this morning.

'I mean... I mean...' He couldn't think what he had intended to say. Anything he said was bound to increase both their discomfort. The woman wanted to be a holy maid, not his future bed companion, even if he kept picturing what she'd look like in the aftermath of their mutually enjoyable coupling. 'I can turn my back.'

She slowly shook her head. 'I'll wait until we reach somewhere safer. My changing will simply slow us down. As you say, we need to put distance between us and Urist.'

His lungs started to work again. 'I agree.'

'You truly mean to do this? Travel with me to Nrurim? You mean to give me protection, not deliver me to my enemies? I never expected... Urist...'

He hated how her voice wavered. She clutched the bundle to her chest, trying to control the shaking. The woman warrior who had surveyed the carnage with a controlled and purposeful air had vanished and her place had been taken by a woman with large, wide eyes and a white pinched mouth.

He wanted to scoop her up and hold her tight, to whisper that all would be well, that he'd survived worse, that the killer was probably some hired sword, not the ruthless assassin he sought, the one who murdered women and their unborn babes in such a brutal fashion, but he refused to give false hope.

The memory of Ingrid as she clung to his hand, her life's blood draining from her, struggling to speak, slammed into him. He'd told her that all would be well and that Brandt would arrive in time, lies he'd believed she'd want to hear. Her lips had turned up at that and she'd shaken her head before she'd whispered her final words. He'd learned that day that offering comfort to the dying provided little comfort to the one who was left behind.

'I've no intention of delivering you to your enemies,' he said instead of explaining the truth—that he needed her more because those attackers could include his quarry.

'Urist betrayed me. And I thought I'd planned so carefully...' She stopped and pressed her face into her bundle of clothes.

'Another mantra to add to your list?'

'If I don't keep trying to be better, how will I ever become better?'

'Sometimes it happens when you're doing something else, rather than planning for it. Be open to refinement and alteration.' He waited for her answering smile, but her eyes were far too wide for his liking. 'My plan currently is to put as much distance as I can between us and that camp.' Sandulf started through the bracken, taking long strides with Vanora following at his heels. 'Your dog agrees.'

She moved far quicker with thick shoes on her feet, lifting her skirt up and revealing a slender calf as she caught up to them. 'Why must we go this way rather than keeping to the road?'

'I need to know how lost we might get if we leave

the road,' he said, choosing his words with care. 'Can you navigate by landmarks? We go east, right? Nearly straight east over the mountains from what my last guide said.'

She paled and clutched the bundle with white fingers. 'Leave the road? You advised against it last night. It is the way through the pass. We might have to go far to the south to go around.'

Last night, he hadn't feared they were about to be attacked. Or followed.

'Better to be alive.' He willed her to understand. 'You have done very well getting here, my lady, but I gave you my word and intend to keep it.'

'I know the landmarks. We head for Ben Mor and keep the loch on our right. There are nine landmarks in total.' She counted them on her fingertips twice, mumbling them under her breath. 'I know all nine. Will you be able to protect us?'

The sound of an owl hooting floated across the heathland, trilling now as it had before. Ceanna froze, her head cocked to one side.

'Should I be worried?'

'Owls in daylight mean treachery and evil are afoot. Remember that and we will be safe.' He forced his voice to sound light. 'But you have a warrior at your side now.'

She gave a tight smile. 'Sandulf Sigurdsson, my protector, the warrior at my side.'

He smiled back at her, impressed with her calmness. 'What good is creating panic where none is required?' he said softly.

She tightened her hold on the bundle and glanced back towards where the campsite lay. 'Will he be all right?

Left here on his own? Perhaps he is in danger if the attackers return?'

Vanora pricked up her ears and gave a small woof. Sandulf nodded, understanding what the dog was trying to say.

He grabbed her hand. 'Come on. Before whoever arrives to collect Urist, be they friend or foe. Vanora agrees with me.'

She rolled her eyes. 'Vanora would. She thinks you are wonderful because you come with an unlimited supply of hard cheese and dried meat. Her judgement is suspect.'

'You've too kind a heart, my lady, for such an unworthy thought about your dog's motivations.'

'I take that as a compliment.'

'Into the woods and through a bog to destroy any scent and then onwards. Can you see the summit of Ben Mor from here?'

She nodded and he saw the slight uncertainty which was instantly replaced by belief. She pointed towards the horizon. 'One set of mountains. One pass through unless we skirt south through the next valley. We head east.'

'Excellent. If I go too fast, let me know.'

She looked down at her sorry dress. 'You promise to stop so I can change where there is shelter? This gown has definitely seen better days.'

'As soon as we are safe.'

They plunged into the heathland, going away from the road and the clearing and up on to the moor. To Sandulf's relief, the sound of owls hooting quickly died behind him and the sun came out.

The going was boggy underfoot until they reached another small wood, but Ceanna's sheer determination to cover as much ground as possible impressed him. She never asked to stop, never once complained her feet hurt or that her gown was a sodden mess—all things he'd expect a woman to do. She had far more backbone than any woman he knew.

When he judged they had gone far enough and no one followed, he slowed the pace. 'When you spot a place which will protect your modesty, we will stop. I've no wish for you to faint.'

'You have a poor idea about me or Pictish women if you think us so weak-livered.'

'But I feel I'm going to learn.'

'A Northman who wants to learn—will wonders never cease?'

Unable to help himself, he burst out laughing.

She screwed up her nose, but her eyes danced with hidden lights. 'Do you think I'm funny?'

'I appreciate your dry wit.'

'People normally think it is something odd.'

'That's their loss.'

She missed a step. Instinctively, Sandulf reached out to steady her. A warm pulse went up his arm and the awareness of her rocked through him. His fingers itched to draw her nearer. A dark tendril of hair cascaded down her neck, pointing towards the gentle swell of her breasts. Her lips parted softly, red and ripe, revealing the pink tip of her tongue. He bent his head.

Vanora gave a sharp bark, breaking the spell. He instantly sobered and let go.

She wanted to be a holy maid, a voice resounded in his mind. He needed her to unlock St Fillans where Lugh the assassin resided.

He knew how such maids were treated in Constantinoplc—the reverence and awe in which they were held. He had no business stealing kisses, even if he thought it a shame that such a lovely creature was going to spend the rest of her life locked away from the gaze of men.

She cradled her arm. Her blue-grey eyes were fringed with thick black lashes. Her mouth trembled. He groaned inwardly as his body responded to her nearness. 'What is going on? Why have we stopped?'

'You nearly fell. Into the mud. I was helping you, but then realised you were capable of standing.' He hoped she wouldn't notice the husky timbre of his voice.

She laughed lightly. 'Balance—or lack of it—is one of my worst failings.'

He rejoiced in her innocence. She had little idea of the agony he was in. 'Take more care.'

Her face fell slightly and he winced. His voice had been too abrupt. 'I will.'

'I might not always be there to catch you.'

Her tongue wet her lips, sending fresh pulses of heat through him. 'We'll be parting company when we arrive in Nrurim.'

He forced his feet to move away from her. He had to stop finding reasons to touch her—that was the path towards madness. Keeping her pure would enable her to meet her self-proclaimed destiny as a holy maid.

He had so nearly succeeded where his brothers were sure he'd fail. He could then seek out Alarr, his middle brother, and most importantly Brandt. The kingdom might be lost, lost due to Brandt's temper, according to Rurik, but his older brothers would have to admit that he was worthy of being one of the fabled sons of Sigurdsson. And he would get justice for Ingrid. He tried to imagine what it would feel like to hear their words when they knew what he'd achieved. The thought of this had sustained him through much danger and difficulty, but this time he found no pleasure in them. Instead he kept thinking about the shape of Ceanna's mouth.

'We need to keep our face away from the sun and go east,' he said, forcing his voice to sound brusque.

'No, that way.' Ceanna pointed to a small hollow where a loch shimmered in the midday heat. 'We go there.'

'I thought the Pass of Brander was back that way.' They would have to cross it at night, in case of prying eyes, but he would worry about that later.

'I spy a small lake. This gown is worse than rags.' Her stomach gave a loud rumble. 'Bother.'

Sandulf forced his face to remain carefully blank. 'Hungry?'

'I don't suppose there is much hope of anything to eat.'

He threw back his head and laughed.

She halted abruptly. 'What now? What have I done?'

'You, only you. Most women —' It was impossible to explain that his mother, aunt and sister-in-law would never have admitted such a thing. Men had appetites, his mother used to say, and women had taste. He was never entirely sure what that meant. 'You're a refreshing change, my Lady Skadi.'

'I am not *your* lady nor this warrior woman you go on about. I'm your unasked-for travelling companion.'

'Truer words were never spoken.' Sandulf recited to himself all the reasons why seducing this woman would be a poor idea—starting with his need to avenge Ingrid's death and ending with her desire to be a holy maid. But the reasons suddenly seemed less important than the way her lips curved up in a smile or how her eyes danced. She was his travelling companion, his way in to the monastery at Nrurim, nothing more. 'But I'll grant your heart's desire anyway. You get changed and I'll see if I can obtain any food beyond the dried meat and hard cheese.'

She wasn't the sort of woman men desired. Ceanna knew that. She accepted her defects and that men were attracted to her dowry before they were attracted to her. It had been part of her reasoning why a holy maid was the perfect vocation for her. It solved many intractable problems if people believed she had deep and meaningful visions. For one thing, it would mean they would listen and protect Dun Ollaigh because it had been her childhood home. Her counsel would be taken because she spoke directly to God. She could declare the people of Dun Ollaigh required the church's protection because they were important.

The tiny knot in her stomach grew heavier. Her plan had to work. No hero waving a flaming sword would come to rescue her or prevent Feradach from preying on the townspeople. Except it was getting harder to maintain the pretence of her otherworldly holiness with Sandulf. She kept wanting to blurt out the full story about her fears and why she was running from her intended groom.

She had to stop thinking that Sandulf would be any different from the rest. He was calling her that name—Skadi—for irony's sake, not because he thought her overwhelmingly attractive or any kind of revered warrior. She knew she was neither.

Circumstance had thrown them together. He had not deliberately sought her out. And it didn't matter that his eyes danced with lights or that he shared her sense of humour. She'd given up looking for men to rescue her years ago. She was getting herself out of this mess. He was... He was...

She pinched the bridge of her nose.

He was irrelevant to her future. She had to cling tightly to her vision of being a holy maid and how being one would help the people who depended on her.

Throwing all that away because she'd woken in a man's arms and felt at once the pleasure and the security of it was wrong. All she needed to do was to keep thinking about the next steps and what would happen when she arrived at Nrurim.

Ceanna regarded the sodden and ripped wedding gown with distaste. She crumpled it in a ball and kicked it away from her. The thing had started making her brain rot, giving her romantic notions. The journey to Nrurim would be the length of their acquaintance, that was all. Then she would begin her new life as a nun, in service to her aunt, in exchange for the protection of her people.

She shivered slightly in the cold as she reached for the russet gown, which was one of her favourites as it gave her freedom of movement and hid the worst of her defects.

Before slipping it on, she carefully secreted the remainder of the gold which she'd stored in the toe of her right boot into a pouch she hung from her waist. Urist had not robbed her completely blind, but she'd seen the hesitation in his eyes. He'd been about to return her to Feradach's deadly embrace.

'It feels good to have proper clothes on again,' she called, coming out from behind the pile of boulders which had screened her from Sandulf after she had fastened a belt about her waist, disguising the pouch.

Sandulf turned from where he sat in front of a small fire. A lock of hair fell over his forehead, giving him an endearing boyish look, even though she knew there wasn't anything boyish about him. His quick thinking had already saved her life on two occasions. He was a man—her body told her that.

From somewhere he'd procured a line and had managed to catch a couple of trout from the loch. He held them out. 'You can move more easily in that. Good. Shall we gut these and cook them?'

'Are you waiting for me to wince squeamishly? I'm afraid disappointment is your destiny.'

He lifted a brow. 'The thought had occurred to me.'

'Your sisters must have loved you. I bet you put spiders down their dresses and beetles in their beds.'

'I don't have any sisters. Just brothers. Four of them. Two full. Two half. They're more than any man could want.'

'That explains it.'

'Explains what?'

'Why you think women are fragile creatures, liable to break at any moment and needing our whims constantly satisfied.'

He drew his lips together. 'Do you want to eat the fish or not?'

'I do.' Ceanna smoothed the pleats of her gown. Whatever this odd feeling was, she liked being on better terms with him. Temporary travelling companions could have a sort of friendship.

'Irritable when hungry, are we?' He regarded her under hooded eyes.

The urge to pat her hair nearly overwhelmed her. She

forced her hands to stay at her sides. 'Happier to breathe freely without worrying about bursting a seam.'

'You have the figure to fill out the other gown. That one is more like a sack.'

'This is my favourite gown,' she said between clenched teeth, unaccountably irritated.

'It is certainly more practical.' He bent his head and started scaling the fish.

'Shall I start a fire?' she said into the silence.

'Yes, I've started collecting some wood, but perhaps you can get some kindling.' He ran his hand through his hair, making it stand on end.

She gulped. 'Hunger makes me quarrelsome. My stepmother used to complain about it, but then she complains about everything I do.' She began collecting small sticks and twigs to start the fire.

'It is nothing.' He waved a hand. 'That colour suits you better, by the way. It brings out the highlights in your hair.'

How to damn with faint praise. Ceanna hated the small bubble of disappointment. She knew she was not beautiful. His words shouldn't hurt. It wasn't as if she wanted compliments, not from him.

'My wedding gown is little more than rags.'

'Best throw it on the fire.'

'The smoke might give us away.'

'Then leave it here. Someone might find a use for it.'

'My stepmother will be more distressed over losing the gown than losing me,' she admitted. 'She kept commenting on its cost. I'm certain that she made the measurements to suit her more than me. Her figure is more slender and she looks excellent in crimson.'

'And that bothers you?'

She tilted her chin upwards. 'Not in the slightest.'

'Then you're a better person than I am.' He gave a half-smile. 'I was furious when my family decided to send me away after my father's death. That anger kept me going for months, if not years. Still does.'

Ceanna stilled. Could that be Sandulf's reason for going to Nrurim? Something to do with his family? An old score to settle, perhaps? 'What did you do about it?'

'That is why I am here.'

'Do you want to speak about it?'

He quickly shook his head. 'I need to cook the fish.'

She pressed her lips together. 'I'll find something to balance the fish on. Be useful rather than decorative.'

'Lady Ceanna, I rarely speak about my family.'

'It is well then that I didn't ask you to,' she replied, stung. He was back to calling her Lady Ceanna again. The ease between them had evaporated. All because of her curiosity. What did it matter to her why he was going to Nrurim? Other people lived there besides the monks and nuns at the abbey. King Aed, his sons and his court had been there recently. It was where he had met his untimely end. From the rumours she'd heard, his murderer remained at large and the boys were missing, presumed dead.

He turned away from her and started gutting the fish, much to Vanora's delight.

As a peace offering, Ceanna hurried down to the loch and discovered two flattish stones that would serve as trenchers. She rinsed them off before she returned to where Sandulf had built a fire.

'Impressive,' she said, nodding towards the fish gently sizzling on a flat rock which was set nearly in the fire. 'I had wondered how you would cook them.'

'I know how to live off the land.' He gestured about him. 'People can starve if they are unaware of the bounty nature provides.'

'Then I'm grateful you know,' she said when she trusted her voice not to scream that she was far from a feather-brained lady who simply did needlework. She held out the flat rocks. 'And now we have something to eat on.'

He nodded. 'Good thinking, but I found some leaves to put the fish on.'

Her heart sank. He seemed more remote than ever. 'We can put the leaves on top of the stones. Saves burnt fingers.'

'We can do that.' He gave one of his smiles that made her heart swoop. 'And I made sure to gather a few extra leaves as it is quite a useful herb, one of the nine herbs Odin gave the world to help with healing.'

'The others are?'

'Mugwort, betony, lamb's cress, mayweed, nettle, crabapple, thyme and fennel. My mother made sure I knew them before I left home for the first time. A warrior must know how to heal as well as how to kill his enemy.'

'She sounds like a good mother—worried about her son.'

Sandulf's mouth became a thin white line. 'She had her moments. Her temper could be swift and ungovernable, though. She always resented my half-brothers and used to try to stop me from following them about. She never succeeded.'

'Your relationship sounds complicated.'

'It is,' he said in a tone which indicated he did not want to discuss it.

Ceanna winced. She had done it again. Her words

were supposed to be friendly. He had taken them as prying.

'I can be too curious,' she said, coming to sit beside him. She carefully put the large leaves on the rocks, two or three leaves to each stone. 'I like to know too many things, like these herbs of Odin. Your family are in your past, not mine.'

'It doesn't matter.' He waved his hand, but took the stones. 'Hunger gnaws at our bellies and never improves anyone's temper. I said I don't want to speak about my family, but with you, I keep finding reasons to mention them. I hadn't thought about the nine herbs in years. But you are right—my mother did…does care about what happens to me.'

'Is she still alive?'

'As far as I know, but she has another life now. A new husband, according to my half-brother. She took his part in a quarrel with my older brother.'

'When my father remarried, he put my stepmother first most of the time. Suddenly she wore many things which had belonged to my mother.' Ceanna stabbed at the fish. 'It hurt. It was as if my mother had ceased to exist and all the ways she had done things were wrong. My father refused to see how she was punishing the loyal servants. When I tried to stop her, I was deemed a nuisance and a bother.'

He put the fish on to a leaf-covered rock and passed it to her. 'Eat the fish, not the plant, Skadi,' he said with a mock-severe look. 'You don't want to make yourself sick and do your stepmother's work for her.'

She took a bite and discovered the fish melted in her

mouth. She might be running for her life towards an uncertain future, but somehow everything seemed easier. 'Food tastes even better when you are really hungry.'

Chapter Six

Sandulf concentrated on the remains of his fish. He'd spoken the truth—he did not like even thinking about his family except to consider about how he'd avenge them. Even in the short time he'd known Ceanna, she had him remembering things he'd buried deep down and each time they hurt a little less. All he knew was that once he had done what he said he would, that dark empty place in the middle of his being would vanish.

'Your friend appeared very eager to help you and blacken my name,' he said when she handed the remains of her fish to Vanora who set about it with a great eagerness, even though the dog had already consumed two fish of her own. Her great jaws crunched the bones with relish.

She shook her head. 'No friend of mine and irredeemably prejudiced against Northmen, I fear.'

Sandulf pressed his lips together. 'I'm discovering many in this part of Alba are.'

'They've cause to be, considering the raids which have happened over the last few years. They even dethroned Constantine, our old King, in the Battle of Dollar until their supply lines became overstretched and they had to retreat back to the Black Pool in Éireann. Who knows when they will begin to raid again? Giric, the new Regent, insists he and his men are more than capable of dealing with the threat.'

Sandulf ground his teeth. One more reason why he was going to need help to get into St Fillans. Marching up to the front door and demanding—as was his inclination—was doomed to failure. 'What precisely is the trouble with your stepmother?'

'My father's second wife is only three years older than I am. She is very beautiful—tall, with a perfect figure and hair as dark as a raven's wing. She was a pupil of my aunt's until about eighteen months ago and was hand-picked for my father.'

'And these days?'

'My father lies abed, sick. He has a wound which refuses to heal combined with a chill and cough that he picked up a month or so ago. My stepmother has declared he is beyond her skill as a healer. Dun Ollaigh must have an able warrior at its helm in these troubled times. She refuses to allow me to see him on his own or get another healer. Either she is present or Captain Feradach lurks.'

'What would your father say if you spoke to him alone?'

Ceanna stared at the gently lapping water of the lake. What would her father say? She'd pondered this for a long time, but she'd come to the conclusion that if he was in his right mind and able to speak beyond grunts and moans, he wouldn't want her dead. He'd never spoken about a marriage between her and Feradach. And in the hurried conversation she'd overheard, she knew her stepmother did not want her aunt to know about the marriage plans until it was too late for her to interfere. It was one of the reasons she believed her aunt would protect her, despite her stepmother having been raised in St Fillans under her aunt's watchful eye. 'I couldn't stay to be offered up as a sacrifice even though I know he may die while I'm gone. I pray for him.'

'Like any holy maid would.'

She ignored the taunt. 'Have you ever seen a body mutilated like that poor dead woman with Urist? The one he dressed up to be me?'

The sound of lapping waves was replaced by unwelcome memories—the torch hitting the rushes, the roar of the fire in the hall and Ingrid's final gasps. He rose and walked to the water's edge. 'Once. A depraved assassin. One of his specialities when he murders women, or so I've been told.'

'Has this murderer been caught?'

Sandulf skimmed a pebble across the lake, making it skip three times, and watched the ripples as it sank. How to answer without frightening Lady Ceanna, without having her beg him to take her anywhere but St Fillans?. Did Lugh have anything to do with the attack on Urist? 'I've no intention of letting him murder again.'

Lady Ceanna took a pebble and attempted to make it skip. It sank instead. 'Do you think the murderer noticed Urist's trick with the corpse? Or did it serve his purpose—the ability to tell my stepmother that I was dead?'

'Skimming stones is all in the wrist.' Sandulf grabbed another pebble and pushed his thoughts about Lugh to one side. He did things in order, not haphazardly. The answer was in Nrurim, he was certain of it, and the most important thing was to get there. If whoever had attacked Urist on the road discovered Lady Ceanna still lived?

Sandulf clenched his jaw. He was enough protection. 'A gentle flick. Shall I show you?'

'If you like. Did someone teach you? One of your brothers?'

'I mastered it myself.' Sandulf remembered how all his brothers had different techniques—Brandt with his determined throws which skipped further, Alarr would do it long and low and pretend the number of skips did not matter as he preferred to practise his sword skills, while the twins Rurik and Danr would vie with each other and gently argue about who was best. He'd idolised them all back then. His big brothers. 'They can all skim stones. None had the time or inclination to help their youngest brother, but then one day, I joined in and skipped a stone nineteen times.'

Sandulf smiled, reliving that rare moment of triumph. The expressions of wonder and pride in his brothers' faces at his achievement. He tightened his grip on the pebble, tossed it and it skipped seven times.

'What happened after that?'

'The fun went out of the game.'

'Or perhaps they became too busy with other things.'

'Perhaps. A pointless exercise, according to Alarr.'

'Not to me. I'd like to learn.'

He stood behind her and was intensely aware of her wildflower scent and the warmth radiating from her body. How alive she felt. Her current gown might conceal her curves, but he knew they were there.

'All in the wrist,' he said, barely recognising his own voice. His fingers closed about her hand. 'Flick it and you will skip the stone. Now you try.'

'Like this.' She skimmed the stone and it skipped twice. She clapped her hands and spun towards him.

Her lips were a breath away and softly parted. He forced himself to step backwards. He could not touch her, have her, if she were to become a holy maid. The last thing he wanted to do was ruin her life.

'Is this why you go to Nrurim?' she asked into the silence which followed her next skim of a pebble.

He pretended to misunderstand. 'To toss pebbles? Is there a good lake there?'

'You hunt a murderer.'

'Is your wish to be a holy maid merely an excuse to avoid the marriage your stepmother planned?'

Ceanna concentrated on rearranging the pleats in her gown. In her excitement at skimming stones, she'd nearly kissed him. And then she'd asked the question she dreaded knowing the answer to, but suspected she did already. Sandulf Sigurdsson was going to Nrurim to hunt down the vile murderer of whom he had spoken before. And now he had asked the question she most wanted to avoid answering. 'Why would it be?'

'It came on you suddenly, probably right after your stepmother decided you were to marry this captain of your father's guard.' He tilted his head to one side. 'You are unlike any of the holy people I've encountered.'

'You, a Northern warrior, have conversed with many holy people? Before or after you slit their throats?'

'Enough to know that they are generally unworldly and have little regard for practical planning. I'm a warrior who kills in battle, rather than slaying unarmed men or women.'

Ceanna stared at her hands. Her nails were short and her palms still bore traces of the dye she'd used with the wool a little over a week ago, a lifetime ago. Everyone thought of her as practical, rather than beautiful or dedicated to God's purpose. Her aunt was bound to see through her ruse. 'Because I'm practical, you think I can have no vocation.'

She took another pebble and attempted to skim it. It fell short. The twinkle in his eye deepened. 'Let us say that I have my reservations, but I'm prepared to learn. Why do you think becoming a holy maid will save you?'

Ceanna swallowed hard. This man had saved her life twice. He deserved the truth. Telling him the truth would not alter anything. She had no intention of waking up in his arms again. Not tomorrow, not any day on this journey and certainly not after the journey ended. Men like him were never interested in women like her. And she wanted to be more than a warm body in the night. 'What other option do I have? I can't become a warrior and go off to foreign lands to sell my sword arm to emperors and traders.'

His gaze roamed over her curves. 'I hadn't really considered it, but I don't suppose you can.'

She picked up another pebble and held it in her hand. It held a gentle warmth from the summer sun. She placed it in the pouch she wore about her waist. 'I'm determined to live my life as I wish.'

'What happens after you make your vows to become a holy maid and dedicate your life to the church?'

'I spend my life praying, doing good works and hoping for more visions.' Ceanna swallowed hard. It sounded even less appealing than it had back in Dun Ollaigh, but she couldn't confess that to this Northman. Becoming a holy maid was the best way to secure protection for the people who depended on her and to save her life. 'My aunt refounded the convent after her husband died several years before I was born. She lives a fulfilling life, I believe.'

'What about the people you have left behind? The people from the estate? Your father?'

Ceanna screwed up her eyes tight. Her father might even now be breathing his last. It had been part of the reason her stepmother had insisted on a hasty wedding—so he could give his blessing from his deathbed. 'If I'm dead, I can't help them.'

'And being locked in a convent ensures their safety? How?'

'They'll come under the church's protection from what I understand. Once I explain my vision to my aunt, she will be forced to act as the request comes from a holy maid. And my dowry will go to the convent along with me. In the past, the Gaelic church has had monks who were warriors. St Columba was a warrior, as was St Aidan.'

'I see.'

Ceanna wrapped her arms about her waist. 'I thought I'd been clever, but it appears someone guessed my intention and took steps. They want me dead and if that happens...'

Her flesh trembled beneath his palm. He tried not to think how warm she'd felt in his arms this morning. Or rejoice in the fact that her heart clearly wasn't committed to the service of her god.

'There are more miles to travel before we sleep tonight. You can pretend I'm your aunt and practise your speech on me as we walk.'

Ceanna glanced up towards where the mountains loomed. They had gone further south than she would have liked and the peak remained barely visible on the horizon. The further south they travelled, the more she risked losing her bearings and having to cross the river somewhere other than at the bridge. Swollen with rain, the river could bear down on the unsuspecting with fury and many had drowned attempting it. She controlled a shudder.

'I don't think that's a good idea. My words are for her ears only.' She wrapped her hands about her waist to contain the shiver. 'We should concentrate on the journey ahead. There are many dangers along the way.'

His eyes turned serious. 'I made my oath and I will protect you. Once we arrive in Nrurim, your aunt will be strong enough to protect you. It is why you are going to her. Nothing which has happened should alter that feeling. Let us not borrow trouble.'

Ceanna wiped her fingers on the remains of the leaves. Sandulf was right. But she wished she could rid herself of the unease that plagued her. 'Then it is best we get there as quickly as possible.'

He gave her a long searching look. 'I'm pleased you see it my way.'

Ceanna curled her fingers into fists. 'What other way is there to see it?'

Ceanna stared at the raging river which stretched out on either side of them, hating it but hating more the unsettled way it made her feel. Her mother and younger brother had lost their lives when they had tried to cross a river in a flood. Her mother had used a ford which was normally safe. The sound of her final screams and her brother's wails sometimes echoed in Ceanna's ears at night. After that she'd always been afraid of rushing water. But here today, with her warrior by her side, she found that the thought of taking risks was exhilarating.

Confessing this to Sandulf was impossible. She wanted to show him that she was better than any simpering lady he'd encountered before. She wanted to live up to the nickname he'd given her earlier. She wanted him to think well of her in a way she had not wanted anyone else to before. It seemed like such a long time since anyone had believed in her, but he did, even if she wasn't brave as he thought.

She dangled her foot over the water, stared at its swirling depths before putting it firmly back on dry land.

'We need to get to the other side as soon as possible,' she said. 'If we keep going inland, the river becomes a giant lake and we'll have to go out of our way to avoid it.'

'Or obtain a boat.'

Boats and rough water? A recipe for disaster. She shivered slightly. 'I would prefer to find a bridge or ford. Crossing here is dangerous.'

'These people who require your death will be watching the nearest places where it is safe to cross.'

'What do you suggest?'

He shaded his eyes, looking up and down the river. 'We go this way, back towards the sea until we reach a ford, but if not, we will reach this fabled bridge of yours.'

'That way? It is towards Dun Ollaigh. We need to keep going away from it.' Ceanna pointed in the opposite direction. 'I say we go towards the loch. Maybe you are right about the boat. We won't be on it long enough to get seasick.'

The corners of his mouth twitched. 'You get seasick? A loch is nothing like the sea.'

'My stomach revolts on a mill pond.'

He instantly sobered. 'You need to take a voyage across the sea. It will settle you, allow you to get your sea legs.'

'Once I am at Nrurim, I will be bound to the monastery and will make no further journeys.'

'You will be a holy maid who spouts wisdom and piety to all who will listen.'

'I have to believe in something.'

'Why not try believing in yourself?'

'You're being impossible.' She started off in the direction of the loch, but Sandulf remained still. At Vanora's whine, she glanced back. 'Will you keep up or not?'

'Either you trust me to protect you, or you don't.'

Ceanna stilled. 'How can it be safer to go back towards Dun Ollaigh?'

'I promised to keep you safe, my lady. As soon as it is safe to cross, we will. If it isn't until the bridge, then we cross at night. You were right in your first thought— we want to keep our presence known to as few people as possible.'

'You said they will be watching the bridge.' She pointed towards where the great loch lay. Her stomach remained sick at the thought of travelling in a boat. She'd never been a good traveller.

'Let me worry about that, Lady Ceanna. My sword arm is strong.'

Ceanna rolled her eyes. She was back to being *my lady*, a sure sign Sandulf was displeased with her attempt to control the situation. 'Very well, I'll bow to your expertise. We head for the bridge.'

Silently she prayed that it was just around the bend and they would not have to use a ford.

He gave a smile which warmed her all the way to her

toes, 'I knew you'd see it my way. It is good to see that you are not completely headstrong and foolhardy, Skadi.'

Headstrong and foolhardy. A combination of words she had never thought would be applied to her. She was known for her caution and prudence. 'I'm not that. These last few days have been unusual.'

A smile tugged at his mouth. 'Someone who likes to take risks now she has discovered the joy it can bring.'

She smiled back at him. 'Maybe.'

'We can cross here,' Sandulf said, pointing to a bend in the river where a large tree had become wedged between several stones. 'There looks to be a reasonable path with stones out to the log and the water is not running nearly as fast.'

'Will that log hold?'

'No reason why it shouldn't.' Sandulf frowned. Ceanna had become very quiet during their journey along the river. He found he missed her light banter. It was a relief from his own sombre thoughts about his failings and the memories of what had happened in Maerr.

She gave a brief nod, but continued to watch the river with trepidation.

'Shall I go first?' He started across the stones, managing to keep his feet dry until he reached the log. As he suspected, it was wedged tight. He rapidly walked across and looked down into the shallows. A series of flat rocks made the rest of the fording simple.

'It is straightforward because the log won't move until the next time the river floods,' he said, returning to where Ceanna stood. If anything, her face wore even more of a pinched look. Once they were clear of the river, they could relax, Sandulf repeated in his mind.

He had no wish for Ceanna to realise the danger he suspected they were in. Anyone who wished to should have no real trouble following their journey, but crossing the river would help solve that problem. 'You need to follow where I put my feet precisely.'

'Precisely?'

'You're more than capable of it. I've seen you in action. Remember, Skadi?'

Without waiting for her answer, Sandulf plunged ahead into the river. The water was moving swiftly, but nothing he was unduly concerned about. By moving from rock to rock, he managed to make it over to the other side with the water merely wetting his boots during the final few steps.

Vanora went in after him and rapidly made it over to the other side, but then gave a slight whimpering noise and started to pace the shore.

He glanced back to where Ceanna stood perched on a rock, about a third of the way across the river, right before the makeshift log bridge. She'd gone a slightly different route and her pathway to the log was completely cut off. The fierce warrior woman of earlier seemed suddenly hugely vulnerable. Droplets of water sparkled on her cheeks—from the river spray or tears? He refused to speculate. His heart, the one several women in Constantinople had accused him of not having, squeezed tight.

'Problem?' he called over the rushing water.

'Maybe we should make for the bridge and the pass.'

Sandulf frowned. 'Vanora made it over. You can do it.'

'Can I really?'

'You were the one who said she liked to take risks,' he said, trying to be encouraging.

'About that... I may have exaggerated a little bit.'

'You'll have to explain after you cross.'

Ceanna concentrated on the swirling water. It was far worse than she had imagined on the shore. It had seemed simple when Sandulf did it and then Vanora had barely got her paws wet. Going forward was not an option and backwards seemed impossible as well. Struggling to get air into her lungs, she knew she should never have misled him about her level of confidence. She should have told him the truth—that she was actually one of those simpering maids who was more at home with her tapestry on her knee than out in the wilderness, that she liked her routine and disliked...well...everything that was uncomfortable and unplanned.

'I'm not sure I can. Oh, help, I beg you!'

Her arms wheeled in the air and she knew in another heartbeat, three at the most, she would be in that river. She closed her eyes and whispered prayers.

Strong arms came about her waist as she felt herself slipping into the churning water. He'd got hold of her before she fell. Her hands clawed at his shoulders. 'Don't let me go. Don't you dare.'

'I've no intention of dropping you.' He tightened his grip on her and started to make his way across the river. His arms were like protective iron bands about her body, holding her against his solid chest. His heart thumped in her ear. The panic which had threatened to overcome her subsided.

She was surprised how easily he crossed the log. She craned her neck to get a better look at the river swirling beneath them. Somehow, with Sandulf holding her against his chest, the raging water was far less terrifying.

'Hold still. Wriggling will only make things difficult. Allow me to keep you safe.'

'Promise?' she whispered, screwing up her eyes tight.

'I promise.' His breath tickled her ear. Warm pulses thrummed through her body.

'I believe you.'

His hands shifted and her feet met with solid ground. 'You're safe, Skadi. Away from the river.'

Her tongue wet her parched lips. She was aware of how his chest rose and fell. If she put out her hand, she'd encounter it. 'Was I? Am I?'

'Yes, you are.' His eyes crinkled at the corners, but he remained next to her. 'Now, tell me what that was all about, Skadi.'

'I've never been good at crossing rivers or any sort of moving water since my mother and brother died,' she said, running her tongue over her dry lips again. 'I should have said earlier but I didn't want you to think the worst of me. I didn't want to be one of those simpering ladies who do little more than bat their lashes while they weave golden ribbons for their dresses.'

'Being afraid of something like that isn't shameful. It is natural. You should have told me.'

'I was afraid you'd laugh at me.'

'How did your mother and brother drown?'

'They were washed away in a ford which was supposed to be safe. It had been raining and the waters came up very quickly. He was in her arms.' She shivered slightly and wrapped her own arms about her waist. 'It was all I could think of when I was on that rock, that the river was rising and you were going to forge ahead without me.'

'Next time just explain instead of trying to be brave when there is no need. We're a team, Skadi, and we go at the pace of the slowest. No one seeks to have sport with the other's fears.' His eyes turned serious. 'You are safe with me.'

Safe with him. She glanced up at his face. He was so close that she could see the faint scarring on his cheeks and the slight cleft in his chin. And his eyes had depth. She wondered that anyone thought them cold.

Without giving herself time to think, she raised up on her toes and brushed his cheek with her lips. 'Thank you. For everything.'

Sandulf swore softly and then lowered his mouth to hers, and his arms drew her against his hard body.

Ceanna started as his warm lips touched her cold ones, giving them life. She'd never known kisses felt like this. She wanted to open her mouth and drink from his lips. She had intended to brush his cheek in thanks, but this had happened. And she wanted more. She wanted to sink into the kiss. She wanted to feel his hands moving up and down her back.

The thought was like the icy river water which had swirled about her ankles a few heartbeats earlier. Kissing him enthusiastically was all wrong for someone whose destiny was to be a holy maid. It demonstrated her lack of pure intent. And she knew her aunt would closely question her on such things.

She forced her feet to move away from him and concentrated on tucking her hair back into the *couvre-chef*. All the while, her cheeks burned. 'I can see Ben Cruachan peeking through the clouds. We've far to go to reach the pass. The sooner we start, the sooner we will get to Nrurim and you can go your own way.'

'Should I beg your pardon, Skadi?' he enquired.

She quickly shook her head. 'I kissed you. I'm not…'

She searched for the right words to explain that men did not desire her. Men desired her dowry, not her body.

'You're not a holy maid yet. You could be wrong about your destiny. The more of the world I see, the more I learn that no one can tell the future. Not even the gods.'

She tumbled into his gaze again and then rapidly concentrated on the clump of blue and yellow wildflowers nodding in the light breeze behind him. 'Do you think my aunt will mind my…exaggeration? My aunt once said to me that if I truly thought I had a vocation, then she would consider taking me, but I must not think about shutting myself away because of fear.'

'Is that what you are doing? Shutting yourself away because of fear?'

'I'm not afraid of the marriage bed, if that is what you are asking. I simply have a great desire to grow old.'

'Ah, Skadi. You've a way with words.'

'Then you understand why I need my aunt to take me in. I am hoping to discover my vocation in earnest before we arrive.'

'So you have not yet felt the calling?'

'It will come. It has to.'

His fingers caught her elbow. A warm pulse rocketed through her. 'A kiss is no reason to abandon your journey to Nrurim. Your aunt will be delighted you favour her establishment for what is sure to be an illustrious career as a holy maid.'

'Abandoning my plans is impossible. My stepmother wishes me dead. Once my father dies, she intends on marrying her lover, the man who was to be my husband. And a man cannot have two living wives.'

'How do you know this with such certainty?'

'I overheard them speaking,' she said and tried for

a nonchalant shrug. At his look, she knew she'd have to give him more. 'It was late and I'd gone back to the great hall for a bone for Vanora. I heard a faint rustling and followed the sound. I encountered them…entwined.'

'You saw them together? Or heard them?'

'Both. In their passion, they did not notice me.' Ceanna scrunched up her face and tried to rid herself of the image—her stepmother bare-breasted and the man naked on his knees before her. 'Here I am, a failed holy maid with no real vocation except the desire to save my life and keep the people who depend on my family safe from my traitorous stepmother. Somehow, I'll have to convince my aunt that my vision of being a holy maid is a true one and hope that my soul is not blackened by the lie. She will offer me sanctuary and take Dun Ollaigh under the church's protection, rather than returning me to Dun Ollaigh, humiliation and death.'

It felt good to say the words out loud and admit it. She wanted to be a nun because she knew no alternative. She envied people who were sure of their path in life, like her cousin who had known since she was a little girl that her destiny lay with the church. Her cousin had spent most of her life in prayer, constantly worrying about what the angels might think of her. Unfortunately, she'd died of a fever shortly after she entered the convent. Ceanna's stepmother had proclaimed that it was because the girl spent so much time on her knees.

She waited for condemnation from Sandulf. He simply whistled and Vanora came bounding up.

'Your dog wants to continue the journey.' He strode off towards the east. Vanora, the traitor, followed at his heels.

'You don't think I'm a terrible person for pretending?' she asked, catching up to them quickly.

'We all have to do what we can to survive.' His mouth twisted. 'I've made enough mistakes in my life and have no wish to compound them by giving advice when I know nothing of your god.'

Ceanna touched her mouth which still faintly tingled from the kiss. She'd think of it as her proper first kiss, not the drunken assault from Feradach at Easter which had made her stomach churn. This was far more pleasant and something to recall in years to come, that once a handsome man had kissed her as though he meant it.

She shook her head. Dreaming had never solved her problems.

Compounding mistakes.

That kiss had been a mistake. The last thing Sandulf wanted was someone like her panting after him. But her heart refused to believe it and longed for it to happen again. Ceanna resolutely started practising that speech that she'd deliver to her aunt. It had never sounded so false.

Chapter Seven

Thoroughly kissing Ceanna had been a strategic error, one which he wanted to repeat, but one which he knew, for the sake of his sanity and her destiny, he had to avoid.

Sandulf resolutely kept his eyes carefully on the rough track as they walked through the bracken. Vanora had given up playing with sticks and mostly trotted at Ceanna's side.

'See,' Ceanna said, pointing towards a faint shimmer off to the right. 'I see the loch. And the two mountains off to our left.'

'Is that good?' Sandulf knew his voice was far too abrupt. At the hint of confusion in her eyes, he swallowed hard and tried again. 'Did you expect to see them?'

She covered her mouth with her hands in quiet joy. 'We're going the correct way. I did find the right track. I'm not totally useless.'

He smiled back at her. 'Your navigation skills are excellent. You should have more faith in your abilities. I do.'

She stopped and looked up at him. Her blue-grey eyes sparkled like sunlight on a lake. 'You do? I wasn't entirely certain. Particularly after we crossed the river. We might be able to avoid the pass by skirting south of the mountains.'

He put his hands on her shoulders, felt the flesh tremble slightly beneath the pads of his fingers. 'You worry too much.'

Her tongue wet her lips. 'Do I?'

'Yes.' He bent his head and brushed his mouth against hers. 'Much too much.'

He gave in to the sensation of her mouth moving under his for one long glorious heartbeat. She tasted of sunshine and warmth, all the good things in life. He let go. He doubted he deserved any of that.

Her fingers explored her mouth.

'Should I beg your pardon?'

She shook her head. 'I thought we'd agreed earlier.'

'Agreed what?'

'I am to be a nun, a holy maid who sees visions.' She gave a half-smile. 'Even if I have not yet had a real one.'

He frowned. 'Out here, you're Skadi, the lady Ceanna, my travelling companion.'

Her eyes became troubled. 'If we'd been acquainted for longer, you would know I am far from the sort from whom men steal kisses. Mostly I'm overlooked and ignored. Far too plump in the bosom.'

He watched her heart-shaped face with her pale rose mouth and upturned nose. 'What is the matter with the men in Dun Ollaigh? Are they blind? I have rarely known a man to complain of such a thing.'

She burst out laughing. 'The Northmen must have different standards.'

He regarded her. The urge to suggest other options for her life besides being a nun in Nrurim nearly overwhelmed him, but he needed to find Lugh and she was his best hope of getting there. After that, he'd assist her if he could. And he had to hope that his gut instinct that anyone attempting to find Ceanna would simply make for the monastery and wait, ready to pounce once she appeared, wasn't accurate. He was taking a calculated risk, but once she reached her aunt's sanctuary, she was no longer his concern. He would have fulfilled his oath.

'Stop listening to your stepmother or whoever else told you that.'

'Marriage proposals have not exactly been thick on the ground, according to my stepmother.'

'Your stepmother seeks to manipulate you.'

'I know the truth, Sandulf. Even before my father married her, I was considered awkward and clumsy.'

He captured her chin between his fingers so that she was forced to look at him. He wanted to slay all of those who had made her feel less than she was. She wasn't conventionally pretty, but once you got to know her, her inner beauty shone through and he wondered how he'd missed it when they first encountered each other. He admired her courage and her vitality. But he also knew he couldn't say those things to her, not yet…and possibly never. She was the sort of woman men married. She was not the sort for a dalliance, however enticingly her mouth had moved against his earlier.

'Nothing happens that you don't wish. We go at your pace and…'

Her eyes blinked at him. 'And what?'

Sandulf abruptly let her chin go and stepped away. Lady Ceanna was an innocent. She had little idea that she'd grown into a highly desirable woman with curves in precisely the right places. She might know things in theory, but she had little idea in practice. She deserved someone better than him to teach her. 'We need to find shelter for tonight before it starts to rain again.'

Ceanna regarded the small cottage. The garden was well tended and there was an air of busy prosperity to it. She hoped that finding a place like this to stay in would get rid of the uneasy air which had sprung up between her and Sandulf.

He had kissed her thoroughly and then strode off without a backward glance. For the rest of the day he'd spoken only when necessary and had gone out of his way to avoid her. She found she missed the little touches, the accidental brushes of their arms, his hand helping her over a muddy puddle. She hadn't realised she'd been looking forward to them until they were gone. She concentrated on the door. Some nun she was going to make.

'Allow me do the talking. Please.'

'Because I'm a Northman.'

'I speak Pict and Gaelic. I've no idea which language they speak in this hut, or if they've suffered at any Northman's hands. You can hardly blame people for being cautious.'

'True enough.' He made a low bow. 'Once again, I will be in your debt, my lady, if you secure us a place to sleep.'

'Where has this formality come from? Are you mocking me?'

'Never. I am prepared to admit that you might be the best thing to have happened to me recently. You are certainly prettier than my other guides on this journey.'

She screwed up her nose. 'There isn't much competition if Urist is anything to go by.'

'I'll admit to not being attracted to Urist in the slightest.' He shrugged.

Ceanna glanced up at the sky with its growing storm clouds. His liking for her, if that was what it was, was friendship, not desire or even love. She had to keep her head out of the dream clouds. Heroes did not come to rescue women like her.

'Then we're agreed that I can approach the lady of the house and ask if she can spare shelter for us and perhaps a morsel of food.'

'I take it you're hungry...again.'

A tiny bubble of happiness rose up inside her. 'You know me so well. My stepmother thinks it a weakness. She says my aunt distrusts people with large appetites as their mind is on earthly pleasures.'

'She was a disciple of your aunt's. Will that cause problems?'

She pressed her hands together. 'My mother was her sister. I believe blood will count for something when my profound vision of holiness is added to the tally in my favour.'

He reached out and pushed a tendril of hair from her face. 'I prefer women who have a healthy appetite for life.'

Ceanna's mouth ached. 'So, you agree. I will speak with the woman.'

'But of course.'

Ceanna coughed loudly as she approached the elderly woman who was seated in the doorway. The woman stopped doing her spinning and stared at her.

'Strangers,' she said in Pict. 'Most go by the pass, rather than taking the long way around.'

'Strangers in search of a place to lay our heads for a

night and something to fill our bellies.' At the woman's puzzled expression, Ceanna reached into her pouch and retrieved a gold coin. 'We're happy to pay.'

The woman gave a silvery laugh which sounded far younger than her white hair suggested. 'What need have I for gold?' she asked in Gaelic. 'The only thing it calls to is thieves and rogues. Keep your money. My hospitality is not for sale.'

She picked up a willow broom and began sweeping.

'We're happy to work. There must be some jobs we can do in exchange for a night's lodging.'

'I've a strong back,' Sandulf added in Gaelic. 'Your firewood runs low.'

The woman stopped her sweeping. 'You interest me, Northman. You've managed to spot my firewood running low without seeing my pile of logs.'

'I find most women on their own are in need of more firewood.'

'And other things besides, hey?' The old woman cackled.

'I always seek to discern a woman's needs.'

The woman looked him up and down and then glanced at Ceanna. 'I can see you do. How do you know I am on my own?'

'You did not call for your man when you spotted us.' He gestured towards the cottage. 'There are a few things which need fixing on the roof and walls, jobs which you would soon set any able-bodied man who lived here to do as you don't appear to be a woman who would suffer idle folk.'

'Aye, you might be right about that.'

Ceanna held up her palm and caught the splash from a raindrop. 'It looks like rain and we have travelled far today. I am willing to help clean the house. I can churn butter and sew a fine seam.'

The woman tilted her head to one side and examined both Ceanna and Sandulf. 'Let me see your hands.'

Ceanna held out her hand.

The woman took it and ran a finger down the palm. She rocked back on her heels. 'You have done some work in the past, but these are the hands of a lady. I see the signs of blisters.'

'I've never been one to allow the servants to work while I rest.' Ceanna jerked her head towards where Sandulf stood next to Vanora. 'I've given all that up.'

The elderly woman's eyes widened. 'For him? I can see why that might be appealing.'

Ceanna felt a tide of red flame mount her face. It was beyond her to explain that she and Sandulf were merely travelling companions. 'Will you be able to accommodate us?'

The woman threw back her head and laughed. 'Aye, my lovely. I can do that. Particularly as your man is willing to split a few logs for me in exchange. I'll admit to finding it harder and harder. And that there dog will be content with a bone, I trust.'

'What does she want?' Sandulf asked. 'She speaks a little faster than I'm used to.'

'For you to chop wood. She needs the firewood more than the gold or other jobs, particularly as you are with me.'

'Tell her that I will consider it an honour for such a lady.'

The woman's withered cheeks burnt rose. 'He is from the North. I can scarce understand his accent, but he is a feast for the eyes. And he no doubt charms the birds from the trees.'

'He means no harm.' Ceanna hoped her voice sounded steady. 'Not all of them are bent on destruction.'

The woman pondered thoughtfully. 'True enough. The dog must stay outside. Cats and an owl make their home with me.'

Ceanna motioned to Vanora to lie down outside while the woman instructed Sandulf where to find the axe and how much wood she wanted chopping. His eyes widened slightly at the size of the log pile, but he started swinging the axe straight away.

A fine stew stood bubbling on the hearth. Everything about the cottage was neat and tidy. The scent of drying herbs filled the air. A black cat opened one eye when Ceanna entered, rose and twined her way about Ceanna's ankles. She bent down and stroked the silky fur. The owl flapped down and watched, then flew out the door. The woman beamed her approval.

'You keep the cottage very well,' Ceanna said in the silence which followed.

'It suits my needs. Some come to seek me out because they think I can cure what ails them.'

'Can you?'

The woman shrugged. 'I help more than I hurt. My animals let me know who to help and who to hinder.'

'I am grateful they approve of me.'

'A fine man, your Northman,' the woman said as she set out several wooden bowls on the table.

'I like to think so.'

'Worth hanging on to by my reckoning. When you have lived as long as I have and have buried five husbands, you get to know these things instinctively.'

'He has proved useful. He helped me to cross the Awe when I panicked.' Ceanna concentrated on the bubbles popping in the stew. The words sounded mealy-mouthed, but she didn't want to go into the full story.

'He cares about you. I could see it in his eyes. He'd have got down on his knees to beg for shelter for you. The good ones are few and far between.'

Ceanna gave a large huff. Cared about her? He barely knew her. She turned away from the stew. 'We...that is...'

'I know what it is like, my dear, when you're young and life calls to you.' The woman's smile grew and it was clear that enlightening her as to the true state of affairs was not going to do anyone any good. 'It reminds me of my third husband. We ran away together. We'd have been happy except...'

'Except what?'

'He died too soon. Before I ever let him know how happy I was.' Her voice broke on the last words. 'It is why I have learned about herbs, so I can help instead of being a foolish woman, wringing my hands.'

Ceanna put a hand on the woman's elbow. 'I'm sure he knows now.'

The woman dabbed her eyes and gave a loud sniff. 'Do you think so? That gives me comfort. I've been thinking so much about him recently. Then seeing how your man looks at you...'

'Can I help you get the pottage ready?' Ceanna moved away from the door. Out of the corner of her eye, she could see that Sandulf had shed his tunic and was still busy chopping wood. Time seemed to stand still. All Ceanna could do was to watch the way the muscles in his back moved and his skin became slick with sweat.

'He does that so that you will notice him. No sane man would do so unless he wanted to catch a woman's eye.' The old woman gave a leering smile. 'I've lived a long time. I know what men are about. If you'd like a potion, I'll give it to you. Something to keep his eyes on you. The young girls sometimes seek out Mother Mildreth for such things. Several have sworn by its effectiveness.'

Ceanna tore her gaze away from Sandulf's rhythmic chopping. A potion to make him love her. It was tempting, but then she'd never know if he truly desired her or if it was purely the herbs. 'He merely wishes to keep his tunic clean.'

'And the potion?'

'Keep it for someone who needs it more than I do.'

Mother Mildreth gave a loud cackling laugh which made the cat jump. 'Youth is wasted on the young. When you're old, you realise how many opportunities you've blithely tossed away because you were afraid of starting.'

'If you can show me where we'll be sleeping, I can put that to rights.'

The twinkle came into the woman's eyes. 'I like the way your mind works, my lady. I've some herbs which will make everything sweet-smelling and ensure good dreams.'

'I'm not...not any longer, that is. Call me Ceanna.'

'Sometimes, it is not about what people call you, but how you see yourself. Anyone can see from your bearing that you are a lady. Now let's see to the bedding.'

Ceanna stared up at the blackened roof and willed morning or a dreamless sleep to come. The stars shone through a slit in the wall turning everything a dull silvery tone. And the dried rosemary, valerian and lavender flowers Mildreth had sprinkled made the hayloft smell delicious. She knew they should help her sleep, but every time she closed her eyes, she thought of the river and the kisses she had shared with Sandulf.

His hair had gleamed in the firelight tonight after he had finished his work and taken a dip in the pond which lay some way from the cottage. She might have refused to accompany him after he jokingly made the suggestion, opting instead for a quick wash in front of the fire, but it had not stopped her imagination from speculating.

If anything, it had been made worse by Mildreth nudging her in the ribs before Ceanna retired to the makeshift bed in the hayloft and wishing her a good evening's sport.

Many solid reasons existed why giving in to her desires must not happen. The first and foremost was that her aunt would never agree to her being a holy maid if she suspected that Ceanna's professed religious devotion was less than it might appear. And, she sighed, who was she fooling? She didn't want to give in to her desires because she was afraid of rejection. He'd kissed her a second time, part of her mind argued, thoroughly and completely. Did that seem like a man who was indifferent? Ceanna clenched her fists.

Beside her Sandulf lay, oblivious to her distress. He had fallen into a deep sleep the instant he closed his eyes.

She turned on to her side and then on to her back again. And then she heard it, a little noise, almost a small whimper. She froze, certain it came from Sandulf. She waited and heard it again, a low keening sound coming from between his lips. His hands lashed out, flailing as he started shouting *No!* over and over.

'Sandulf?' she whispered, shaking him. 'Are you all right?'

'Ingrid? You're alive.'

'It is me, Skadi. Wake up. A bad dream. You are safe here in Mother Mildreth's hut.'

The flailing ceased. He shifted on to his side. His contorted features were silver in the pale light. His eyes blinked open. 'Ceanna? Is something wrong?'

'You cried out in your sleep. You kept saying no. You were obviously dreaming about being somewhere else.'

She listened to the steady sound of his breath and wondered if he had drifted off to sleep.

His hand brushed hers. 'I didn't mean to disturb you. Bad dreams are terrible when they come.'

'Do you know what the dream was?'

'My dreams are always the same—the day my father and sister-in-law were murdered. I'm sorry to disturb you.' He started to rise. 'I'll go and sit by the hearth. Sleep will be beyond me now.'

'You didn't disturb me. I was awake.' Ceanna put a restraining hand out. 'Stay. We don't want to break Mildreth's illusion about us.'

'What is her illusion?'

'She has a romantic heart. She believes we're lovers escaping from some disapproving parent. There was nothing I could say to dissuade her. The very notion, eh?'

The words came out in a great rush. She felt all her muscles tense as she waited for his derisive laughter at the mistake.

'Do you often find it difficult to sleep?' he asked rather than enlightening her as to his views about their supposed romance.

'I must be overtired. I always find it difficult to sleep

when I'm exhausted,' she said, forcing the bubble of disappointment back down her throat. 'I keep thinking about Urist and the poor woman from the village with the knife in her belly.'

'You slept well last night.'

'That was before,' she said with a weak laugh. She really did not want to think about waking up in his arms or the kisses they had shared throughout the day any more. They had obsessed her every time she closed her eyes. She should be thinking about other things, things which people with true vocations considered right and proper, like long bouts of prayer on hard stone floors. She sighed. Such things held little appeal. She was going to be hopeless and her aunt would instantly see through her ploy. 'I hope it wasn't my restlessness which caused your unpleasant dream.'

'It comes more frequently than I'd like. I hate the powerlessness I felt when Ingrid died. My eldest brother was right. I froze when I should have acted.'

Her heart knocked. 'This Ingrid, she is the one whose murderer you chase.'

'Yes.'

'I am sorry for you. And for Ingrid.'

He cupped her face with his hand.

'Do you think he is in Nrurim, this murderer of yours?'

His hand fell away. 'Annis, my new sister-in-law, led me to believe it. Either he is hiding there, his treacherous heart waiting for another opportunity, or it is possible he may have wished to atone for his many sins, as you Christians would say.'

'If he was responsible in any way for the assault on Urist's group, then he hasn't,' Ceanna whispered. 'My aunt may even be in danger. She could be harbouring a viper who will strike without warning.'

'Perhaps. He may not even be there.'

'Was he responsible for the deaths of all your family?'

'Of my sister-in-law? Most certainly. He also may know the identity of the man who killed my father. My new sister-in-law did not think he had time to kill both my father and Ingrid. Someone would have claimed the honour of bringing down such a fearsome warrior and my half-brother Rurik said no one had done, not to King Fcann who organised the attack to avenge his sister's honour. And he would have showered them with gold if they had.' Sandulf explained rapidly about the massacre at Maerr and its aftermath.

Ceanna listened with growing sympathy. 'Why aren't you with your brothers, trying to discover exactly what happened?'

'I was sent away, sent east on a trading ship of my aunt's new husband, but Brandt would have banished me in any case. He took his wife's death badly and he blamed me because I should have protected her. I am alive and she is not, and I should have given my life for her. I heard it in his voice and so I went.'

'But you are searching now, by yourself. Why?'

'Without me, the assassin Lugh will never be held to account for his crimes against Ingrid. I alone saw his face with the shooting-star scar. I know what the man is capable of.'

Ceanna heard the barely suppressed anger in his voice and wondered who it was directed towards—the assassin or his brothers. Or himself?

'Your father made many enemies.'

He sighed. 'My father made no secret of his ambi-

tion and lust for power. He ruled through fear instead of
through love and respect. Once I had wanted to be like
him, but on my travels I learned there were many ways
to be a leader of men, ways which build men up instead
of tearing them down. Should I ever become a leader
of men, I have vowed to be different from my father.'

'How did you know where to look for this man?'

'I left Maerr on board my Uncle Thorfinn's ship, but
about a week into the voyage, a man called Rangr sidled
up to me and said he'd heard I was Sigurd's youngest and
he had a story to tell me, but to keep it quiet. The captain
shouted it was my turn to row and so we couldn't talk.'

Sandulf fell silent. Ceanna nudged him. 'You can't
stop now, you are getting to the interesting part.'

'After my shift, I went to meet this Rangr, but as I
went near him I spied a partly concealed knife in his
hand. One of the helmsmen shouted to have a care and
told me to turn around, but I had seen the knife. Rangr
lunged forward, intent on killing me and, together with
the helmsman, I managed to tip him overboard.'

'I presume he died. What happened to you? Were
you punished?'

'Afterwards, the captain told me Thorfinn's personal
guard had declared Rangr was prone to sudden intense
rage and to keep an eye out for any trouble. Before that
incident, he had had a go at another of the crew. It was
good riddance, but I would have to do double shifts of
rowing from then on as punishment for costing them a
rower. I went to Rangr's place on the rowing benches
and discovered a gold pendant, very like the one my father had given my mother when I was born, concealed
by one of the loose boards.'

'You thought she had hired this man to look after you and you accidentally killed him?'

'She could have done. My mother worried about me. But if he was supposed to be protecting me, who wanted me dead on that ship? And why did he change his mind and try to put a knife between my ribs? After Rangr's death, they worked me hard enough to kill me. The whole incident made me jumpy, so I escaped as soon as we docked in Kaupang and gave my oath to another captain who was travelling east.'

'You said your mother could have hired the man? Why do you doubt it?'

'I discovered another pendant—a golden arrow like the one which my mother was given for Brandt's birth— around the neck of a man in lodgings in Constantinople. I recognised him and his companion as two of the Saxons who had carried out the massacre at the longhouse, the ones who had slit the throat of Vigmarr, the father of the woman my middle brother Alarr was to marry. Vigmarr was one of the best warriors in the north. I gained the trust of one of them before I enacted my vengeance. Before he died, he showed me the pendant and said it was payment for that job. I had to wonder—what if *both* pendants were given by my mother as payment to get rid of my father?'

Ceanna stared into the darkness, trying to discern his features. 'You think your mother had something to do with the attack on your father? They could have been stolen. You said everything was in confusion.'

'You don't know my parents. My father, he was obsessed with power and gold, far more concerned with amassing both than with his family, and he was willing to sacrifice everything, including his honour, to get it.

My mother worried that he was going to divorce her and make another alliance. They were either arguing or icily ignoring each other's existence in the months before the attack. My mother is a proud woman and she may have had enough. But arranging for all of what happened to my family... I hope not. I hope she did not orchestrate the attack. Her potentially dishonourable blood runs in my veins.'

'And I know their son, who has saved me several times over in the last few days. Someone taught you that sort of honour.'

He moved so he was lying on his back. Their bodies barely touched in the narrow loft. 'That came from my brothers.'

'Tell me about her, your brother's wife, the woman who died.' She hesitated, remembering how touchy he'd been on the subject earlier. 'It might make it easier to sleep if you remember the good things, rather than dwelling on the bad.'

'There's some truth in that.' Sandulf described his eldest brother Brandt and how he'd worshipped the ground he walked on. And how when Brandt had married, he'd worshipped his wife as well. How he'd hoped to marry someone like her—golden-haired, tall, with a beautiful smile and an even sweeter temper.

This dead woman sounded like everything *she* wasn't, Ceanna thought with a pang. She had no wish to marry Sandulf. She simply wanted to get to Nrurim and restart her life. Even though the prospect of a life immured in a convent held less appeal than ever.

'She sounds wonderful,' Ceanna said, injecting real warmth into her voice. Hating a dead woman was not something worthy of a holy maid.

'Ingrid was lovely. Beautiful on the inside as well as on the outside. I was supposed to be looking after her that day. She was carrying her first child. Her feet ached, and she didn't want to stand for the whole ceremony and maybe shame the family. We'd gone into the longhouse because I had suggested it as everyone in my family was sure to come back there after the ceremony. No one would know, you see. I'd even ensured she had a dish of honeyed plums before she asked, in case she was hungry. She often appears in my dreams, all bloodied, demanding I fulfil my oath.' His voice trailed away.

'And you are. You're doing what is required. Tell her to hush so you can focus on your quest.' She gave a small yawn. 'I have to hope I can rest.'

'Sleep will come soon enough.' He sighed. 'Now, what is your trouble that keeps you from sleep?'

'Mildreth thinks we are…lovers,' she blurted out before she had time to consider the implications. 'What if she asks how it was for me? How do I answer without giving the truth away?'

He turned on to his back and stared up at the faint starlight peeking through the cracks in the ceiling for so long she thought he must have fallen asleep.

'We're friends, Ceanna, which is better,' he said as she opened her mouth to whisper his name. 'Tell her it is none of her business, but you slept very well indeed.'

Friends. Her heart panged a little. She hadn't realised until he said the word that in many ways she had hoped the decision would be taken from her. That he would kiss her and things would go beyond the point of no return, that she wouldn't have to think about the half-truths that she'd told and the lies she would have to tell when she reached Nrurim. Pretending to be a holy maid with a profound vision was a sensible plan, one which ensured Dun Ollaigh's safety. Glaring flaws existed, she knew that, but the good intention was there.

While her heart grieved, the sensible part of her rejoiced. She wouldn't have to lie to her aunt about her purity.

'Is it better to be friends?' she whispered around the lump in her throat.

'I've had many lovers, but my friends I count on the fingers of one hand, particularly my friends who are women.'

'Are you trying to insult me?'

He reached over and smoothed the tendrils of hair from her forehead. 'No, to honour you. I've bedded many women, Skadi, but can scarce recall a single one. I want to remember you.'

Ceanna worried her bottom lip. It was a new thing for her as well. She wished he'd pull her into his arms and kiss her senseless, but she wanted to be more than a warm body. She wanted him to remember her. 'And you remember your friends?'

'True friends are never forgotten. I'm a dangerous man to my enemies, Skadi, not my friends.'

'I see.' She paused and kept her heart from rejoicing. He considered her a true friend. And he was right—a friend was far more important to have. One could count on friends. She was determined to prove her friendship by helping him in his quest to find his sister-in-law's murderer. Perhaps her aunt would know something.

Her throat went tight. Such a creature could threaten her aunt and all those who lived in the monastery, but travellers stayed there all the time and it could have been merely that he was passing through. Ceanna could barely make out Sandulf's features. She wasn't sure if it was the intimacy of the darkness which had made him confess or because they were becoming friends. Summoning up her courage, she touched her lips to his forehead. 'You might be dangerous to your enemies, but you are a good man. I'm grateful for your friendship.'

A drop of moisture ran down her cheek. She wiped it away with a quiet finger.

'Sleep. You don't have any ghosts to keep you awake. I envy you that,' he said in a rough voice and turned his back to her.

Sandulf lay in the darkness and listened to the soft sound of Ceanna sleeping. Friends, not lovers. The dull aching in his groin at her nearness showed what a lie that was. Luckily, she was far too innocent to understand—he wanted to be much more than her friend. What sort of rogue would he be if he took her innocence when she was about to enter a holy life?

If he'd been anything like Danr, Rurik's twin, he would have seduced her by now and got her out of his system. Danr was the one brother who could charm women out of trees and who never lacked for female companionship. He had a quick quip for any situation and had diffused more arguments with their father with a joke than Sandulf liked to count.

Sandulf had sought to emulate him in the past, particularly where women were concerned, but with Ceanna, heartless seduction was impossible. He respected her far too much. He did want her friendship. It had been far too long since he had laughed with anyone, yet Skadi and her dog kept finding ways.

'I will protect you,' he said softly into the night.

When she met her aunt, he wanted her to be able to say that she was as chaste as a nun should be. He wanted to give her a chance at the life she desired without regrets.

It did not make it any easier, though, particularly as she snuggled closer. He put his arm about her and knew he would not sleep for the rest of night. He'd lied to her. He'd had his usual dream about Lugh and the killing spree, but this time, the woman he held as her lifeblood had streamed from her had been Ceanna, not Ingrid.

He forced himself to think of killing Lugh rather than the warm body lying next to him. The thoughts were not as comforting as they normally were. If he failed, Ceanna would be in danger and protecting her had suddenly become more important than avenging Ingrid's death.

Sandulf forced himself to concentrate. He had not come this far on his quest, suffered that much, only to give up. Ceanna was important because she could take him to Nrurim.

Lugh had to be at Nrurim—or he had been there recently—like Rurik's new wife had said. Once he had dealt with the man, then he'd confront Brandt, give him Ingrid's last words and regain his rightful place as one of the sons of Sigurd. Whatever that place was.

He wrapped a tendril of Ceanna's hair about his finger. The prospect did not excite him as it once had.

Chapter Eight

When Ceanna woke the next morning, sunlight filtered through the gaps in the thatched roof and the space beside her was empty. The only indication that Sandulf had been there was the faint indentation in the straw. She ran her hand over it, but it was cold, as if he'd been up for hours

Ceanna rapidly dressed and discovered Sandulf sitting at the table. Vanora lay at his feet and Mildreth plied them both with food while the owl slumbered on a rafter. The cat was nowhere to be seen.

'I overslept,' she said and immediately the heat rose on her cheeks. 'I thought… I thought you didn't allow dogs in the house.'

Mildreth gave her a large wink. 'Thanks to your man's promise of doing extra chores last night, your dog slept beside the hearth and has been perfectly well behaved.'

Sandulf choked on his food. 'I was up early chopping wood. Our hostess will not need to worry about that particular chore for a while.'

Up early? Had he even gone back to sleep after his nightmare?

'I must have been more tired than I imagined. I can't remember the last time I slept for so long. Normally I'm up before sunrise as there are always jobs to be done.'

'Sometimes it is good to sleep,' Sandulf said.

'Particularly after exercise.' Mildreth gave a high-pitched laugh.

Ceanna knew her cheeks burned worse than ever, much to Mildreth's cackling delight. She quickly concentrated on the table rather than meeting Sandulf's eyes. It made it all the worse as a large part of her had wanted to do exactly what Mildreth thought she had last night.

In the cold light of day, she was pleased that his sensible head had prevailed and that she'd done nothing to jeopardise her chances of becoming a holy maid. And she'd continue to do that. She wished the thought filled her with more pleasure. Deep in her heart, she knew she had been able to resist temptation because no temptation had been offered. Sandulf had believed her when she'd explained it was the best thing for her future. She wished she knew that for certain.

'We should get going,' she said. 'I'd like to get to Nrurim as quickly as possible. My legs are fresh, Sandulf.'

'You should go by the high road,' Mildreth said, wrinkling her nose. 'This track will eventually take you to it, but I know a short cut, one which ensures you miss the pass. It'll take several days off your journey.'

'We'd be grateful for any assistance,' Sandulf said. 'We both wish to get to Nrurim as speedily as possible.'

Ceanna's heart clunked. She had wanted that yesterday, but getting there would mean the end of her time with Sandulf.

Mildreth stood up. 'Once your woman finishes her

meal, then we will go. She'll need to keep her strength up for the night-time. I have a few things I need to get.'

She bustled out of the room before Ceanna could object.

'She believes we…' Ceanna whispered. 'About us. Our relationship.'

'It makes her happy to think about a little romance,' Sandulf said in a low voice.

Ceanna concentrated on her pottage. 'But we know the truth. Friends, not lovers.'

He squeezed her hand and the gleam in his eyes deepened. 'We do indeed.'

She withdrew her hand, hating how the warm pulse travelled up her arm. 'Friends. We are both entirely too sensible to be anything else.'

He put his fingers against her lips. 'Hush. She returns. And I doubt anyone but you considers me sensible.'

Ceanna turned towards the door. Her mouth tingled from his light touch.

Mildreth put a cloth-wrapped package in front of Ceanna. 'For you, my lady. Take a drink of this here tea every morning.'

Ceanna glanced inside the package. It was filled with sweet-smelling herbs. She recognised raspberry leaf and rue. She swallowed hard. 'And this is for…?'

Mildreth lowered her voice. 'You aren't wed, are you? The tea will keep a baby from settling in your womb.'

Settling in her womb.

Ceanna instinctively put her hand to her stomach. The words to proclaim it was impossible rose in her throat, but she forced them back down and took the package, tucking it into the pouch she had fastened to her waist. 'I'll be sure to take steps.'

'My remedies are highly sought after, I'll have you know,' Mother Mildreth said with a decisive nod. 'Many a day I've had a queue of women and men making their way here. Some I choose not to serve.'

'I'm honoured.'

'Shall we go and discover that short cut?' Sandulf proclaimed in a loud voice, clearly embarrassed by the whispered conversation.

'Yes, I'm most anxious to get to Nrurim,' Ceanna said and silently vowed that she would dispose of the tea as soon as possible. If her aunt discovered it, it might lead to awkward questions about her purity.

She silenced the little voice which asked her why not take the risk and seduce him? She had always tried to avoid taking risks which would end in abject humiliation, but maybe her warrior was worth it?

'You've been silent since we left Mother Mildreth's.' Sandulf bent down to retrieve Vanora's stick. Unlike yesterday, Ceanna had not kept up a steady stream of conversation. He discovered he missed it. 'Have I upset you? Is there something I failed to do? I thought you'd have been pleased to sleep.'

'Why would you think that?'

'You and silence are not natural partners. When you are quiet, you hum.'

Ceanna kicked a stone which went skittering along the path. 'You barely know me. I can keep quiet when the occasion requires.'

'Don't get me wrong, I enjoy it. I thought I liked silence, but right now...'

'You'd like some relief from your thoughts?'

He had to resist drawing her into his arms and kissing her senseless. He forced himself to pick up a stick and toss it for the dog. 'Precisely.'

'I wanted to let you know I never asked her about the tea to prevent babies.'

'Ah, that.' Sandulf concentrated on the stick.

'I'll teach you Pictish to pass the time.'

'Do you think I will have a need of it where I'm going?'

'You never can tell.'

He threw the stick again. 'I am good at picking up languages.' Sandulf tossed the stick further and harder than he intended. A talent which would have remained uncovered if he'd stayed in Maerr. 'I discovered it on the way to Constantinople.'

'It can be difficult. The Gaels rarely try beyond a few words.'

'But I want to.' He pointed to a tree. 'What is the name for that? Will I have to pay a forfeit if I get it wrong?'

She ducked her head. 'You are starting to sound like Mother Mildreth.'

'Perish the thought. And I'll teach you some of my language in return. You never know when you might have a need of Norse.'

'We made it,' Ceanna said staring down at the wooden walls of the monastery. Like most of the buildings in the Kingdom of Strathclyde, the monastery was fashioned from wood and set behind a palisade in case of attack from marauders.

A few short days ago she had thought seeing the monastery would be like coming home, except now with the silver-birch logs towering over her, it felt more like she was entering a prison.

Arriving here meant that she would have to say good-bye to Sandulf and she wasn't ready to do that. She'd grown accustomed to his banter and his quiet helping hand under her elbow when she needed it. She struggled to think of anyone she'd rather have had as a travelling companion. They had discussed so many things since they had left Mother Mildreth's, arguing in a light-hearted manner and setting the world to rights. She had started teaching him to speak Pictish and was surprised at how quickly he was learning it while he had taught her a few words of Norse. She'd ignored his repeated suggestions of meaningful forfeits as being teasing designed to make her blush.

Ceanna had begun to see that Sandulf was correct—they were friends. She felt as if she could confide practically anything to him. Everything but her growing feelings towards him—those she knew would have to be kept as a dark secret.

Friends, not lovers.

The last thing she wanted on this bright sunshiny morning was to go into those darkened buildings and devote her life to prayer. She tried to remind herself of all the reasons why this was the correct thing to do—her life, her people, honour and pride—and why she should be pleased at taking this step. Her attempted deception felt very wrong suddenly.

'I thought it would take longer,' she said when she noticed Sandulf looking at her with a quizzical expression. She was going to miss his little looks and asides.

'It took less time than I worried it might,' Sandulf said.

Ceanna wrapped her arms about her waist. She had nearly flung them about his neck and begged him to take her away from here. There was something about the place which gave her an unsettled feeling which curled about her insides and refused to let go. 'We seemed to have escaped whoever attacked Urist's camp.'

He paused for a long while before answering. 'I know.'

'It worries you.'

'Given the carnage back there, it surprises me. Something's not right. I dislike surprises when lives are at stake.'

'But you do like them at other times.'

The light in his eyes deepened. 'It depends on the nature of the surprise.'

'I normally like my life to be well ordered and safe. Once I choose a course, I tend to keep it. This time has been unsettling—I keep having to alter my plans.'

'Some plans are worth altering.'

'And others you hold fast to.'

A smile hovered on his lips. 'I've kept my end of the bargain—protection until you reach safety.'

Ceanna concentrated on smoothing the folds of her gown between her fingers rather than watching his mouth. It wasn't his fault that those kisses they had shared had haunted her sleep over the last few nights and she wanted more. He had made it very clear that he was respecting her wishes. Keeping herself pure was essential in those seeking to become a holy maid and she knew her aunt would be able to tell any sort of lie. 'I'm aware of that.'

'Do you wish to go on alone? Are you asking me to wait here until you can return? I can take care of Vanora for you.'

Ceanna stared up at the clouds scurrying across the sky. Her aunt had no great love for Northmen or dogs, but she knew she'd feel safer with Sandulf at her side. And Vanora was non-negotiable. Once her aunt had seen the great joy Vanora could bring, Ceanna hoped she'd be allowed to stay. She swore softly. She would never abandon Vanora.

'We go together. My aunt will understand things better once she hears about my journey with you. She will be overcome with gratitude and will be able to assist in your search for this Lugh, this assassin.' The knot in Ceanna's stomach grew. On a good day her aunt would be overjoyed, but the last time Ceanna had seen her things had not gone entirely as Ceanna had planned.

'That is something to hope for.'

'I've practised my speech over and over until I have it down perfectly. I did have a vision—a vision of my death if I stayed.' She clapped her hands together which made Vanora, who was inspecting a stick, jump. 'I'll make an oath to you in return—to find your sister-in-law's murderer. I promise. A thank you for what you've done for me.'

His gaze seemed to pierce Ceanna's soul. 'If you can't keep the promise, I won't hold you to it.'

'We're friends, after all, and friends keep their promises.'

'They do.' A muscle jumped in his jaw.

Ceanna raised her chin. 'Whoever destroyed Urist's camp won't be in this monastery. If this man with the shooting star on his face is here, I'll find him for you and allow you to do the rest.'

Sandulf's mouth became a thin white line. 'You're not to search him out. Let me do that.'

Ceanna winced. 'I've no wish to quarrel with you. I'm trying to assist you in your quest. All I know is that if you go in making demands, they'll turn against you and seek to protect someone who deserves no protection. Do it my way…for the sake of the language lessons I gave you.'

Rather than answering her, Sandulf stared at the monastery and the small town which had sprung up around it, nestling within the shelter of its walls. 'We'd best be going, then.'

She wished she could grab his hand and run far away from there. Already she missed the ease they had had on the road.

He caught her hand and raised it to his lips. A warm thrill went through her at his touch. 'Thank you.'

She folded her fingers about the kiss and tried to hold it. 'I've done nothing.'

'You've been my friend and you believe my story. I'd forgotten what companionship feels like.'

The finality of his words washed over her, dampening her mood further. Was it her fault that she wished for something more? For it not to be over? She firmed her mouth. She'd given up wishing for impossible things.

When they reached the outskirts of the town, a guard stopped them. 'State your business.'

'I go to my aunt, the abbess, Mother Abbe.' Ceanna put her head to one side. The town appeared nearly deserted instead of the bustling place she remembered from the last time she had visited. And the guards were busy stopping everyone who entered the garth, checking baskets and carts. 'Is there some sort of trouble?'

'The old King died here.' The guard sniffed as if she was beneath his notice for making such a remark. 'The assassin remains at large. The new King and his advisors endeavour to keep the peace.'

'That was several months ago. The culprit has surely been discovered or is long departed,' Ceanna said in an overly sweet way, the voice she used to coax her father into eating his pottage. She thought about what she knew. Her cousin, King Aed, had been brutally murdered while hunting near Nrurim, but the assassin had escaped in the confusion. Aed's two young sons had also disappeared when the new King and his Regent took over. Rumours ran rife about where the sons of Aed could possibly be. Some had it that they had been kidnapped, others that they had been murdered by Giric, the new Regent.

The guard did not meet her gaze. 'We serve at the Regent Giric's pleasure, my lady, not anyone else's. Recent intelligence indicates the culprit might be returning.'

Ceanna and Sandulf exchanged glances. 'Recent intelligence? How recent?'

The guard's gaze narrowed. 'I'm not sure I should be saying such things to strangers, particularly not Northmen.'

'I'm from Dun Ollaigh,' Ceanna said. 'And Mother Abbe will be pleased to see me. I am her niece, Lady Ceanna.'

'I have no idea who you are, my lady, but you can speak Pictish as if you were born to the language.'

'Because I was. In Dun Ollaigh, on the coast.'

Sandulf held out his hands. 'King Aed died before I ever entered this country.'

The guard appeared to consider both statements. 'I'll take you to the monastery. That way neither of you can get into mischief.'

'I can assure you that neither of us plan any sort of trouble,' Ceanna said firmly.

'For Mother Abbe's sake, I hope you are who you say you are.' He glanced down at Vanora. 'Mother Abbe is not overly fond of dogs, but then I suspect you know that, being her niece and all.'

Sandulf merely raised a brow at the guard's tone. Vanora slunk next to Sandulf and gave a low growl. Ceanna concentrated on the cobblestones and tried to keep her temper in check.

The last time her aunt had encountered Vanora, it had not gone well. Perhaps she'd been optimistic in bringing her dog with her, but there was no way she would have left her behind.

'If my aunt objects to Vanora, will you…?' she said in a low voice to Sandulf.

'Stop borrowing trouble,' he replied. 'All will be well. I have promised to see you to safety and I will.'

'To Nrurim, that is what we agreed.' She hated that her voice caught on the final word.

'Until you reached safety is what I agreed.'

'Am I not safe here?'

'We shall see, my lady. We shall see.'

When they arrived at the bustling monastery, a young friar hurried towards them. 'Lady Ceanna? Is that you? You probably don't remember me—Brother Malcolm? I had the honour of giving you a tour of the scriptorium the last time you were here. We've been so worried.'

Ceanna froze. Why should they be worried about her? 'Were you expecting me?'

Brother Malcolm drew himself up like a startled hen. 'A message reached us two days ago that you'd been kidnapped. Your aunt feared you'd become one of the disappeared, taken by raiders from the North because of your headstrong behaviour.'

Ceanna ignored Sandulf's swift exclamation. After they had escaped Urist and the false ambush, Sandulf had predicted something like this. Her easy assurance that her stepmother would never dare contact her aunt because she would oppose the proposed marriage tasted like ash in her mouth.

'The messenger was mistaken.' Ceanna tried for a reassuring laugh. Behind the friar, various nuns stopped tilling the soil and stared open-mouthed at her. When she looked back, they rapidly dropped their gaze and started labouring with great intensity. The austerity about this place pressed down on her soul. But it was just nerves. This place was home now, not Dun Olliagh. But already her soul longed for the sound of the sea and the wind which pervaded every part of Dun Ollaigh, the way the sunlight danced on the waves of the harbour in the early morning and the coolness of the stones against her feet— things she'd never encounter again. 'Very much mistaken.'

'Was he?' Brother Malcolm queried.

'You can see I'm perfectly well. Ever since I left Dun Ollaigh, I've been travelling towards here of my own free will. I haven't taken a detour or escaped from some botched kidnapping. And my reason for travel remains serious.'

Brother Malcolm tugged at the neck of his robe. 'And your companion? He looks fierce with that dog of his.'

'The dog is mine.'

'Mother Abbe is not fond of strange dogs, but I suppose since it is yours… I take it your visit will not be long in light of these rumours?' Brother Malcolm held his robes away from Vanora's inquisitive nose.

Ceanna pressed her lips together. Her aunt's dog smelt and tended to be sick on the rushes after her aunt fed it too many sweetmeats from the table. Blurting out her new vocation to Brother Malcolm would not be a good idea. She would wait until she saw her aunt.

Brother Malcolm lowered his voice. 'Has your companion come to raid or to pray?'

'He's hardly a raider! Why would he bring me here and protect me, if he intended kidnapping me and selling me across the seas?'

Brother Malcolm tucked his hands into the sleeves of his robe. 'Tales can get tangled in the telling. That much is true. You're here now. Praise all the angels and saints in heaven.'

'Lady Ceanna intends to stay,' Sandulf said.

'You are going to remain here!'

Ceanna glared at Sandulf. 'I wish to discuss this with my aunt first. Her views are paramount.'

'Mother Abbe. Good idea.' Brother Malcolm started to scurry away. 'I see. I wasn't told about that. I thought you would return to your home immediately, to the safety of your family, if you actually arrived here.'

Return. Ceanna's heart sank. Someone had indeed been here, sowing the seeds of her destruction. Immediately the difficulty of her task increased. What was worse, this place held little appeal. She kept thinking about the reasons why she had detested it the last time she had visited.

'Allow me to see my aunt,' Ceanna called after him. 'She will want to see my miraculous arrival for herself. See that her prayers were answered.'

The friar's shoulders twitched. 'You had best wait in the guests' antechamber. It would be more seemly.' He looked Sandulf up and down. 'You and your companion do understand that singular honour?'

She knew if she caught Sandulf's eye, she'd dissolve into highly inappropriate laughter or, worse, frustrated screaming. She covered her mouth and regained control of her emotions before she threw away any lingering chance of being a holy maid. 'Of course, Brother, of course we do.'

'A heathen here, at St Fillans,' Brother Malcolm muttered. 'I know it was foretold, but will wonders never cease. I never believed Brother Mattios's predictions before, but I must now. I shall let him know when he returns. I've become a true believer.'

'Well?' Sandulf asked. 'Will you do as Lady Ceanna requests or will you explain to her aunt why you have prolonged her agony, instead blathering on about predictions from a missing monk?'

The colour drained from Brother Malcolm's face. 'I didn't realise men from the North could speak our language so well. And the Mother Abbess's great confidant, Brother Matthios, is far above the average monk. He is a learned man from St Benedict Biscop's Abbey in Jarrow where St Bede wrote his famous histories.'

'It's amazing what people, even if they are heathen, can learn, isn't it?' Sandulf retorted in perfect Pictish.

'Wait in there, both of you…and that creature.' Brother Malcolm ushered them into a small antechamber and left them. Ceanna heard the lock turning. Vanora immediately settled, putting her head on her paws.

Ceanna knelt beside her and whispered that everything would all right, that she would refuse to give her up. Vanora peaked at her with one eye.

'What is troubling you, Ceanna?' Sandulf asked in a low voice.

'He locked us in.'

'We were not planning on leaving.'

'Someone reached here before us.' Ceanna put her hand on Vanora's neck. 'They were sent, in case I made it here alive. And if not, the story would be that I acted in a headstrong manner and brought ruin on myself. I was not supposed to make it here. I was supposed to become one of the disappeared, vanishing into the mists, never to be seen again.'

Sandulf pursed his lips. 'It looks that way.'

'You don't seem surprised.'

'I saw what happened to Urist's group. I suspected they might take precautions. Urist might even have said that you were taken by a Northman.'

Her mouth dropped open. Sandulf had anticipated this, that someone would arrive before them. 'But you didn't think to warn me? We could have found a way to travel faster. Walked at night. Found horses. Something.'

'Would it have made a difference if I had? You were determined to come here, to be a holy maid. No other alternative, you said.' He gave a half-smile. 'Where would we have found ponies? Other than Mother Mildreth, we barely saw a soul. Your stepmother likely dispatched someone as soon as she realised you were missing—before the ambush.'

Ceanna balled her fists. She had been certain her stepmother would not dare admit her scheme to the abbess of marrying Ceanna off to Feradach. It had been an arrogant assumption. Of course her aunt's abbey was the most logical place for her to run to. She needed to come up with a plan quickly, something to convince her aunt that she should stay here. She paced the room. Would explaining about her profound vision at prayer be enough?

Vanora shook her head at Ceanna's agitation and pointedly went to sit beside Sandulf. She settled with a long-suffering sigh, as if she knew the last place Ceanna wanted to be was here.

'Goodness knows what tale they have told my aunt, then. Probably that I might arrive here with some wild story about my stepmother. They are very manipulative, my stepmother and her lover.'

'You've said.'

'You do believe me. I'm not given to fantasy or headstrong behaviour as Brother Malcolm implied.'

'I saw what happened to Urist and his friends. I've come to know you, Lady Ceanna. You don't run to flights of imagination. The opposite, in fact. You possess a purely practical frame of mind.'

'Practical and pragmatic. Good for being a nun.'

Sandulf stroked Vanora's ears. The dog leant into him. 'Something like that. I've little experience with nuns. They spend much time on their knees in prayer and I'm uncertain if that actually helps.'

'Good for the soul.' Her laugh sounded strangled to her ears. Her stomach knotted. Being here reminded her of all the reasons why she had initially considered becoming a nun would not suit her. But it had been a choice between living under her aunt's thumb and death. She froze. What if there was another way?

She regarded Sandulf. They were friends. Might he help if she asked? She'd only get one chance to ask.

'What do you anticipate will happen next? Will your aunt take you in?'

'I leave foretelling the future to others, but I know going back home will mean my death. As I said, I heard them plotting.'

'Will your aunt believe you?'

Ceanna stopped mid-stride. Her aunt's devotion to the need to secure Dun Ollaigh's future was only second to her devotion to the church. If she considered Ceanna's vocation was less than sincere, or didn't believe her tale about the plot to end her life, then she might put it down to a case of pre-wedding nerves. Her aunt had not favoured her as a child after Ceanna had once asked her when her wings were going to sprout. She remembered hearing about girls her aunt had sent back to their parents after branding them unsuited to the contemplative life.

'I once overheard—' She stopped and glared at him as he sought to hide a smile. 'What is amusing you? Please share the joke.'

'You do seem to overhear a lot.' He shrugged. 'That is all. It reminds me of when I was young. My cousin always seemed to be the one overhearing things. He constantly raced around to tell everyone, but the trouble was he kept telling the wrong people. None of us ever cared for him. Me in particular as our mothers kept trying to make us play together and I wanted to be with my brothers.'

'I never had a cousin. And my father kept me away from my aunt after my mother and younger brother died in the flood. She looked far too much like my mother for his grief. She and my father rarely agreed, but she respected my mother's right to marry whom she chose.'

'What does your mother have to do with it?'

'In the absence of a son, under Pictish law, the inheritance goes to the eldest daughter. My grandfather did not have any sons. My aunt wanted the church after her husband died, so my mother had to marry.'

'Does your father have any sons?'

'My brother died with my mother. With my father's current state of health, I fear it is beyond him to get any more children.'

'You'll have to marry if you wish to keep your lands safe from raiders. Your stepmother was right about that.'

Ceanna hugged her arms about her waist. The people at this monastery, they couldn't lift swords or fight. Back in her great-great-grandfather's day, the monks of Iona were trained in war, but not the ones at St Fillans. 'Once my father goes, I'll be dead within the week.'

'How ill is your father?'

'My father was very healthy until my stepmother's lover arrived. Then the wound he received when he fought off raiders fifteen months ago refused to heal. In recent weeks, he grows worse, despite my stepmother's devoted attention. He barely recognised me when I whispered goodbye.' She banged her fists together rather than giving in to tears over her father and how she might never see him again. Her heart grieved for the man he'd been before her mother and brother died. 'I won't be sacrificed on the altar of my stepmother's ambition.'

Sandulf raised his brow and Ceanna belatedly realised that she'd been shouting. She continued in a calmer voice. 'I hoped to persuade my aunt to accept me as a young woman who knows her own mind, someone who truly does wish to take the veil instead of a silly girl who ran away from an important strategic alliance.'

'You fear your aunt will see through the ruse immediately.'

The weight on Ceanna's chest lifted. 'I don't fear marriage in the abstract, Sandulf, but I do fear losing my life.'

'You remain under my protection until you reach a safe haven.'

'Why, my gallant warrior, are you making an offer of marriage?' she teased with a strangled laugh, hating how her heart leapt. They were friends, not lovers. He'd made that perfectly clear.

His eyes slid away from her. 'It won't come to that.'

'No, it won't.' Ceanna's heart sank. He had a life elsewhere, a family, dreams, ambitions, to which he would return after he completed this quest to find his sister-in-law's murderer. He'd been her companion for the journey, not the hero who was going to save her future. 'I'll manage, Sandulf. I'll find a way.'

He put his hand on her arm. Warmth radiated through her. She turned to move away, but tumbled into his gaze instead. 'What do you need me to do?'

She wet her parched lips. What she needed was his touch. 'My desires are not important; only my life. This place must be more congenial than it appears to my nervous eyes.'

He raised a brow. 'The friar seemed less than keen about Vanora.'

At the sound of her name, Vanora thumped her tail. It sounded like a drum in the all-pervading quiet of the room.

'My aunt will find a place for her once she understands how useful Vanora is.'

He shrugged. 'You're the one who knows her. I have some misgivings, but I'm willing to be wrong.'

Something was clearly going on and she was beginning to doubt whether fleeing to her aunt had been a good idea after all. Could she beg him to take her away from here? Where could she go? But instead all she said was, 'My aunt will do what is right. She is a stickler for order and tradition.'

'And here I was, thinking you delight in creating chaos. How will you get on here?'

'That is unfair. What chaos have I created?'

'You've turned my life upside down.'

'Normally I'm very restrained and orderly. Ask anyone.' His answering smile warmed her to her toes. 'But I stand a far better chance of seeing my next birthday here than I would at Dun Ollaigh. Being alive means that some day I might have the chance to fight back against my stepmother's machinations.'

'Do you want to spend your life in this place where you will be under the control of your aunt, where you will be on your knees day and night, no freedom to come and go as you please?'

'Every corner of this abbey hums like a beehive,' Ceanna said to his chest. She knew it wasn't an answer, but bringing herself to voice her sudden disquiet was beyond her. Out in the garth she had seen a handful of women toiling in the soil and being chastised for speaking and it made her blood run cold. She knew, despite her earlier bravado, being a nun was the last thing she wanted. 'Even if it is an awfully silent hive.' She sighed, but turned abruptly when the door was suddenly thrust open.

'What is going on here? Ceanna, why are you here,

instead of at Dun Ollaigh where you are supposed to be?' her aunt's voice thundered from the doorway. 'The marriage alliance between you and Feradach is of the upmost importance to this family's continued prosperity, according to your lady stepmother.'

Chapter Nine

At the sound of her aunt's voice, Ceanna jumped away from Sandulf. Her cheeks burned as if she had been standing in front of a hot cooking fire. Ceanna rapidly straightened the folds of her gown and tried to concentrate. Her aunt's words confirmed her worst fears. She had failed.

Sandulf gave her an unrepentant look before he stepped away.

'Aunt.' Ceanna stuffed the nerves back down her throat and held out her arms. 'How I've longed to see you. Come, do not be stand-offish. Let us hug. I've travelled a long way to see you.'

'Niece, it is really you.' Her aunt awkwardly caught her to her bosom. Her aunt smelt of wildflowers and incense, but it wasn't a comforting scent, more overpowering and cloying. 'I feared for you, child. What were you thinking, coming all this way? You should have sent word that you wished my counsel instead of making the journey on your own.'

'I needed to see you, Aunt. I wanted to explain in person…why I've taken this course.' The words that she wanted to become a holy maid stuck in her throat. She might have practised the speech many times in her head, but saying the words aloud was impossible. Lying to her aunt was wrong. And in this holy place, too! If she could see any other future, she'd take it, particularly after witnessing the silence the sisters were forced to endure. 'I wanted your advice on my future.'

Her aunt released her and stepped away. Her face became remote and fearsome. Ceanna sighed inwardly. She'd conveniently forgotten what her aunt could be like—it was her way or no way, her mother used to say.

'I do hope you're not going to be tiresome, Ceanna. You know I'll advocate you doing your duty. Always. Prayerful contemplation—something which you've been singularly lacking in—always grants me my solutions.'

Ceanna crossed her arms. 'My duty as I see it, or what my stepmother thinks is my duty?'

Her aunt's thin lips turned up. 'Your father has your best interests at heart, Niece, even if his ways can seem brusque. Your stepmother is devoted to me. She would never counsel anything I'd disapprove of.'

It was worse than Ceanna had imagined. Her aunt had already made up her mind. She was going to return Ceanna to Dun Ollaigh without listening to Ceanna's side. But she couldn't give up so easily, not when her life was at stake. Ceanna cleared her throat and began again.

'With respect, Aunt, my father is dangerously ill. Or weren't you aware that he can barely string a coherent sentence together? His frame shakes when he coughs. His brow burns with fever?'

'Your stepmother keeps me informed with regular messages. If there was a real problem, she'd send for one of my priests. This monastery has an excellent reputation for healing the sick.'

'My stepmother has changed greatly in the past fifteen months. Feradach, my father's new captain of the guards, has rapidly wormed his way into her confidence. Why are you willing to believe her messages over your own flesh and blood who has faced danger to speak with you and plead for her life?'

'You're being tiresome, Ceanna. Again.'

'I doubt Lady Ceanna is ever tiresome.' A muscle in Sandulf's jaw jumped. 'Please listen to what she says. She speaks the truth. I'm a witness to the destruction.'

'Indeed.' Her aunt's gaze flickered over Sandulf and widened when she saw Vanora, who gave a small growl in the back of her throat.

She raised her brow and Sandulf gave an unrepentant shrug while Vanora settled back down at his feet.

'I can fight my own battles, Sandulf.' She turned back to her aunt, took a breath and started again. 'Aunt—'

Her aunt held up her hand. 'Spare me the pretty speeches. Why are you here, Ceanna? You don't have a devotional bone in your body. I remember the time when you were six and refused to be quiet during mass.'

Ceanna clenched her fists. 'I've no desire to marry Feradach because he will be terrible for Dun Ollaigh. He seeks power for himself and will destroy everything we hold dear. He has burnt farms and demands far too much tribute. My father will listen to your counsel when you tell him this marriage is against the best interests of all concerned.'

Her aunt's brows drew together. 'Feradach has an excellent reputation, which is why I recommended him for the post of captain of the guards. His younger brother,

Brother Mattios, has proved to be a most able asset to our little community.'

'With the greatest respect, Aunt, he is not the sort of man—'

'I hope you're not starting to take after your mother, Ceanna. Very frivolous and flighty in her youth, she was also stupidly stubborn. Once she had acquired a notion, it remained stuck in her head.'

'Frivolous and flighty are two words which have never been applied to Lady Ceanna,' Sandulf remarked. Vanora gave an approving bark. 'Without her steadfastness, we would have perished on our journey. Your niece is to be commended, Mother Abbe, rather than berated.'

Her aunt's frown increased. 'Be that as it may, I know your father has your best interests at heart.'

'He may do, but I doubt my stepmother does.'

Her aunt gave a disapproving sniff. 'You're his only living child. You must consider what is best for Dun Ollaigh. I can be of little assistance in this matter. I'd hoped you had grown out of your wilful ways after your mother died, but I can see you have retained some aspects of her stubbornness.'

'My mother was your sister. You and I are blood. My stepmother wants to take control of Dun Ollaigh along with her lover, Feradach. She seeks to deceive you.'

'What is it with women and their stepmothers? You are far from the first person to come to me with this problem, bleating complaints about the woman their father married.'

Ceanna slammed her fists together. Vanora hid her nose under her paws. 'Please listen to me, Aunt. My stepmother wishes me dead so that she can rule Dun Ollaigh.'

'That does not sound like Mhairi at all. She was always a pliable creature, keen to please, the perfect sort of wife for your father, in my view and Brother Mattios's.'

'The guide I was supposed to use to come here was attacked and left for dead and a woman dressed in my travelling cloak was stabbed.' Ceanna ticked the points off on her fingers. 'Someone sent you a false rumour that I'd been kidnapped by a Northman. If such a thing had happened to me, would I be here, in the company of a Northman? I suspect that I'd be bundled away on the North Sea, bound for Éireann or even further west to that new colony of Iceland.'

Her aunt's mouth snapped open and shut several times. 'There'll be a logical explanation for the message. The most likely one for your disappearance was a raid. You know the troubles we've suffered since the Heathen Horde appeared on these shores.' She cleared her throat. 'Whatever the cause, I'm pleased you've turned up safe from your little adventure. Mhairi will also be pleased to learn the good news. It is well your father's messengers chose to remain at St Fillans for another day.'

Ceanna stared at the floor. Unless she did something very quickly, she would be unceremoniously shipped back to Dun Ollaigh and would not emerge alive. Her aunt was clearly predisposed to believe her stepmother over her. Why had she not thought more carefully about the connection before? But then, where would she have gone? There was nowhere else. She glanced towards Sandulf, solid and real by her side. 'I wish to marry another, Aunt. My lady stepmother would not approve because she wished me to marry her lover. It is really that simple.'

She was clutching at straws when she needed to be weaving a complete tale, but it was the best she could do. She willed Sandulf to remain silent and not to point out the obvious flaws in her story.

'Another?' Her aunt's eyes widened. 'Is this man suitable? I can't see your father refusing permission if the man was suitable, Ceanna. I know how he has longed to have you settled. Until the proposed alliance with Feradach, marriage proposals were lacking, I was led to believe. I blame the freedom he gave you.'

'Why else would I want to marry him unless he was suitable in ways Feradach can never be? I am hardly devoid of common sense, whatever tales my stepmother has spun.' Ceanna held out her hands. Her stomach trembled. She would keep as close to the truth as possible and hope that she could avoid mentioning Sandulf by name before she had had a chance to speak with him and offer a proposition. Inheriting Dun Ollaigh through his wife, becoming its lord, had to be worth something. 'My chosen husband will be better for Dun Ollaigh than Feradach ever could be.'

'And you know what is best for Dun Ollaigh, do you?'

'Listen to me, Aunt, I beg of you. I will explain everything Feradach has done.' Ceanna rapidly told her aunt about all the evil doings she had uncovered in recent weeks—from selling off wheat and livestock and then claiming they were stolen to demanding time with young maids, and all the ways the people were suffering.

When she came to the end of her list, she went down on her knees. She had to hope her aunt believed her and agreed that Feradach was completely unsuitable.

If her aunt took her side, then the other potentially larger problem of finding a suitable bridegroom quickly loomed. She glanced at Sandulf. He'd remained silent during her recital of the ills which had befallen Dun

Ollaigh and his face appeared carved from stone. Without knowing his precise thoughts, she could not declare an intention to marry him, even if she'd implied it. He was just as likely to denounce her and then she'd be in a worse position than ever.

Her aunt motioned for her to stand. 'And you travelled here to repeat all this…this tavern gossip?'

'No, Lady Ceanna travelled here so you could meet me and listen to my tale.' Sandulf held out his hand. 'Sandulf Sigurdsson at your service, Mother Abbe.'

Her aunt sat down on the stool with a bump. 'You wish to marry this man! I know nothing about him except he is obviously a heathen raider and therefore our enemy.'

Ceanna stared at Sandulf. At her look, he gave a small nod. It was impossible to tell what he meant precisely. She slowly rose and tried to keep her excitement from mounting. He understood what she was doing and why. 'Do you think it is wrong I should seek my aunt's blessing in what I wish to do with my future?'

'Why has your stepmother not mentioned him before? What does your father think of him? What *is* wrong with him?'

'Why would she mention him if she wishes me to marry Feradach?'

Her aunt's gaze narrowed. 'He appears to be one of those heathen Northerners. I refuse to believe you have brought a heathen such as this one to a place like this. Or that you are seriously contemplating joining with him.'

'I'd far rather join with him, as you put it, Aunt, than with Feradach who churns my gut.'

A flash of hurt shone in Sandulf's eyes but was quickly masked. 'You've such a way with words,' he said in a low voice. 'I've important reasons for being here or I'd leave you to your fate.'

Ceanna clapped her hand against her mouth. 'I beg your pardon, that came out wrong.'

Sandulf gave a brief nod to show he understood.

Her aunt coughed pointedly. 'Anything else before I call your father's guards? You're the same as you always were, Ceanna—given to daydreams and imaginings. I can't believe I was persuaded to think otherwise through stories of your good behaviour.'

Ceanna shuddered. This was going far worse than she'd imagined. Sandulf was about to walk out on her and she was going to be sent unceremoniously back to Dun Ollaigh, to her wedding and her death. The least she could do was to find Sandulf's quarry—the man who had killed his sister-in-law and whom he believed had taken refuge in these walls. She drew a deep breath. 'Aunt, your walls harbour a ruthless killer.'

'Who told you that?' The abbess jerked her head towards Sandulf. 'That one?'

'It is why he has travelled here—to warn you. It is how we encountered each other originally.'

'You come here with one tale, Ceanna, about marriage and your stepmother, and now you wish to spin another.' Her aunt lifted her hands towards the ceiling.

'Lady Ceanna speaks the truth,' Sandulf said. 'If you will listen, I can explain. I have proof.'

Her aunt gave one of her snorts which always reminded Ceanna of a disgruntled cow.

'Aunt, listen, please. The entire monastery might be in danger if someone has hidden his past in this fashion.'

'What are you talking about, my dear? What do the past lives of my flock matter? That is something between them and the confessional. They are all honest hard-working people now. I will not have you impugning their character on the say-so of a Northman.'

Ceanna's heart sank. She had made a mess of it. 'The truth,' she whispered. 'About this.'

Sandulf reached into his pouch and withdrew a sheet of vellum. 'My brother's wife had the priest write down a list of the crimes as she suspected you would not believe a Northman. She is willing to vouch that my tale is true.'

Her aunt briefly glanced at the sheet of vellum before tucking it into her sleeve. 'I recognise the seal. We have had dealings in the past, a long time ago. I will make enquiries in due course. If such a person is here, then he should be given the opportunity to explain.'

A muscle in Sandulf's jaw twitched and Ceanna knew he was close to erupting.

'I would suggest you do that straight away, Aunt.'

'I wish to finalise plans for your impending nuptials. I won't be distracted with tales of a murderer.'

'I will speak of nothing until you investigate this man's claim.'

Ceanna's gaze warred with her aunt's. Her aunt was the first to look away.

'Very well, I will have my scribe look through the rolls to see if someone named...'

'Lugh, son of Aidan.' Sandulf gestured with his hand. 'It is all on the vellum. I'm given to understand that he is here and has been here for at least eighteen months.'

Her aunt retrieved the vellum and looked at it more closely. 'I will see what can be done as it is Annis of Glannoventa who asks. It won't take very long, but I must assure you that I know of no man with that name here. If he is indeed as evil as this document suggests, then he must answer for his crimes.'

'Sandulf Sigurdsson will be willing to wait until you have made your enquiries.'

'We will speak further about your future, Ceanna.' Her aunt nodded and left the room.

'I wanted to do things differently,' Sandulf said in a low voice. 'Your aunt has taken against you.'

Ceanna raised a brow. 'My aunt wouldn't listen to a Northman. You saw. She barely glanced at the piece of vellum you shoved under her nose. Something is wrong here, something I can't quite put my finger on.'

'Do you think she will actually check the rolls?'

'My aunt is a stickler for correctness. If she says she will do a thing, she does it.'

'But...'

'Men from the North burned down this monastery six years ago. They tried again last summer.'

'I've never done anything against this place and I've every intention of saving them from harm. Lugh is a ruthless killer, Ceanna. I've seen his work.'

There was something in his voice which made her pause. 'Are you keeping something from me?'

His gaze slid away from hers. 'I guessed they'd be waiting for you. This is the worst place you could have gone to. I should have said something days ago. Given you the choice.'

Ceanna examined the rushes. 'I had to try and I wouldn't have listened to you anyway. I miscalculated my stepmother's closeness to my aunt.'

'Your aunt won't allow you to become a nun. She won't believe you are a holy maid. You allowed her to think you and I wish to marry.'

'I needed some time. I will explain that she made an error in her assumptions. I will find a way to resist being returned to Dun Ollaigh. If I don't, I'm sure I will not see next spring.'

'Marry me.'

The words hung in the air. Ceanna was certain she'd misheard. He was asking her to marry him! Not because he had any feelings for her, but because he thought the alternative would be her death. If he'd truly wanted to marry her, why had he waited until she had no hope left?

'Marry you? Is this a serious offer?'

'I can take a heavy hint.' His voice deepened to a husky note. 'I will not allow you to be sacrificed for your aunt's ambition or your stepmother's inclination. I saw what happened to Urist's caravan. Someone is searching for you, Ceanna. I gave you my word that I would protect you until you reach safety and I will. We both know you are not safe here. Marriage to me will protect you.'

She ran her tongue over her lips and tried to blot out the horrible image of the mutilated corpse. Sandulf was right. Someone had tried to kill her and they would try again. That someone could be related to the assassin he hunted, a little voice reminded her. 'You want to marry me to offer me protection? What do you get out of it?'

'This.' He leant forward and brushed her mouth with his. She moaned slightly in the back of her throat and he deepened the kiss. Her hands went about his neck and she clung on, drinking in his mouth, revelling in the way his tongue moved against hers. Standing like this, she could almost believe that he actually wanted her rather than that he had been forced into it.

He lifted his mouth from hers. 'Will you?'

Ceanna ran her tongue over her aching lips. Her mind

focused on the bow shape of his mouth. The many reasons why she should refuse circled her brain. He had not really answered her question about what he hoped to gain from marrying her. There was no guarantee that she could ever reclaim Dun Ollaigh after her father died. 'I... I...'

'What is going on here?'

Ceanna started to move away, but Sandulf's arm twined about her waist and hauled her against him. Her body hit his hard planes with a thud.

Behind her aunt, she recognised several of her father's guard. Men who had supposedly been going on an expedition several days before the wedding. Sandulf was right—someone had betrayed her...or perhaps they had just anticipated her escape attempt. She should have known that it had been far too easy.

'Lady Ceanna and I intend to marry today,' Sandulf said in a commanding voice when a faint strangled squeak emerged from Ceanna's throat. 'Her wish. My desire. My only question for you is—do we marry with the blessing of her church or do we marry in the fashion of my people?'

'What say you, Ceanna?' her aunt asked pointedly. 'I thought this man was a stranger you picked up on the road. That this foolishness about marrying him was a ruse to compel me to keep you here as one of my flock. What evidence do you have of his ability to defend Dun Ollaigh in its time of need? Can he even use a sword?'

Her aunt made it sound as though Sandulf was akin to the dirt under her shoe.

Ceanna leant against Sandulf and drew strength. As far as marriage proposals went, it had not been softened by fine words and noble sentiments. He was doing this to protect her and because her tongue had forced this on him, not because he had any depth of feeling for her and she had no idea about his plans or prospects. But she could either take a chance on him or return to certain death at her stepmother's hands, and that was no choice at all. Her girlish dreams of a hero who worshipped the ground she walked on and saved Dun Ollaigh from all its enemies were never going to happen.

She moved out of the protective circle of his arms.

'I intend to marry the man I've chosen, Aunt. You can either help me or our family will lose control of Dun Ollaigh. You haven't visited the estate in some time and are relying on a person who has every reason to lie to you. Dun Ollaigh has been in our family for many generations. Why do you wish to surrender it?'

Her aunt's face contorted. 'You know I will always do everything in my power to ensure that Dun Ollaigh remains in our family. It must. You will do as your stepmother commands.'

'My stepmother is not blood kin. She seeks to manipulate for her own ends. Why were you not invited to the wedding ceremony? Could it be because my stepmother wished to keep the news from you until it was too late?'

Her aunt was silent for a long moment. 'She is married to your father and owes him her loyalty.'

'Yes, she does. But he does not have it. Trust my judgement. Allow me to marry Sandulf Sigurdsson today in your church with your blessing.'

Her aunt sighed. 'You look exactly like my dear sister with that determined thrust of your jaw. I could never refuse her anything. Too headstrong for your own good, the pair of you.'

Ceanna threw her arms about her aunt. 'Thank you.'

Her aunt gave her an awkward hug back before putting Ceanna away from her. Her lip curled. 'But I warn you, child, do not come crying to me, begging for a place in my monastery, when this man abandons you.'

A muscle twitched in Sandulf's cheek. 'I have no intention of doing such a thing.'

Her aunt cleared her throat. 'I give my reluctant blessing to this match, Ceanna. Now, may I speak to you alone?'

'After we are married,' Sandulf said, eyeing the guards. 'Until then, Ceanna remains at my side. I won't have her spirited away.'

'You distrust me.'

Sandulf shrugged. 'I have heard of such things happening.'

Her aunt turned a faint crimson colour. Ceanna wondered when anyone had last successfully defied her. Her late mother, most likely.

'I agree with Sandulf's caution, Aunt. I will not be returning to Dun Ollaigh to do my stepmother's bidding. I will be getting married. Today.'

Her aunt's mouth became a thin white line. 'Very well.' She snapped her fingers. 'Get me the priest. Get it done. Then we speak, Ceanna, and you will see what I was trying to say about Northmen and their ways. I hope you know what you are doing.'

Chapter Ten

The church at St Fillans had a distinct and forbidding chill to it, reminding Sandulf why he actively tried to avoid such places. He had first gone to one when he arrived in Constantinople and had not enjoyed the experience, but the man he'd been guarding at the time had insisted. Its lingering smell of incense and stale air reminded him of death and the many failings that had dogged him in his life and for which he felt great responsibility.

Going to church never became any easier, but he was willing to endure this for his Skadi and that very fact unnerved him. Lady Ceanna had become important to him in a way that he hadn't anticipated. Somewhere between Dun Ollaigh and here he had begun to think of her as his and he wasn't prepared to see her suffer.

The marriage would offer her immediate protection from the threat of being forcibly returned, married to her stepmother's lover and then murdered in her sleep. He refused to allow her to be dragged back to her old life. He knew the fate which waited if she should ever seek to return to Dun Ollaigh. And the future?

He'd given up trying to see the future.

Sandulf forced his words to be calm and measured in answer to the priest. The man raised a brow at discovering Sandulf could speak a rudimentary Latin. Sandulf did not bother to enlighten him about his time in the east. It simply amused him that he could confound expectations.

Married. A state he'd never looked for since the massacre, and to Ceanna, the woman he counted as a friend. He wanted to shout that she deserved better, that she deserved someone who could truly protect her instead of him—the man who had frozen when the need arose.

As he mouthed the words, he knew he had not told her the full truth—he had no right to such a woman as her. But he desired her with every fibre of his being.

'I will,' Ceanna said, finishing her vows.

She looked up at him with a luminous expectation and absolute sincerity. Every instinct told him to gather her into his arms. He forced his hands to remain at his sides.

A tiny frown puckered her brows and she started to turn away. Less than a heartbeat and he'd already disappointed her.

'I'm sorry,' he muttered, capturing her chin with his fingers and lowering his mouth.

The kiss was supposed to be a brush of his lips against hers, but one brief touch proved impossible. The desire to linger and sample the delight of her mouth nearly overwhelmed him. Too soon she'd look at him with eyes of disappointment and loathing. For what he had to do. For what he'd failed to do. And he hated that he wanted to be better than his father as a husband and very much feared that he would end up being worse.

How could he protect her from the assassin he was

pretty sure had been hired to kill to her when he didn't even know where he was? How could he rescue her people when he was committed to finding Lugh and demanding justice for an innocent woman?

For now, he drank in her mouth, welcomed her touch and tried to forget the future he must face.

'Sandulf Sigurdsson keeps secrets, you know. I can always tell,' Ceanna's aunt said to her when they were alone together after the brief marriage ceremony. She had lent them a bedchamber for the night and had insisted on preparing Ceanna for the marriage bed. 'He knew every word in the ceremony. An oddity for a heathen warrior, don't you think?'

'He did travel to Constantinople and served the emperor. He will have learned it there. I thought you'd be pleased that he was willing to go through a baptism as well.'

Her aunt shook herself like a disgruntled hen. 'Were you convinced of his sincerity? Only time will tell. He twists the truth about other matters, so why not in this, too?'

'It's impressive that you know his secrets within an afternoon of meeting him.' Ceanna forced her voice to be light.

'I know his type, Ceanna. Don't be impudent. And keep still. Your hair is in a terrible tangle. Unless you braid it carefully, you'll never be presentable.'

'Maybe I like it wild and free.'

'Allow me to do this for you, Ceanna. Your mother should have been the one. I can honour her in this way.'

Her aunt combed out Ceanna's hair until it shone and fell about her in a silken cloud. The tenderness with which her aunt did this surprised Ceanna. It was almost as if she cared.

Ceanna stared at the bed and tried not to think of the night which lay before her. It was entirely possible that Sandulf would treat her as he had always done—as a friend rather than a lover. She remembered the agreement they made about friendship the night they spent in the hayloft. 'Twists the truth about what? What other secrets has he kept hidden? What have you uncovered?'

'His reason for coming here. I fear a much darker purpose.' Her aunt put down the comb with a sigh. 'You are so like your dear departed mother. You will not listen to reason, but please know that should you ever require it, a place can be found for you here, despite what I said earlier. I'll look past your indiscretions provided you do proper penance. When Brother Mattios returns from his travels, he'll be able to advise me.'

Ceanna silently vowed that she'd starve first. Her aunt simply wanted to unnerve her. Ceanna remembered how her mother had often dissolved into tears after one of her aunt's more pointed barbs. She wondered how she'd forgotten that little fact, in her haste to find a refuge here. No, she hadn't really forgotten it; she'd just had nowhere else to go.

'You don't trust my judgement of him,' she said instead.

'No man by the name he gave resides at this place. Never has done. Why did your new husband want to come here so badly? Why does he lie? The obvious reason is that he seeks some holy treasure. It is what Brother Mattios predicted.' Her aunt coughed pointedly. 'There is still time to get the marriage annulled before the bedding. Think about it, child.'

Ceanna stilled. Someone had given Sandulf the wrong information. His coming here had all been a wild goose chase, most likely concocted by his new sister-in-law, this Annis of Glannoventa. She might have reasons why she had wanted to send Sandulf on a fruitless and time-consuming quest. Her heart sank. She'd had a half-formed plan of getting Sandulf to fight for Dun Ollaigh. Now, it would appear, his quest would have to continue in a different direction.

'No man by that name. Are you certain?'

'My scribes checked the rolls three times. The only man who could possibly even fit the description your husband gave is Brother Mattios, a man with an impeccable reputation and who is beyond reproach. You should have seen the scrolls he brought from the Jarrow monastery.'

'Perhaps this Lugh took a different name before he arrived.'

Her aunt frowned. 'So you prefer to believe your Northman's pretty words. Some day you will be wiser about men and their ways, my dear. I've had Brother Malcolm inform him about the lack of any evidence in the records. Your Northman may very well decide to leave before ever gracing your bed or seeing you. At least, that was what Brother Malcolm predicted.'

A hard knot formed in the base of Ceanna's stomach. Sandulf wouldn't abandon her, would he? 'Brother Malcolm doesn't know my husband.'

'It would be a blessing in many ways if it happened. An unconsummated marriage and a deserted bride…an annulment would be merely a formality.'

'If you are so against him, why did you allow us to marry?'

'I don't know, child. You looked at me like your mother used to and I found I couldn't refuse. But I thought you ought to know my disquiet despite your obvious enthralment with this man.'

Ceanna rolled her eyes. Enthralled. She had to hope that Sandulf hadn't noticed. And that he paid no attention to Brother Malcolm's helpful suggestion of abandoning her.

'Has anyone come here lately asking to join the order? Anyone whose motives were questionable, anyone who was refused?'

Her aunt started to shake her head when her assistant, who had been preparing the bed with fresh linens, gave a squeak. 'There was a man several weeks ago who was refused.'

'Out with it, Sister. What man?'

'Brother Mattios was speaking to him in the yard when you had that bad headache. He swore me to secrecy. He spoke of dire things happening if anyone knew. Could this be the man your new husband is looking for?'

Her aunt sighed. 'Sister, Brother Mattios would have told me if there was anyone untoward who came here while I was indisposed.'

The nun made a curtsy and mumbled that Mother Abbe must be right.

'Where is this Brother Mattios, Aunt? You've spoken of him several times. I should like to meet him, this man who would tell you if a stranger visited, who arrived about the time my husband was told this Lugh the assassin would have arrived.'

'He is away on some business for the monastery. Nothing for you to be concerned about.' She tapped the comb against her teeth. 'I had thought he was being overly cautious about something, but…he may have been right. Secrets can harm, my dear, and your new husband has far too many.'

Ceanna could scarcely contain her frustration. 'What was this Brother Mattios right about? You are the one keeping secrets, Aunt, not Sandulf.'

Her aunt cleared her throat. 'Brother Mattios predicted an assassin, a Northman, would come to harm some people I care about.'

'Whom do you fear he wishes to kill? You?'

'The royal children, the ones who have been here since King Aed's murder,' the young nun burst out and then clapped her hands over her mouth.

'There are reasons why I enforce the rule of silence, Sister. You gave your oath on the relics.'

Ceanna examined the rushes. Her aunt was also keeping her share of secrets. She was hiding the late King's sons here in the monastery! She should have seen it before—the increased guards and her aunt's reluctance to speak. 'You're the one responsible for keeping the missing sons of Aed hidden.'

'How could I refuse a dying kinsman's wish?'

'Where are the sons of Aed now? With this paragon of virtue who fears an assassin from the North?'

'Under Brother Mattios's care. In a place of safety. Where they should have gone in the first place, had I not listened to Giric, the Regent. He wanted them to take the tonsure in due course—a noble ambition. And I thought why not here? It would bring honour to this house. Brother Mattios agreed with me, but then…'

Ceanna went cold. Taking the tonsure would ensure neither boy could make a claim for the kingdom. There was more to this than her aunt wanted to say. 'He has taken them to my stepmother and his brother Feradach, hasn't he? It is not just Dun Ollaigh they desire. They're going to use them as counters to gain control of the entire kingdom.'

'You do like to spin your fantasies, Ceanna,' her aunt said, but Ceanna did not miss the troubled look crossing her brow.

Her aunt then deftly turned the subject towards what Ceanna might expect during the wedding night, which was a marked change from her earlier attempts to persuade Ceanna to put aside her husband of only a few hours. What was going on?

'Lie back and allow the man to have his way. It is the most practical advice I have heard on the subject,' she said, reaching the end of her recital. 'It worked with my late husband, not that he lasted long. He caught a chill and died a month after our marriage.'

Ceanna forced a smile. There was little point in explaining that she had already had this lecture from her stepmother. Her aunt had made the process sound even less appealing than her stepmother had. Ceanna put her hand on her stomach and thought about the way Sandulf made her feel. His touch was very different from Feradach's.

The noise grew from the corridor. 'Your bridegroom arrives. Brother Malcom's news obviously has not sent him on his way. I can't say I don't wish he had left in pursuit of this phantom assassin. But if you change your mind, cry out. I shall check the sheet in the morning.' Her aunt and the young nun swept from the room.

Sandulf entered with Vanora at his side. The dog quickly settled in a corner and closed her eyes.

'I felt it best if she remained with us.'

Ceanna kept her back straight and tried not to look at the bed or think about what needed to pass between them. The rush lamps her aunt had left gave off a weak flickering light, causing strange shadows to dance on the rough plastered walls. 'You did right. Vanora frets if she is outside at night. She won't move a muscle now until morning.'

A warmth started in her loins, driving all thoughts about politics and the mysterious Brother Mattios from her mind. Ceanna pressed her hands against her eyes and tried to look anywhere but at him, except inevitably her gaze went back to his broad shoulders and how his chest tapered down to a trim waist.

She had little idea of his expectations about this sudden marriage. She had to hope that he had not done this out of pity. She had to do something to make her marriage more than simply one of convenience.

She wasn't a prospective holy maid any longer, nor the prospective heiress to a large fortress to be married off at her stepmother's whim, she had become someone else. She had become a wife, Sandulf's possession, someone she hoped Sandulf would see as indispensable to his quest. She tightened her jaw. She could do it—she could become that woman. He had saved her from being murdered at Feradach's hands after their wedding, so she could find the assassin Sandulf sought and then surely he would have to see that they could have the sort of marriage she'd dreamed of. She could twist herself into becoming that person far easier than being a holy maid.

'You seem concerned about something,' he said, breaking the silence before she had worked out her scheme of how she was going to accomplish this. 'I take it you know about the failure to discover Lugh. Brother

Malcolm took delight in informing me about it. The fool seemed to think I would want to leave and annul the marriage. I refrained from hitting him, but I came close.'

Ceanna stifled a relieved laugh. 'I can well imagine.'

'Tomorrow I will decide on my next course. Tonight—' he laced his fingers through hers '—tonight is for other things. Has your aunt said something, anything, which alters things between you and me?'

'It is probably nothing.' Ceanna told him what she'd learnt about the sons of King Aed. She was aware that her voice was picking up speed, but she couldn't slow down. Her words came to an abrupt shuddering halt at his incredulous expression. 'You know what this means. What I must do.'

'Are you asking to go back to Dun Ollaigh? We married to keep you from that place. You return there and you will die. We both will. Shall we annul this marriage so that you can return? It would give your aunt no end of pleasure.'

Ceanna wrapped her arms about her middle. She had done it wrong already. He was disappointed with her and the marriage had not yet truly begun. She had to try harder or her aunt would inspect the sheet in the morning and discover that Ceanna remained a maid. But confessing this might mean he made love to her out of pity and she most definitely did not want that. She slowly shook her head. 'I want to be married to you. I choose that.'

He lifted her chin so that she looked into the shifting colours of his eyes. A woman could drown in those eyes. 'Good. Then let us stop seeking reasons why you should go back to Dun Ollaigh. We have other things to do that are more important right now.'

She licked her parched lips. 'Enlighten me.'

'I came in here with seduction on my mind.' He ran his hands down her arms. 'I told you once that we go at your pace, not mine. I want you to enjoy yourself. It increases my pleasure.'

'I thought we had agreed to be friends rather than lovers.' She retreated a step away from the enticing touch of his hand. The bed dug into the back of her legs. Her aunt's warnings about men and their ravenous appetites came back to her. While the older woman had been speaking, Ceanna had decided she wanted to be someone who enjoyed such things, rather than someone who lay there and endured.

'We're married now.' He crossed the room to her. He shed his tunic and stood in the flickering light from the rush lamps. 'I don't have to worry about ruining your chances of becoming a holy maid. Destroying your future. I want you to have a future, Ceanna. I want you to live. It is why I married you.'

'That's what stopped you before? At Mildreth's—'

He gathered a strand of hair. 'Your hair falls like a cloud about your face.'

'My aunt gave me a list of instructions about how to be a bride in our marriage bed. We are supposed to pray first, but I am not certain how effective that will be.' Her voice had become less than a reed singing in the wind. She swallowed hard and tried again. 'I don't know what to do so you will have to show me.'

He cupped her face with his long fingers and lowered his mouth. 'Trust your instincts, Skadi, not your aunt.'

The use of her nickname calmed her. His lips met hers and she gave herself up to his kiss. Their tongues met, touched and tangled. The warmth in her belly ignited, infusing her.

He gently eased her back against the soft bedcoverings.

He ran a finger down the side of her face, sending tingles through her. 'Shall I blow the lamps out?' he asked.

Slowly she shook her head. 'I like looking at you.'

He gave a very husky laugh. 'I bear scars.'

She traced several of the silver scars on his chest. There was one particularly vicious one near his heart. Her hand ran over its almost unnatural silky smoothness. 'How?'

'Someone wanted me dead in Constantinople. I objected.'

'I am glad you did.' She ran her hands further down his chest, encountering his nipples which hardened to points under the pads of her fingers.

He caught her questing hands and held them above her head. His tongue nuzzled circles on her neck, making her writhe under him. A hard bulge pressed between her thighs. Her thin gown had become plastered against her body, leaving little to the imagination.

'Tell me you crave this.' He gently bit her earlobe and the heat surged between her thighs, making her slick. Her body arched upwards towards the bulge. 'Tell me that your dreams have been full of me, like mine have been full of you.'

'I… I…thought you were not interested,' she admitted.

The admission earned her a quick kiss and a laugh. 'You have much to learn about men, Skadi, particularly me. I've been hot for you since the day we met.' He tugged at her shift. 'May I? I've imagined you like this.'

She nodded, scarcely able to speak. His hands gently removed the garment so that her naked body was open to his gaze in the faltering light. She instinctively tried to hide her breasts with her hands, but he shook his head.

'There is no need to hide from me, Skadi. I have long wanted to feast on your beauty.'

'My beauty?'

He ran gentle fingers down her side. 'You are more desirable than I ever imagined.'

He bent his head and took a nipple in his mouth. His tongue went round and round its point until a sharp stab of heat radiated out through her. Her body arched upwards, seeking his touch. She made a mewling noise in the back of her throat as she fought to remain still.

He lifted his head and gave a very masculine laugh. 'Do you like this? You must say something if you don't. Your pleasure is mine.'

'I've never—' she said. 'That is to say—everyone said I must lie completely still, never moving.'

'They are wrong. Do what your body tells you to.'

She touched her tongue to her bottom lip. 'I've never done this before.'

He pushed the hair back from her forehead. 'I know. It means I have a great responsibly to ensure you enjoy this.'

'You are staying dressed?'

'For now. I don't want this to be over before it truly begins.' He put a finger against her lips. 'Let me feast. Please.'

Despite his words, she resolved to lie still until she worked out what to do. His probing mouth made the flames fan higher. She gripped his shoulders before tangling her hands in his hair and holding him against her breast. A deep shuddering went through her.

He raised his head and looked at her.

'Is that everything?' she whispered.

'No, there is more. Much more.' He placed kisses down her skin. His mouth moved inexorably lower to the nest of curls at the apex of her thighs. He slipped a finger in between her thighs, stroked, round and round, sometimes slipping into that place within her. Each time he did that the warm heat within her grew. Her thighs parted. He placed his palm against her while his fingers danced against her secret place.

Her body arched upwards again. The heat which had been growing again within her exploded. And she knew she craved more than his fingers there.

'Please.'

He took off his trousers, allowing his rampant manhood to spring free. He was far larger than she'd considered.

'See how I want you,' he growled in her ear. 'Touch me. Hold me.'

She closed her hand around his hot silken hardness. He groaned deep in his throat. 'Put me where you want me. Hurry.'

Instinctively she guided him to between her thighs, to her secret place which ached for his most intimate touch.

He sighed in the back of his throat as his tip nudged her, making the heat ripple through her again.

'I'm sorry, Ceanna, but this will hurt,' he said against her ear.

She nodded, unable to speak. Her stepmother and aunt had both emphasised the pain, but neither of them had spoken about the pleasure infusing her body. The brief intense pain caused her to sharply gasp. But her body opened and the pain subsided, as if it had never been.

'Hush.' He kissed the side of her temple. He lay completely still, embedded within her. Her hips began to move with a primitive rhythm. He answered her tentative movement and the wondrous heat filled her again, engulfing her.

At her joyous cry, he gave a great shudder and drove deeper.

When she came back to earth, she found he was looking at her as the rush lamp gave out its final glimmer of light.

He smoothed the damp tendrils of hair from her forehead. 'I'm sorry. It is never very good the first time.'

'You mean it gets better than this?'

He rolled off her and laughed, making the bed shake. 'You always surprise me, Skadi.'

He quickly left and the air cooled. In a heartbeat he was back beside her.

'This will help.'

He placed a cool cloth between her thighs and gently cleaned her. The coolness contrasted with the earlier heat and soothed the faint stinging sensation.

'It will make it easier to sleep,' he said.

He retrieved her shift and helped her to pull it over her head.

'Is that all?' she asked unable to keep the plaintive note out of her voice.

'We have had a long day,' he said, settling down next to her and pulling her into the circle of his arms. She laid her head on his chest and heard the steady thump of his heart. 'I want do this again, but you need time to recover. You have used new muscles.'

Do it again. Ceanna hugged the words to her and wriggled her toes. Her body had a lovely floating feeling as if she were on a cloud and her mind started to spin dreams. 'That would be very pleasant indeed.'

Sandulf lay in the dark and listened to the sound of Ceanna sleeping softly and the gentle snores of her wolf-hound. The depth of feeling that ran through him both surprised and worried him.

Every other time he had joined with a woman, he had been looking to find a way to end the encounter, but with Ceanna, he knew he would never tire of her. Perhaps that was a good thing, given she was his wife. Despite knowing that her body needed time to recover, the ache had already grown within him.

He started to understand Brandt's howling grief at Ingrid's death. Had his older brother felt this way about his wife? Wanting her in all ways? And what morning gift could he offer his new wife? He had nothing but what he carried in his pack. It needed to be something which would mean, if anything happened to him, she wouldn't starve.

It wouldn't be anything like the golden gift his father had arranged for Ingrid, a token of the family's affection he proclaimed in his booming voice when the couple had finally emerged from their seclusion. His mother had rolled her eyes and mentioned it should be the groom who gives the gift, not the father-in-law and that once again Sigurd had to be at the centre of things. Sandulf remembered Brandt glowering at the golden Valkyrie pendant, but Ingrid had accepted it graciously. One of the last things he remembered about his father was him bellowing at Ingrid to wear her golden Valkyrie and be sharp about it, not to disgrace the family.

Sandulf frowned and tightened his hold on Ceanna's

slumbering form. From what he could recall it had not been found on Ingrid's body. But that was a mystery for another day.

All he knew was that he wanted to protect Ceanna in a way that he never had for any woman before and it frightened him. He had begun to depend on her. He knew the danger they faced—and how quickly a beloved wife could be ripped away—and Ceanna had only begun to guess at it. If he could do one thing, it would be to keep her in ignorance of the evil he faced and to keep her well away from any danger. But his quest was leading him towards danger. He had no idea how to keep her safe and keep her with him at the same time. And he had no one he could trust to help him.

Ceanna gave a small whimper in her sleep as if something distressed her. Sandulf instantly drew her tighter into his arms. 'What is wrong?'

Her sleep-filled eyes opened. 'Stay with me. Always.'

'I'm here.'

She snuggled closer. 'Good. I like you being here with me.'

She could have little idea what she was asking. He knew what was coming, who he'd have to meet. She needed to stay elsewhere. Safe.

Rurik and his new wife might take her in, or he could go cap in hand to his middle brother, Alarr, in Éireann. Rurik said that he'd done well and was now a king or on the verge of becoming a king. Surely Alarr would not refuse his request to look after his wife while he pursued Lugh. His gut twisted. He wanted to be with Ceanna and see her smile. He wanted to wake up with her in his arms.

'I will keep you safe, Ceanna,' he whispered. 'That is the most important thing.'

Chapter Eleven

Ceanna woke to sunlight streaming into the room. Her head rested on Sandulf's chest. She lay and listened to his heartbeat. She should be happy. This was something that she had never considered could happen to her—waking in the arms of a handsome husband with a bright future ahead of them. Except, like a maggot uncurling from an otherwise perfect apple, the thought was doomed, an illusion like the heroes she used to dream up. She had about as much chance of keeping a man like Sandulf happy and contented as she did being able to catch the sunbeam which highlighted his stubble against her fingers.

She raised her hand. His arms immediately tightened.

'Good morning, sleepyhead,' he said with a laugh. 'Once again, you failed to wake before me.'

'You rarely sleep.'

'I might make an exception if you promise to stay in my arms every night.'

She basked in the nonsensical lovers' talk. Ceanna levered her elbow against his chest in order to sit up. He made no effort to hold her. 'Have you been awake long?'

'Long enough.' He gestured. 'Vanora would like her second breakfast, but I could stay here all day.'

'She has already had her first one?'

'I took her out earlier, but you slept through it and, when I returned, you looked so delectable that I couldn't resist getting back in bed with you and waiting until you woke.'

Her face flamed and she said with embarrassment, 'I dare say my aunt will want to inspect the sheets to ensure we are properly married. She mentioned something about it as she left last night.'

'At least she waited until we are ready.'

She swung her legs over the bed and muscles she didn't know she had until that instant protested. She collapsed back against him. 'I ache all over.'

His laugh rumbled against her ear. 'Is that a problem? My brother Brandt took three full days before he emerged with Ingrid.'

'Our marriage is different. We need to find this Lugh before he strikes again. We have little time to waste.'

'Yes, I do need to find him.'

There was no mistaking the word *I* rather than the *we* she'd expected to hear. Ceanna tightened her jaw.

He reached behind him and held out a golden arm ring. 'For you as the morning gift. It will have to do for now.'

'My morning gift?'

All laughter vanished from his eyes. 'If something happens to me, I'll not have you starve. I'll not have you abandoned without anything. It is what men in my family do—look after their brides. I had it made after my first successful voyage. The other one I wear belonged to Lugh. I grew tired of explaining why I only wore one arm ring.'

Ceanna hated the finality of his words. She stared at the intricately marked arm ring. He was going to find an excuse to leave her behind, claiming that it was for her own safety. No one could force her to return to Dun Ollaigh, he'd say. He had kept that side of their bargain, but she was determined to have more. She would demonstrate to him that she was an equal partner in this relationship. Indispensable. She rolled the word around on her tongue. A good word, a word to aspire to, rather than concentrating on the forgettable woman she knew she was. She took the arm ring and put it beside her on the pillow. 'Thank you. I will treasure it.'

'My pleasure.'

At his questioning look, she cleared her throat and started on her 'Make Ceanna Indispensable to Sandulf' scheme. 'I thought to ask my aunt if I could inspect the rolls. There might be something there about Brother Mattios   the monk who suddenly left when he heard a Northman was coming.'

'You seem obsessed by this Brother Mattios and those missing children. Your aunt has given her assurance that he is bona fide, a valuable member of Jarrow before coming here.' Sandulf put his hands on the top of his head as if that ended the discussion. 'I can't believe my sister-in-law Annis lied to me, but she may have misheard the rumour about Lugh's intentions. She'd little liking for the man. It could be there are more clues in Glannoventa which she and Rurik are unaware of. We start towards there tomorrow, due south to avoid Dun Ollaigh.'

'What if Brother Mattios actually feared you? What if he used the children as an excuse to get away from the Northern assassin who was coming here?' she asked, ignoring the little flip her heart did that Sandulf's immediate plans included them both.

'Or what if they were his real target?' Sandulf asked softly.

'He has been here for eighteen months. I doubt anyone plans that far in the future. He seized an opportunity.' She balled her fists and hit the bedclothes. 'I know he isn't genuine, deep inside me.'

His fingers tightened about hers and he raised them to his lips. 'It is good that you are so passionate. If you are frightened of travelling south because of the rivers, there may be another way for our marriage to proceed.'

'Another way.' Her throat closed. What had passed between them last night meant everything to her and nothing to him. He had given her protection and the means to buy a future for a little while. She eyed the arm ring with increased distaste. It was what she got for wanting to believe in heroes again. She swallowed the large lump which was forming in her throat. 'What other way?'

'You remain here and I'll return when I can. You are a married woman now. Your aunt will not have any cause to send you back. If you prefer, you could go to Mother Mildreth and live with her. Leave word which you decide if you remain undecided by the time I depart.'

Ceanna resisted the urge to throw the arm ring against the wall. Her plan to be indispensable was an unmitigated failure. How could she prove he needed her if they were apart? 'But why can't I be by your side? I can cross any river or ocean that you want if we are together.'

The warmth drained out of his eyes, leaving her chilled. 'That is your choice, but never say that I refused you the option of remaining behind on dry land.'

* * *

While Sandulf took Vanora outside for some exercise, her aunt came in and inspected the bedding. The older woman proclaimed that the marriage had been well and truly consummated and, in a lower voice, she told Ceanna that with luck she might not have to endure such a traumatic night again.

'Did Brother Mattios leave anything behind, Aunt?' Ceanna asked in desperation, trying to halt the awkward conversation about her marriage rites, and to stop from spilling her heart out about her worries. 'Anything at all for you to look after?'

'Why do you keep asking about Brother Mattios, Ceanna? He has nothing to do with you or your new husband.' Her aunt peered at her hard.

'Does he have any personal possessions? Anything that might give a clue to his previous life? Are you sure he is everything he said he is? I'd like to question him myself, but that is impossible.' Ceanna put her hands against her eyes and tried to think rapidly. It was a gamble, but she had to follow her instinct and show Sandulf she could assist him before he ordered her to stay behind.

'Why are you obsessed with Brother Mattios, Niece?' She blew out a breath of air. 'He came from Jarrow, St Bede and Benedict Biscop's old monastery. We were fortunate he decided to favour us and stay, rather than returning to his former home.'

'And he left, claiming that a Northman assassin would arrive.' Ceanna reviewed the situation. 'As my new husband is a Northman and the only one to arrive recently, something which no one should be bothered about, naturally I wonder why a monk felt the need to flee. And now I consider it, it is highly unusual for a monk from

Northumbria to travel so far north. Why did he leave Jarrow?'

'Because he did.' Her aunt waved a hand. 'It is uncommon for a monk to change orders, but he said he admired the way I ran this double monastery and had created a place of such contemplation.'

'Why did he come here in the first place?'

'He had heard rumours of our library. Less extensive than the one at Jarrow, of course, but we've one or two excellent manuscripts. The Kings of Strathclyde, particularly King Aed's father, were generous benefactors.'

Ceanna raised her brow. Her aunt wore the same expression her mother had done when she was trying to get Ceanna to believe in heroes who would rescue her. 'Humour me, Aunt, and I won't bother you about this again. I will leave with Sandulf and start my new life well away from here.'

Her aunt's sigh reverberated off the walls. 'When a person dedicates his or her life to the order, they give their possessions away. We take a vow of poverty, Ceanna dear.'

'But you have the tapestries from Dun Ollaigh, The ones my mother said you always loved even as a child. I spied them in your room earlier.'

Her aunt's mouth flattened into a thin white line. 'What are you trying to imply? Perhaps it is as well you decided not to join my order. Your trouble with obedience continues to astonish.'

'When did he suggest taking the late King's children away from this place of safety?' she asked, trying another tack. 'After my father's messengers arrived? Or before?'

For the first time, her aunt appeared uneasy. 'I suppose it was after, now that you mention it.'

'Shall we ask them?' Ceanna straightened her gown, enjoying the rush of confidence. She gave her aunt her best imperious stare. 'I assume they have not vanished in the night.'

Her aunt was the first to look away. 'I will summon them to my scriptorium. It would not be suitable here in this bedchamber.'

The scriptorium smelt of ink, vellum and dust. The area was now vacant except for Ceanna and Sandulf with Vanora at their feet. Ceanna had gone and discovered him in the physic garden once her aunt had agreed to the meeting with the guards. Although Sandulf was impatient to leave and return to Northumbria, he did agree to wait until Ceanna had finished her enquiries. Her stomach knotted. Her gamble had to be right.

She heaved a sigh of relief when one of the guards—one of her father's more faithful retainers—entered in her aunt's wake. He immediately knelt before Ceanna.

'My lady! Good that you are well. We heard rumours. Then you refused to speak to us and insisted on marrying a heathen. I feared the worst.'

'I've married. But my husband is a good man, Ecgbert.'

He gave Sandulf a wary look and said in Pictish. 'Is he really a good man? Did you do this of your own free will?'

'One of the best,' Ceanna replied in Gaelic, aware that Sandulf was trying to follow the conversation. His Pictish had improved, but he still had some way to go.

'Your stepmother will be unhappy,' the guard continued in Pictish. 'She is a very determined woman. She desired this match between you and Captain Feradach.'

'My aunt has given us her blessing.' Ceanna marvelled that she could say the words without her voice trembling. 'I hope I can count on your loyalty to me and my new husband.'

'We are loyal to you and your father.'

Sandulf tilted his head to one side. 'Do you think you can speak in Gaelic so I can understand?'

'I will have to redouble my efforts in teaching you Pictish,' Ceanna said in a low voice. 'But all is well. This man is loyal to a point.'

'I look forward to your instruction, then.' The husky undertone to his voice did strange things to her insides.

'Good,' she said, making her voice sound brisk, but knowing that her cheeks had suddenly become heated. 'Before you go, Ecgbert, what I wanted to know is whether you were tasked with a special message for Brother Mattios as well as one for my aunt.'

'Captain Feradach's brother?' the guard said, switching to Gaelic. 'Funny you should mention him. Brother Mattios was most insistent that there must be a message from his brother and followed me about asking and asking. When we arrived here, the vellum with the message on could not be found, but the most junior member of my team said that Captain Feradach had made him repeat the message five times over because vellum had a way of going missing.'

'What was the message?' Sandulf asked.

'*A Northman asks the way to Nrurim. I've need of your skill. Leave immediately, but have a care.*' I could not make sense of it, but then Captain Feradach and I have not seen eye to eye for a long time.'

Ceanna's neck muscles eased. She had done it. She had shown there was a connection. The next time, maybe Sandulf would not be so quick to dismiss how important it was to have her at his side. She could prove her worth to him. She could be his Skadi in truth, his warrior woman.

'Feradach sent this message to his brother? Why wasn't I informed of this earlier?' her aunt asked sharply. 'Why is Captain Feradach ordering my monk about? I am the one who decides who can leave and who can go.'

The guard bowed deeply. 'Yes, my lady abbess. Brother Mattios went whiter than snow and rushed off to find you. I thought you knew.'

Her aunt put her hand to her throat. 'I don't know what to say. Brother Mattios told me quite another tale about the sons of King Aed needing to depart. He became agitated, but he persuaded me with his argument.'

'And you let him leave with them?'

'Yes. They are to go to their aunt in Éireann, away from the whims of the new King or his Regent. He promised.'

'Now will you allow Brother Mattios's possessions to be examined? Please,' Ceanna said.

'For what purpose?'

'Because if he is who my wife and I think he is, he will have kept one or two trinkets from his past exploits,' Sandulf said very slowly. 'One of his fellow conspirators said that the man I seek always did. From the victims he particularly enjoyed killing.'

Her aunt gave an exasperated sigh.

'I suppose there is no harm in it. Brother Mattios is not here to defend his reputation, but I suspect the mystery will be easily solved. He did, as I recall, put a few small trinkets to one side, safekeeping for his brother in the advent of his death.'

Sandulf squeezed Ceanna's shoulder after her aunt left. 'Thank you for your persistence, Skadi, for ensuring that this happens. I was wrong to dismiss your instincts earlier. I'm sorry. You knew how to handle your aunt far better than I could ever have done.'

'You are welcome, Husband.' She inclined her head as the dreams started to grow. 'If Brother Mattios is who we think he is, those royal children are in grave danger. They may already be dead.'

Her aunt returned with a small, intricately carved wooden casket. 'Brother Mattios left this with strict instructions that it must go to his brother if he failed to return from his mission. It appears he secured it with beeswax and a seal of some sort.' She shook it. 'It sounds as if there is something in there. Make of it what you will. I am beginning to wonder if there is not something in your tale, Northman, and I would like the matter resolved.'

'Thank you.' Sandulf took the box from the nun. His stomach knotted. He owed Ceanna a great deal. Her swift thinking had made this possible. He had nearly left for Glannoventa without her. It was like the man who had saved his life on board the ship explained—assassins are like Loki, double dealing and entirely untrustworthy.

He broke the wax seals, opened it and started to shake. On the top of a folded linen cloth lay a small gold figurine, holding out a shield, slightly battered but as shiny as when his father had first shown it to him. He stared up at the ceiling, struggling to get hold of his emotions.

The memories from that day when Ingrid was first given it flooded his brain—his father's preening at the figure's sheer weight in gold; Brandt's look of absolute horror and fury when his father presented it to Ingrid in a brief ceremony; his mother's anger that her husband should seek to embarrass their son in such a fashion through offering a morning gift to his daughter-in-law as if his eldest son possessed nothing; and how Ingrid had smoothed everything over with a few well-chosen words.

When he felt he could trust his emotions, he handed the box back to Mother Abbe.

'Satisfied?' The old woman gave a disingenuous smile, holding her hand out for the box to be given back to her. 'Ceanna, you must return with your father's men. Your husband—'

'Turn that gold figurine over, please,' he said. 'I want you to do it, not me. You saw I only looked at it, but did not touch it or turn it over.'

'The statue? I must say it is an odd interpretation of Our Lady, but who am I to argue? It was important to Brother Mattios.'

'If you look closely, you will see that it is a Valkyrie with a shield. She has cats at her feet. On the back will be the rune for Ingrid, the wife of my eldest brother. The figurine belonged to my sister-in-law, who sometimes wore it as a pendant. It was her morning gift after their marriage. I am certain of it.'

With a faintly trembling hand and an over-confident smile, the abbess plucked the ornament from the box. Her smile faded to nothing. 'I can't quite make it out, but something is there. I do not know how to read runes.'

'May I see it?' Ceanna took the gold figurine from her aunt and held it up to one of the torches. 'There are definitely markings on the back. Can you scratch the ones for Ingrid in the dust, Sandulf? I want my aunt to see the truth. I want the scales to drop from her eyes.'

He didn't deserve a woman like Ceanna. She'd believed in him. His sense of responsibility towards her filled him, pressing down on his lungs with a choking certainty. He picked up a stick and quickly scratched the runes.

'See, Aunt.' Ceanna passed the figurine to her aunt. 'Sandulf has scratched the runes in the dust. They match precisely with what is on the figurine's reverse. There is no way he could have seen them.'

'I… They…could be the same markings.' The abbess's voice was little more than a thread on the wind. 'You mean it is not Our Lady, but some heathen idol?'

'It seems mighty peculiar to me that someone as devoted as Brother Mattios held such store by something which is so blatantly heathen. Maybe he didn't want anyone to know and that is why he sealed the box.' Ceanna tilted her head to one side. 'What do the runes mean, Sandulf?'

'They mean *I belong to Ingrid*. My father gave the figurine to my eldest brother's wife as a morning gift from the family. My father said it was because a woman would need the heart of a warrior to breed strong sons from his eldest son.'

Ceanna looked down at the ground, her cheeks flaming. 'I see.'

'I carved the runes myself during the night. Something for a younger brother to do on the occasion of his eldest brother's wedding, or so my father proclaimed.' Sandulf forced a smile. Brandt had shouted at him when he discovered Sandulf's part in it, but Ingrid had been understanding about why he hadn't defied his father. It was then she had really won his heart—telling him to ignore Brandt's cross words. 'Ingrid thought it sweet of me, but kept it locked away, saying it was far too expensive to wear every day. My father insisted on her wearing it the day of the massacre as my eldest brother had been called away.'

'Was it lost in the massacre?' Ceanna asked.

Sandulf concentrated and brought the terrible scene to mind. Blood everywhere. Ingrid's clothes ripped. He could not remember seeing it then. Or even earlier, now that he came to think of it. Ingrid had kept a shawl wrapped about her body even as they sat in the longhouse. 'I don't remember it on her corpse, but she would have been wearing it; she won't have wanted to risk my father's temper on such an important occasion for my family. She was like that, always eager to ensure things ran smoothly.'

Ceanna took the figurine from her aunt's hands and placed it back in the box. She handed the box to Sandulf. 'This belongs to you and your family, not to the man who calls himself Brother Mattios.'

His throat closed with the emotion. With his fingers tightening about the box, he nodded.

'Do you have an explanation, Aunt, for how this could have come into Brother Mattios's possession?' Ceanna crossed her arms and gave her aunt her hardest stare. 'Or may I finally draw the obvious conclusion? Brother Mattios was not the same Brother Mattios who left Jarrow. Sandulf's intelligence was accurate after all—you have unwittingly been harbouring a fearsome assassin.'

The abbess shook her head and took a step backwards. The colour had drained from her face, leaving her pale and shaking. 'He had the correct papers. We were anticipating his arrival, you see, to view a manuscript whose provenance was in dispute. Father Callum warned me that he was not all he seemed, that his Latin was not very good for a scholar sent on such a mission, but then Father Callum unexpectedly sickened and died. You must understand that Brother Matt—that *that man* was utterly charming. So devoted to prayer. So dedicated to silence. Seemingly gentle despite that awful scar on his face.'

'No one told me about a scar.' Every sinew in Sandulf's being tightened. 'Was it in the shape of a shooting star?'

'He called it his angel's kiss,' her aunt said. 'And said it made him more devoted. I liked that about him, that he saw God's hand in everything.'

'Ingrid's murderer, Lugh, had a scar on his face which resembled a shooting star,' Sandulf said.

The abbess's hands shook. 'Maybe it could be called a star, a double star with a cross.'

'Who nursed this Father Callum in his last days?' Ceanna asked. 'I take it that he was very healthy until Brother Mattios arrived.'

'Your stepmother and Brother M—' The abbess sank to her knees. 'May God and all the angels forgive me. Father Callum was a good soul. You must take the box far away from here. Destroy it. It must be cursed.'

'That heathen idol, as you called it, meant a great deal to my father,' Sandulf said, unable to prevent the words spilling out. 'Any curse came from the assassin you sheltered.'

Ceanna put out her hand. 'Sandulf!'

Sandulf gave an unrepentant bow. 'I do beg your pardon, my lady, for my words. It would be my pleasure to take this back on behalf of my family, for whom it has great value, Lady Abbess.'

The old woman turned her face away.

'Helping us will ensure Father Callum gets some justice,' Ceanna said softly. 'Something which has been denied to him.'

The woman's skin turned the colour of old parchment. 'From what your husband has been saying about this killer, those little boys are probably dead. I thought I had been firm in doing my duty, but I have been betrayed. Miserably. In my arrogance, I sent them to their deaths, Ceanna.'

'Did you know Captain Feradach before this Brother Mattios arrived?'

'He came to visit…the man who claimed to be Brother Mattios shortly after he arrived from Jarrow. He said that Feradach was his brother. It was why I recommended him for advancement with your father.'

'I see.' Ceanna stood up straighter—a lady demanding justice prevail in every sense of the word. 'You appear to have made a number of grave errors, Aunt. There is every reason to believe this Mattios—or Lugh, as Sandulf calls him—will be headed towards Dun Ollaigh, seeking to use those little boys for his own gain rather than delivering them to their aunt in Éireann as he promised.'

Sandulf ground his teeth. Dun Ollaigh—the one place where she'd be in the most danger. The danger from her stepmother and this Feradach had increased immeasurably. His stomach churned. He wanted her with him, but he had to be sensible. He would fight better knowing that she was safe and that somewhere safe had to be here. He silenced the little voice deep within which protested. Once everything was resolved and he had earned the reward of a better life, then he could return here and start their marriage together properly.

'Aunt, what say you?'

'I hadn't realised the danger,' the old woman admitted, her body crumpling. 'I was fooled by his devout prayer and his charm. I was so worried about you and I wanted the boys to be elsewhere. They were very noisy, you see. I missed the peace and quiet.'

Ceanna rolled her eyes heavenwards. 'It is well that I am leaving, Aunt. You would discover I enjoy talking far too much.'

Sandulf firmed his mouth. Ceanna made it sound as if she was going off with him, hunting Lugh. 'I'll travel much more swiftly on my own. You should remain here.'

The hurt in Ceanna's eyes made his insides twist. It was for the best. Her safety above all things. What could he offer her really? Until he'd made peace with his brothers, he could not consider anyone or anything else. He'd been fooling himself earlier.

'I will go with you,' Ceanna said. 'I know Dun Ollaigh and its ways.'

'You will be safer here. Your aunt understands that now.'

'Are you already disobeying an order from your husband, Niece?'

'Aunt, will you excuse us for a brief time? I need to speak with my husband alone. He can be pig-headed at times.'

'You are the one who was insistent on marrying him.'

'I know and I have no regrets about that.'

'Take as long as you like.'

She ushered the sisters and guards out of the scriptorium.

In the silence which followed her aunt's departure, Ceanna struggled to hang on to her temper. Her insides felt as if they had been torn out. She knew he worried for her safety, but she felt as though he was abandoning her at the first opportunity. Her husband did not think she would be able to contribute anything in the hunt for the assassin.

She firmed her mouth. He wasn't thinking straight. Seeing that golden Valkyrie had upset him. The terrible look he'd given it had showed her all she needed to know about the state of his heart. He cared for the dead woman far more than he could ever care for her. He'd never made any sort of promises about that. He had promised to be her husband, but he had only ever promised her friendship. She was emphatically not someone he was in love with. The knowledge made her chest ache all the harder because she knew she was rapidly falling in love with him.

'See the matter from my perspective. I have a duty towards you as your husband.' He put his hands behind his back. 'Knowing you remain safe will enable me to fight harder. If you return to Dun Ollaigh, then you put yourself into danger. You wanted to be at the monastery before we arrived here.'

A small part of her knew she had to fight the temptation to remain safe and secure behind the high walls of the monastery. It was what she had set out to do—find sanctuary from her stepmother. She would be safe here, if there was safety in being a prisoner. In the past few days she'd felt more alive than she had done since long before her mother and brother had died.

Ceanna the Indispensable. The words rolled about in her brain again. Sandulf didn't see her as such yet, but she'd make him see it. 'You need me, Sandulf. More than ever, you need me.'

A muscle jumped in his jaw and his brows lowered. 'I don't need anyone, particularly not you. I'm perfectly capable of dealing with Lugh on my own. When I was growing up, my brothers always told me I was incapable of handling things by myself, even when it was easy to see that I could. You need to remain here and stay safe. It is the best way you can help.'

His words stabbed her, but she kept her back straight. 'You have only a limited knowledge of Dun Ollaigh or its inhabitants. I have all the knowledge you will need. However, we won't know what you need until you need it. It is why I must go with you.'

He put a heavy hand under her elbow, but she shook it off with an impatient gesture. 'I want to keep you safe. Safe means remaining here in this monastery.'

She raised herself up on her tiptoes and brushed his lips with hers. 'You protected me all the way here. Why shouldn't I put my trust in your sword arm?'

'Because—because I am looking out for your welfare.' He ran a hand through his hair, making it stand up on end. 'For once in my life, I am attempting to do the right thing. Be reasonable, Skadi.'

'I know you are trying to protect me, but you will need to be with me to provide that protection. I don't trust anyone but you.'

He made a face. 'And if I am useless at it?'

'What happened to Ingrid was not your fault. It was the fault of the assassin, the man you are trying to prevent from murdering again.' She put her hands against his chest. 'You will have to accept that I am going to return to Dun Ollaigh and bring this man and his brother to justice. I will not be left behind to wonder and worry.'

His arms went around her and held her tight. He rested his chin on top of her head. 'Goodness knows what sort of mischief you and Vanora would discover without me guiding your steps.'

'Perish the thought.'

He laughed. The muscles in Ceanna's neck eased. The storm had passed, after a fashion. 'If there is any fighting to be done, you make sure you are far away.'

'I will do my best.'

'I mean it, Skadi. I will not have the death of another innocent woman on my conscience.'

Ceanna knew from the tone of his voice that she'd won. Her heart squeezed. It scared her how much she cared for this man and she knew that she had to be willing to let him run headlong into danger to complete his mission. He had saved her by marrying her and now she must do all she could to help him find the assassin. It was the terms of their deal.

She marched to the door and pulled it open. Her aunt tumbled in. 'I think my father's messengers had best remain here with you, Aunt. The element of surprise will be key to discovering the truth about Lugh.'

Sandulf stroked his chin. 'My wife speaks true. The messengers can remain a while longer under your excellent hospitality.'

The guards protested loudly, but Ceanna was relieved when her aunt smiled, the first genuine smile Ceanna had seen. 'I think my niece makes an excellent suggestion.'

'Aunt, when we find the boys, I will ensure they go to their relations in Éireann. I give you my word.'

'You hate travelling over water, they tell me. Ever since your mother and brother died.'

Ceanna glanced at Sandulf, who nodded. 'Some things are more important than my irrational fears. This is one of them. Watch for my message.'

'Despite my reservations, marriage appears to be good for you, Niece.'

Ceanna firmed her mouth. She would be a widow before long if Sandulf did not succeed. But she could not bear to be abandoned, even though she would finally be safe. She only wanted to be by his side, to be his Skadi in truth, even if it meant watching her beloved husband die at the hands of the treacherous assassin who had massacred his family, or dying alongside him.

Chapter Twelve

They made the bridge by the River Orchy by the time
the summer glimmer had started to light the insects who
danced in the sky, making brief glints of gold appear.
The blackbirds and thrushes chattered in the bushes
which lined the track while the wind rustled the pines.
Everything was at peace. Ceanna glanced over to Sandulf. Everything was at peace except him.

He had barely spoken a word since they had departed
and the ease which had been between them on the journey to Nrurim seemed to have vanished.

'Shall we stop here for the night?' she asked, injecting
a determined cheerfulness in her voice as she gestured
to where a small hut stood nestled in a wooded glade.
'It would provide shelter.'

'If you wish.' Sandulf swung down from his mount.
'No one is here.'

'We should be safe, then.' Ceanna dismounted and
inspected the panniers which were attached to her pony.
'My aunt packed us a good supply of food. She was concerned about our welfare.'

He raised a brow upwards.

She pushed a stray lock of hair behind her ear. Her cheeks burnt. 'What's wrong? We have pies, cheese, cold meat and even several pieces of the honey sweetmeat that my aunt adores.'

'Trust you to think of food.'

'And you are thinking of something else?'

'Yes.' He came over to her and gathered her into his arms. 'This.'

His kiss was fierce and untamed, banishing all the worries and concerns she had had earlier. He took her hand and put it against the front of his trousers. She felt him, hard and firm.

'See what you do to me?' he growled in her ear. 'What appetites you unleash?'

The heat grew within her, flaming higher. Last night had been more than some misplaced sense of duty. She knew she didn't want to be the way her aunt suggested— quiet, obedient, dutiful. She wanted fire and passion and love. 'Food can wait.'

His smile transformed his face. 'Good.'

He picked her up, went into the small hut and set her down on the table.

'Here?'

'I intend to feast on your body.' His hands roamed over the contours of her legs, sending little prickles of heat radiating outwards. He leant forward so that his lips nuzzled her earlobe. 'And invite you to feast on mine.'

'You want us to join? In the daylight?'

His eyes danced. She knew she could spend a life-time studying those eyes and never fully discern their many colours. 'Why wait for the cover of darkness when we are alone?'

Her response was to wrap her arms about his neck and pull him down into her embrace.

Sandulf watched Ceanna sleep. Her lashes made half-moons on her pale cheeks. He ran a finger down one of them.

She might be tiny, but she was fierce. She'd firmly woven herself into his heartstrings. She'd given him her body and allowed him those blissful moments of peace in her arms.

He knew beyond everything that he had to keep her safe. She had become important to him, almost as important as his heart beating. But he hadn't done enough to deserve her.

He stared up at the darkened beams. This time he wouldn't fail. He had to prove his worth as a husband and that meant finding Lugh before he realised Sandulf was on his trail. And the thought frightened him to the core of his being.

An unnatural hush clung to the entire village which perched between the sea and the great fortress of Dun Ollaigh, the sort Ceanna struggled to remember hearing except after the death of her mother.

The familiarity of the buildings and its scents washed over Ceanna. She'd missed it in ways she hadn't quite been aware of until she returned. Everywhere her gaze brought on the rush of another memory, but as long as her stepmother and Feradach remained in control, this place was dangerous for her. For them both.

'Where to now?' Sandulf asked in a quiet voice.

Ceanna adjusted the hood of her cloak, keeping her

face concealed. 'The tavern is impossible. My step-mother is sure to have spies there. Shall we try Urist?'

'He tried to betray you.'

'Did he? Do we really know that?'

'What do you mean?'

'No one came after us. He acquired that corpse which he pretended was me. And the messengers left before the ambush, but…' At Sandulf's gentle cough, she paused. 'What?'

'I thought you were the one who hated taking risks.'

'I'm learning that I'm rather better at this than I could have imagined.' She cocked her head to one side. The air was far too still. She couldn't even hear the fishwives calling out their wares besides the harbour as they always did at this time of day. 'Something is wrong. I can't quite put my finger on it. There seems to be a certain sadness hanging over the village.' A shiver ran down her spine. 'Probably my over-active imagination. I hope it isn't anything to do with my father. I hope he remains alive…' Tears stung at the back of her throat. 'I want to see him again, Sandulf. I want him to meet you and bless our union.'

He gave her a sideways glance. 'I know what your imagination is like.'

A warm bubble of happiness filled Ceanna, banishing her fears for her father. When he said things like that, she could almost believe that their marriage stood a chance of being a happy one.

Sandulf shaded his eyes. 'I can hear shouting. Can you make out what they are saying?'

'Kill the heathen who murdered Our Lady.' Ceanna wrinkled her nose. 'Which lady? Do you think someone tried to steal the statue of Mary from the church? It will surely be drunk lads from the fishing boats. They are always doing daft things like that. At least it is not about my father's death.'

Sandulf gave her a look. 'Since when can anyone kill a statue? Who else is their lady?'

She placed a hand on her stomach. The full horror of it washed over her. 'They are blaming some poor innocent for my death. How could this be? Did Urist pass that body off as me? Could he do that? Why would he? I should—'

His fingers closed tight about her arm. 'Should what? Show yourself? Ruin any hope of surprising your stepmother and this Feradach? Alert Lugh? You've no idea what trick Urist played, but it was certainly not designed to assist you escape. You might as well march into the middle of Dun Ollaigh begging for your death at the top of your voice.'

She jerked her arm away, hating that his words contained some small measure of truth. 'I can't have an innocent's blood on my conscience.'

Sandulf glared at her, obviously expecting her to back down. He gave a long sigh 'You're right. Something must be done. Keep in the shadows. Do not reveal yourself unless it becomes absolutely necessary.'

'What are we going to do?' she asked before he could stride away.

His glance flickered over her. 'What makes you think I will need help? You stay here with Vanora. I will report back after I have worked out what is happening.'

'We're a partnership, Sandulf. You need me whether you like it or not. You are far from fluent in Pictish despite your practice.'

He sighed heavily. 'Why do you make it so difficult

for me to protect you? Where has the woman gone who hated taking risks?'

'She ceased to exist not long after she encountered you.'

She gestured towards where a crowd gathered. A sort of mute rumbling roar filled the village, driving out the quiet, but it, too, was an unnatural sound.

'Those are the people I grew up with. They mourn my death. But not my father. Not my father, Sandulf. He lives.' Her heart leapt. All the way here, she'd tried not to hope that he might still breathe and that she could see him again, but even still, a faint hope about rescuing her father had taken hold inside of her. It had started as something small like a warm ember, but had since grown to a steady flame. With Sandulf's help, she knew they could rescue him after the plotters were exposed. Then maybe her father would grow strong and they could become closer again.

'They may be your people, but they can also be your undoing. You spoke true—leaving you in the shadows would be a mistake. Follow my lead. But revealing yourself to the crowd will be a last resort.' After Ceanna's unsteady nod, Sandulf crouched down in the dust and rapidly sketched out his plan. 'Our main objective is to determine who is being held and if he is worth saving.'

'He has been captured and abused because of me. Of course he is worth saving.'

'If it were Lugh or Feradach, would you feel the same way?'

Ceanna hugged her arms about her waist. 'Everyone is entitled to a fair hearing, but you are right, I wouldn't risk my life for either of those two.'

'Sense from my Skadi.' He dropped a kiss on her lips.

Ceanna hated that her heart turned over. She knew in that heartbeat that she loved him and wanted to be by his side for the rest of her life. He hadn't asked for her love and she had little idea how he'd react if he knew he had it. The marriage had been foisted on him, after all.

Ceanna stabbed at Sandulf's sketch with her finger. 'You have drawn the square, but not the whipping post. Whoever this man is will be tied there, waiting for justice. We need to go there and see who this poor unfortunate is, before they tear him apart.'

'I am hoping to pass unnoticed.' He jammed a hat he'd procured from the monastery down on his head. 'Ready to brave the howling mob?'

'Try to shuffle like a peasant rather than striding like a warrior.'

'Always the practical one.'

'Always.' She covered her head with a shawl and hunched her shoulders. 'We will succeed, won't we?'

He regarded her for a long heartbeat. 'We leave Vanora here. The fewer questions, the better.'

Ceanna chucked Vanora under the chin. 'She is rather memorable, isn't she?'

Ceanna motioned for Vanora to stay by where the ponies were tethered. The dog gave her a baleful look, but settled down with her head on her paws. 'Shall we have at it, then? Find out what's going on?'

Sandulf led the way through the baying throng. It seemed to part in front of him as if people sensed that he was not the sort of person to cross. Several people gave them curious stares, but no one stopped them.

Sandulf's muscles relaxed, but he couldn't help keeping an eye on Ceanna's slow progress. With her body swathed in a thick cloak and the hood pulled firmly down so her face was shielded, she walked more like a pregnant duck than a lady. A few people shoved her, buffeting her about, but she kept her lips pressed tightly together.

When she noticed his stare, she made a little circle with her hand to tell him to turn around and concentrate. Ceanna was being sensible and there was every chance this man could be ignored until they had dealt with the true problem—Feradach and his brother.

'They are bringing him along this way towards the square,' Ceanna murmured, sidling up to his elbow. 'We should get a good vantage point there.'

She pointed to a little alley in the shadow of two houses. The crowd was thinner there. And a disused barrel stood to one side.

They ducked into the alleyway. The crowd surged past with the prisoner. Sandulf lifted Ceanna up on to the barrel to improve her view, then he turned his attention to the prisoner, a man more dead than alive.

Despite the dirt and the evidence of the beating, the cut of his fine woollen clothes proclaimed him as being a Northman like himself. His blond hair hung about his face as he was dragged along, his legs bumping on the ground. Every muscle in Sandulf's body tensed. His mouth went dry.

What in the name of everything was Danr doing here?

He pressed his hands to his eyes and hoped he'd seen wrong. Perhaps he was the one with the over-active imagination now. A trick of the light. There was no way the prisoner should be Danr. He was safe in Éireann with Sandulf's other brothers.

Then the man screamed in Gaelic that he'd never

seen this lady of theirs and a dagger of ice went through Sandulf.

He gave a low moan in the back of his throat. Danr had obviously come in search of him, only to find himself caught up in the mess Sandulf had left behind in Dun Ollaigh.

A great red mist descended. Rurik had obviously told the others, a counsel of war had been held and Danr had been dispatched to bring the incompetent brother back to the family in disgrace, except it had not worked out as they had planned. But he'd make good—starting with Danr's rescue. This was the chance he'd been waiting for his entire life. He'd demonstrate once and for all time that he was indeed worthy of being their brother, one of the fabled Sons of Sigurd.

He stepped forward. Someone grabbed on to his tunic, hauling him backwards. He looked at Ceanna in incomprehension. He put up an arm to knock her away. 'I must get out there. I must. Do you understand?'

'Sandulf!' Ceanna jumped down from the barrel, grabbed his arm with fierce fingers and pinned him against the building. 'We're here to watch, not to act without thought, remember? Who is that man? One of your countrymen?'

'Danr.'

'Your brother?' Her grip loosened. 'Oh, no, Sandulf, how can that be? What is he doing here?'

'I can't tell for sure. I haven't spoken to him since I left Maerr.'

'But what are we going to do about it?'

'There is no we. I alone will do it. I have to. My brothers turned their backs on me after what happened in Maerr and this is my chance to redeem myself in their eyes, to prove I am a man, that I am worthy of being their brother.'

Her hands clawed at his arms. 'You have to remain with me until you start thinking logically. I refuse to allow you to do something which will endanger everything and everyone.'

'You will stop me?'

'By physical force if necessary. I'll sit on you and pin you down.'

'Sit on me?' The red mist cleared and he let out a small laugh. He saw her stricken face peering up at him. She had prevented him from making a mistake of immense proportions, the kind that had got him his reputation with his brothers in the first place. He put his fingers about her face and whispered in a softer voice, 'Let me go. I have to go.'

'No. You have to remain here. With me in this alley. We consider our options. We make our plan. We execute it together when the time is right.'

'But my brother suffers,' he bit out in a furious undertone. 'Let me go and save him. I must. Stay here if you wish, but I can't just stand aside and watch him die for something they think I did.'

She manoeuvred herself in front of him. 'Hold true to your earlier arguments. Danr will understand why you did not rush in waving your sword when we free him. He will want to find this Lugh as much as you. He will want everyone punished. Believe that the rule of law still exists around Dun Ollaigh. He'll survive until we rescue him. Go now and you will ruin the best chance you have of catching Lugh.'

He collapsed against her. His frame was tense with

the internal struggle he faced. Her arms came about him and held him tight.

'I know. I know,' she murmured in his ear.

'We must rescue him. Somehow. Before everything else.'

'Agreed, but what you said earlier about keeping my presence a secret must be so.' Her calm measured voice made his heart ease.

'So what do we do now?'

'Wait until the cover of darkness. They have had their fun. They will leave him tied to the post. The petition against him will have to be presented to my father. I know these people, I know how things are done here.' Ceanna bristled. 'We do not simply enact rough and ready justice in this kingdom. There is a rule of law and procedures to be followed. Even Feradach and my stepmother will want to see lip service paid to the law. Time is on our side. Just.'

'And if we can't rescue him that way?'

'When did you become such a doubter? Rescuing people is what you do.'

Like the first taste of cloudberries or the song of the first blackbird outside the longhouse in spring, a nearly forgotten but oddly familiar warmth spread through Sandulf. He'd passed through the winter solitude of suffering and now he bathed in the light of someone who truly believed in him and his ability. 'Together?'

'I guarantee it.' She pulled his hat further down over his forehead. 'If you're ready, we make our way back to Vanora and wait.'

He glanced once more at where his brother was tied to the post. 'What will happen today?'

'Normally they'll keep him tied to the post until the

lord can make his judgement, provided my father is well enough. As your brother is a foreigner, they might even need the permission of Giric, the King's Regent. Danr will survive until then. If he is your brother, then he is as hard as tempered steel, just like you.'

Sandulf watched the now-empty street. The shouts had subsided. What Ceanna said made sense. Law and order existed here. It was not the anarchy of battle. With patience, it was possible he could achieve both his aims.

He took her hand, clung to it like a drowning man clings to a spar and raised it to his lips. 'Thank you.'

Although there were days in the summer when it never became truly dark, now that it was autumn the days were starting to draw in. She had seen the fields they travelled through and knew it should be a decent harvest, but the crops had not been brought in, as they should have been. If her father were still alive, he wasn't commanding his stewards in the way he had once done.

She pushed her thoughts about management of Dun Ollaigh away and racked her brain to come up with a plan of how to rescue Danr. Sandulf was going to need her help. And she wanted to give it, no longer because she wanted to be indispensable, but because she had seen the naked longing in Sandulf's face. She knew what it was like to lose a brother.

When they came to where the ponies were tethered, Vanora was nowhere to be seen.

'Vanora!' Ceanna called softly. 'Come here, girl.'

Ceanna heard a low whine and desperate yipping. She followed the sound to where Vanora was tied up outside the tavern. She rapidly undid the rope and turned to go.

'My lady! It is you! By all the saints in heaven! We

thought you were dead. Your father came out of Dun Ollaigh for the first time in months for your funeral. That
was three days ago, then this here dog of yours turns up
without a by your leave and takes one of my pies and
I hardly dared to hope. It can't be Lady Ceanna in her
grave without her dog, I told myself. Where that dog is,
you will find her. It is a bad business if they put someone
else in your grave and made your father weep like that.'

Ceanna pivoted to see Bertana, the tavern keeper's
wife, standing there, behind her. 'But who said I was
dead?'

The woman enveloped her in a tight hug. 'We have
been so worried. Urist told a tale about an ambush with
you being attacked, but I knew about that corpse he'd
taken and how that lady who died in childbirth hadn't
been buried. And I wondered... And your poor father
weeping. I thought he'd expire from the trauma of it all
and they'd be having another funeral in a matter of days.
But my husband told me I was being foolish.'

Ceanna looked up at the skittering clouds. Her father
was alive three days ago and well enough to attend his
daughter's funeral. She blinked rapidly until she had her
emotions under control. 'You knew about the corpse, the
one Urist used as a decoy? But said nothing to my father?'

The woman shrugged. 'Urist's woman always had a
big mouth. She told me after you left. Urist always has
an eye for the main chance, but this scheme has him living in Dun Ollaigh and dining on the choicest meats, according to my cousin. I told my sister that he is playing
both ends against the middle and for his own advantage,
make no mistake. I thought you must be in trouble if you
had made a bargain with him. Listen to me, babbling on.
I am like a brook in flood, never knowing when to stop.'

Ceanna shot a sideways glance at Sandulf. To her relief, he stayed silent, watching with hooded eyes. 'Urist made a dreadful error, throwing his lot in with those people.'

'A mistake. A terrible one.' Bertana's mouth firmed. 'I can see that—you being alive and here.'

'Who is the prisoner? And how did they come to accuse him?' Ceanna asked as an idea began to grow in her brain. Urist might hate all Northmen with a passion and see this as a chance to strike a blow, but if he saw Sandulf there instead of Danr, what would he do? Excitement filled her throat.

'I don't know, but he faces judgement tomorrow morning. Urist is not well enough to be moved today and remains at Dun Ollaigh under Lady Mhairi's care. In the morning, he and your lady stepmother are coming to view the prisoner.' She worried her chatelaine's belt, making the various keys and scissors jangle. 'My lady, I am not sure what is for the best, but my cousin said that something peculiar was happening up at Dun Ollaigh. That Feradach has been taking your father's place, acting as though it belongs to him. All I can say is that I'm sorry from the bottom of my heart. You were right to go when you did and I was wrong to allow my man to send that boy to tell on you...only he were found tied up. It is all most confusing.'

'And is Captain Feradach's brother, the monk, at Dun Ollaigh?' Sandulf asked, breaking into the conversation in heavily accented Pictish. Ceanna gave him a quelling look, but he nodded.

Bertana stopped and stared at Sandulf, taking in the obvious foreignness of his sword and colouring. 'You look familiar. Weren't you here that day Lady Ceanna left, or am I mistaking you for someone else?'

'This is my husband. We married at Nrurim with my aunt's blessing.'

The woman's brow furrowed. 'The lady abbess sanctioned your marriage to a Northman? Will wonders never cease. Feradach's brother has been saying masses for your soul. Night and day. They say it won't be long until your father follows you…that is, well I don't know…but I think he is alive.'

'You explain,' Sandulf said in an undertone. 'I doubt my Pictish is sufficient yet.'

Ceanna nodded, agreeing with his assessment. They were going to have to move quickly to rescue Sandulf's brother and were going to need help. She had to trust Bertana and rapidly told the woman about the attack, her distrust of Urist's intentions and the missing sons of the late King Aed. Her eyes grew wide.

'I have never liked that Feradach and I know your stepmother is a great lady and all, but something's going on and I don't like it,' Bertana said when Ceanna finished her brief recital. 'Two boys, you say? Now that I come to think of it, there were two boys crying their eyes out in one of the chambers, according to my cousin, the one who works in the kitchen up at the keep. I thought she were exaggerating, like. Why would Lady Mhairi have any children there, seeing how ill her lord was and that begging your pardon, my lady, her stepdaughter had been foully murdered.'

'I've promised my aunt I will see them to safety. I intend to keep that promise.'

Bertana put a hand on Ceanna's shoulder when she finished. 'I know what you have done for everyone around here. You carried on doing what your mother did before you, looking after everyone, but your stepmother has a different approach. Those bairns, if they are the ones my cousin saw, my blood chills to think about what could have happened to them. I want to help, my lady, and make amends for sending my boy to tell on you.'

A lump grew in Ceanna's throat. Her efforts had not gone unnoticed. 'Then you will keep my secret until I decide what is for the best.'

Bertana gave a sideways glance at Sandulf. 'Only thing is, if you were in trouble, my lady, you should have come to your friends first and explained instead of throwing your lot in with a Northman.'

'Northman or not, Sandulf Sigurdsson is my chosen husband. A true friend to… Dun Ollaigh. Remember that.'

Bertana gave a quick curtsy. 'I don't mean no disrespect, but if he were such a friend, you should have told us afore you left. My sister Mildreth ran away with the man she loved, but she told me afore she did it so I didn't worry. I don't know what happened to her.'

Silently Ceanna resolved that if she could, she would pass on news of how Mother Mildreth was faring and strive to bring them face to face. She pressed her lips together. She hoped she would still be here to do it. The same with the harvest. Her destiny lay with her husband, but these people commanded part of her soul.

'You grow solemn,' Sandulf said. 'Is everything well? A new complication?'

She gave him a quick smile, banishing the thoughts as problems for the future. 'Our luck holds. We can rescue your brother before confronting Feradach and Lugh.'

'If we rescue my brother, this will let everyone know what is happening. There is much more at stake here. Do you want Lugh and Feradach to steal your lands?'

Ceanna frowned. 'I've been working on a plan.'

Sandulf's eyes narrowed.

'This is a good one, I promise.'

'You will be taking far too many risks for a start, whatever this plan of yours is.'

She smiled back at him. 'Calculated risks. Nothing is going to go wrong. I'll have your sword with me when I reveal myself, but in order for my scheme to work, you must take your brother's place.'

Sandulf's eyes gleamed. 'We don't look much alike.'

'To the Picts you will. One man from the North appears much the same as another. But scrubbing your face with dirt will help.'

To her relief, Sandulf smiled. 'Freeing my brother is the most important thing. Discovering how he was captured.'

'Feradach and his brother are sure to be in the square when Urist makes his accusation. They won't be looking for a move from the prisoner.'

'I want to know why the fool travelled here. I had everything under control,' He shook his head. 'Despite everything he said, Rurik doesn't trust me to accomplish this on my own.'

'You don't know that.'

'I do. I know what my brothers are like. I'm the baby of the family for ever, toddling around behind them. A wooden sword clutched in my fist, never a steel one. They do not see the warrior I've become, the things I have achieved and all the things I am capable of achieving in the future.'

'Yet you long to be a part of the brotherhood.'

Sandulf was silent for a long heartbeat. 'I do. More than anything.'

Chapter Thirteen

Sandulf was pleased that they would be operating under cover of darkness. He had to admit that Ceanna's plan was a sound one. There were flaws—not the least her being in the square rather than waiting safely with Bertana back at the tavern. But he had accepted that he would need help getting Danr back if he was going to take his place.

She was asking him to trust that the villagers would rise up in support of her once they had gathered to see Urist's viewing of the prisoner. But he didn't have a better plan and he did know time was of the essence. In his mind, he could hear his brothers arguing and he knew what each of them would say about the scheme. Brandt would counsel that it was far too risky. Alarr would warn him against being caught without a weapon. Rurik would scout out the lie of the land and have three other backup plans. Danr, well, he'd notice Ceanna's ankles and tell him that he was being a fool for not telling her how he felt. But how could he when he had this hanging over him?

'Are you ready? Do you have enough dirt on your

face?' Ceanna asked, lifting her hood. 'Have we thought of every eventuality?'

'I will take a dagger. Just in case it is not a fair hearing as you think it will be.'

'It would be highly unusual for my father to behave in any other way. He will want his daughter's murderer punished according to the law.'

'Nevertheless, I remain cautious. I would be a fool to be caught without one.' Sandulf slipped the slender blade into a special pocket in his right boot. He'd purchased the boots in Constantinople, after he'd seen how the hidden dagger in a friend's pair had saved both their lives.

It had struck him at the time that of all his brothers, Danr would be the most envious of the boots. Danr was fond of his clothes and said that it was the cut of his boots that endeared him to the many women who fell at his feet.

An unaccustomed throb of pain went through Sandulf. He wanted to hear Danr joke again. He missed his brother's teasing jests; he missed the faint pause after his outrageous statements as if Danr was waiting to judge the reaction; mostly he'd missed the sound of his brother's voice.

'We will free him,' Ceanna said.

He gave a quick smile and squeezed her hand. 'Yes, we will. Together.'

She answered his attempt at a smile with a genuine one of her own. His heart ached afresh.

Whose happiness would he put first—his wife's or his brother's? He pushed the thought away. It wouldn't come to that. He had to survive first.

The faint silver of moonlight lit the market square, silhouetting the post. Ceanna stifled a cry. Sandulf's brother had collapsed against the wooden spar, with sagging knees and hands held over his head.

'Stay here,' Sandulf said in a low voice. 'Until I give the order. There may be watchers.'

Ceanna sighed. 'How can I help if I remain in the shadows?'

'Ceanna!'

She rolled her eyes.

'Do this for me. Please.' Sandulf hurried over to where his brother was slumped. 'We will get you out of here alive, Danr.'

Danr groaned. Ceanna saw Sandulf wince and fumble with the ropes. There was no way Danr would be able to walk on his own towards her.

Ignoring Sandulf's earlier order, Ceanna ran over to them. He raised his brow.

'You need another pair of hands.'

He nodded. 'When I release the ropes, keep his head from touching the ground.'

'I've got him.'

He carefully undid the ropes, muttering a curse as one of the knots stuck but he persisted. It finally gave way suddenly. Danr slumped. Staggering under the weight, Ceanna managed to lower him down gently.

Up close, the resemblance to Sandulf was apparent. Even if she hadn't known of the relationship, she would have guessed they were related.

He nodded his thanks to Ceanna.

'All right, Danr? Your baby brother has nearly rescued you.'

His brother gave a faint groan which sounded like, 'Took your time, you fumbling idiot.'

'I don't know why I ever expected thanks from you, Danr. Maybe I should leave you here to die.'

Danr opened one eye. 'It is you, Sandulf. Rurik said you were here when he sent me north. I half-doubted him. You know what Rurik can be like. Then these crazy people claimed I murdered the daughter of their lord. Never saw the woman in my life. Now you turn up and I know it must be all your fault.'

'Rurik is happy with his lady?'

Danr closed his eyes. 'Utterly.'

'We need to get him away from here. Before anyone realises what is happening,' Ceanna said in a hoarse whisper.

'Ceanna, I may not get the chance again.'

Ceanna forced a smile, trying to banish the sudden clench of fear at the risk Sandulf was taking. 'You *will* have a chance. Our plan will work. Now get the ropes about your wrists before someone comes.'

Saying the words out loud helped and the sheer nauseating panic which had choked her subsided.

'Ceanna? I think I was supposed to have murdered a Lady Ceanna,' Danr said.

'This is Lady Ceanna, my wife, and she is very much alive.'

'That figures.'

Ceanna put an arm around Danr and helped him to rise. She started to lead him away, but he stumbled and his heavy weight fell into her. A low moan escaped her throat. She gritted her teeth and redoubled her efforts, but his bulk prevented her from moving very fast.

Sandulf put an arm around Danr's other shoulder and pulled him off her. 'Let's get you gone before the ropes go on my wrists.'

Danr shrugged him off. 'I can walk. Give me a chance to get the blood moving in my feet. Always in a hurry, you.'

'My fault, not his,' Ceanna whispered. 'My ankle turned.'

'You go with my wife,' Sandulf said in a low voice. 'When we are done here, we will speak properly. How in the name of Sigurd you got yourself in this situation, I will never know!'

Danr put his hands on his knees. Sweat poured from his brow. 'Everything you do, Sandulf.'

Sandulf's jaw jutted forward. 'Everything I do what?'

Ceanna braced herself for a fight between the brothers.

Danr paused and then smiled. 'Everything you do is different from how I'd do it. I can walk now.'

Sandulf clapped him on the back. 'Good. Go.'

Ceanna shook her head. 'Are all your brothers like this?'

'Brandt is far worse. Always gave me grief. He wanted things done precisely his way. He was very like our father in that respect.'

'Still is,' Danr said.

She rolled her eyes. 'Is it any wonder you took the first opportunity to escape?'

'That's one way of thinking about it.' Sandulf leant forward and brushed a kiss against the corner of her mouth. The touch sent a pulse thrumming through her. 'Take my battered hulk of a brother to safety. Let me handle the rest. I can do the ropes on my own.'

Ceanna knew there was much she wanted to say to him, but now was not the time. It amazed her that she had ever stopped believing in heroes when the man in front of her was doing a very good imitation of one.

'I love you,' she whispered before her nerve failed.

In the dim light his eyes burned. 'Don't say that. Don't ever say that.'

Ceanna reeled back as if he had struck her. 'I understand.'

Did she love him? Did she really love him? Sandulf found it impossible to banish the stricken look on Ceanna's face from his mind. He wasn't worthy of her love, not yet, maybe not ever. His brothers clearly didn't think so. But he was going to try.

Sandulf's arms ached from where he'd tied them on the post. The ropes were loose enough for him to move when he had to, but he needed the element of surprise to work in his favour. He kept his face against the post and contented himself with running through all he had to do and how he would keep Ceanna from doing anything rash.

By Ceanna's reckoning, Feradach and his brother would make their move about noon, when everyone was gathered and the judgement would begin. However, they arrived when the rose hue of dawn had barely lit up the square and all remained quiet. Urist, a well-dressed woman and the two brothers—one in the costume of a guard and the other dressed as monk—entered. Sandulf glimpsed them out of the corner of his eye. Despite the temptation, he kept his eyes trained on a knot in the wood and went over the plan he'd agreed with Ceanna. To take all of them, he needed his sword, the sword which Ceanna would bring with her. His dagger would only work against one assailant. Which brother would give him the best chance of success?

'It needs to be done carefully,' the well-dressed woman said. He assumed it was Mhairi, Ceanna's stepmother. There was a faint nasal twang to her words. Her shoes rang out against the cobbles, stopping a little way from where he was tied. 'We want justice done. You can recognise the culprit, can't you, Urist ab Urist? When the time comes?'

Urist gave a loud belch. 'His features are emblazoned on my mind, my Lady Mhairi. I will not make that sort of mistake. I will do you proud. This man murdered your stepdaughter. He made such a mess of her that it weren't right for you or her father to see her corpse. Right vicious he was. Captain Feradach agreed with me.'

Urist peered at Sandulf. His jaw dropped. Sandulf mouthed *Ceanna is here* and Urist took a step backwards.

'For the sake of Lady Ceanna I will identify the culprit,' Urist said. 'I promise. I won't let her down. I will proclaim the truth at the judgement. Now let me go. I need more ale. I don't need to see any more.'

'He won't have gone far,' Lady Mhairi said after the footsteps died away. 'Your guards can fetch him from the nearest ale house when the case will be tried.'

'It would be better if the witness was not drunk,' a man said. 'Can we sober him up in time?'

'Don't worry. It will all work out. You will see—the shock of the trial combined with the funeral will kill the old fool.'

'You shouldn't have come here, Lugh. You should have stayed to ensure your job was done,' Feradach said.

'You sent word about a Northman asking the way

to Nrurim. My angel from Glannoventa might be in danger.'

'You should never have accepted that commission from Glannoventa. What did you gain from it? Nothing.'

'I met my angel, a sweeter and kinder woman you could not ask for.'

'And nearly blew everything because this Annis of yours had the eyes of an angel and must not get blood on her hands. Dealings in the kingdom of the Northmen to bring fabulous wealth, Lugh? You killed what? Two women? A sure way to get yourself killed to my mind. Your ugly face even acquired a new scar.'

'My angel gave me a cloth to stem the bleeding when the ship was pulling away. It's why I call my scar my angel's kiss.'

'Spare us any more about your blessed angel,' Feradach said. 'It's all you've gone on about since you got back and I'm sick of hearing about it. Keep to the business at hand.'

Sandulf's fingers itched to grab the knife in his boot, but he resisted. Striking now would achieve little.

'I'd feel happier if we hadn't used that body from your little ambush,' Lady Mhairi said. 'You were far too heavy with your sword that night. Thankfully, no one has questioned about that missing woman.'

'That drunken sot gave his oath with a sword held to his son's throat. I should have run him through. He insisted that Lady Ceanna was certainly dead out in the forest and you needed a funeral. You said your husband would collapse on the coffin and never rise. He seems stronger than ever since he learned of her death. Since he put his head on that coffin and the crowd roared their approval.'

'The depth of the feeling towards her has surprised me. I had no idea that she was that beloved,' Lady Mhairi said. 'If anyone thinks I had anything to do with it, it could be the end of all our hopes, Feradach.'

'You're far too nervous, my dear. Even if this idiot has double-crossed us, Ceanna is long gone from here.' Feradach gave a harsh laugh. 'I doubt she'd survive for long. The woman wouldn't say boo to a goose, terrified of her own shadow.'

'I hope you are right.'

'See.' Rough hands jerked Sandulf's head back and a fetid scent assaulted his senses. 'This man will be the right sacrifice. I should slit his throat right now and be done with it. Who mourns for one from the North? Certainly not I.'

'Look! Isn't that your arm ring he wears, Brother? The one you lost on that expedition.'

'That he does. Well, well, it would appear *all* our problems are about to be solved, Feradach. My angel will be on her knees, thanking me for it, and I look forward to her thanks no end.'

When they returned to the stable, Ceanna set about cleaning the worst of Danr's wounds, despite his protests that he was fine. The wounds appeared to be mainly bruising from the beating and superficial cuts and scratches rather than anything more serious. Keeping busy with little practical jobs rather than thinking about Sandulf's rejection of her love made it possible for her to hold her hands steady.

Sandulf had never made any secret of the reasoning behind their marriage. And she had been under no illusions that she had cornered him in the interview with her aunt, forcing his hand. The one time they had discussed it, at Mother Mildreth's cottage, he had firmly but kindly promised her friendship and nothing else.

'Remain here with Bertana as your nurse,' Ceanna said to Danr when she'd finished tending him. 'Sandulf and I have the plan worked out to the last detail. I go back, show myself when a crowd of enough size has gathered and Sandulf will do the rest. Bertana has done well, spreading rumours about my death being false.'

Danr blocked the door. 'With the greatest respect, you have that wrong. No son of Sigurd is a coward. I will join this fight. I will be at your side.'

'You've been beaten. You've hung from a post for nearly a day.'

'All the more reason for me to fight.' He put his hands together. 'Give me a weapon, any weapon. Allow me to help. I'm grateful for what you both have done so far, but he tempts the Norns who control his destiny too much. These men are determined to kill him and he lacks his sword.'

'It goes with me. For later. We've worked it out.'

Danr blanched. 'My very foolish baby brother. Will he never learn?'

'He has a dagger in his boot. He said you'd approve of his boots.'

A wry smile crossed Danr's face. 'I knew I liked the cut of his boots.'

'He thinks well of all his brothers. He wants them to think well of him.'

'Rurik told me what he'd done to the other killers. The boy has to stop doing things all on his own.' Danr shook his head. 'It is how he gets himself into serious trouble. You should have seen him the summer before our father died. He rushed the enemy and was out on his own, down on one knee. We thought he was off to Valhalla for certain that day. Brandt fought his way to him to rescue him and received no thanks for it.'

'My husband is not the impetuous boy bent on glory you remember.' Ceanna quivered with righteous indignation. 'He is a man, he is my husband and you will treat him with respect.'

Danr gave a low bow. 'Aye, my lady. I beg your pardon.'

'Granted.' She graciously lowered her head. 'It has preyed on his mind for a long time that he can't measure up to his brothers. He told me about the skipping stone contests and how he always came last.'

'Until the day he came first.' Danr shook his head, laughing. 'We must have another contest.'

'I think he would welcome that.'

'He was alone in the longhouse that day, looking after our sister-in-law,' Danr said. 'If he'd had help, who knows what might have happened. One young warrior against the four assassins who managed to murder our father and Vigmarr—two of the best warriors in the North—before people even understood what was happening? He is lucky to have emerged with his life.'

'I'd understood that his brothers were all away, except for his middle brother Alarr who was severely injured in the fight outside the hall.'

'There was one brother who wasn't there who should have been.' Danr's cheeks flushed and he rapidly examined his boots. 'I have to live with that, my lady. The knowledge remains with me always. I swear to you that I have changed my ways.'

'Where were you?'

'With a woman. Some forgettable warm body with accommodating thighs.' His mouth twisted. 'I'm not proud of what happened, my lady, but I want a chance to put the matter right. Please let me have that chance. Let me assist in whatever Sandulf has planned. He cannot bear this burden alone.'

She watched the shifting shadows. Danr and Sandulf were much alike—neither wanted the other one hurt.

'Call me Ceanna, please. I'm your sister.'

'I hadn't considered that. I have acquired three sisters in a matter of months. All of them excellent women.' He sobered. 'I love my little brother dearly, my—Ceanna. He is fun to tease. I can see he has grown up beyond all recognition in our time apart. I knew the boy and want very much to know the man. Will you allow me the honour and privilege of fighting alongside him and you? Will you allow me to do what I failed to do all those years ago?'

'He gave me specific orders where you were concerned.'

'And if I fail to protect you, my new sister-in-law, what will that make me? Don't you think I carry enough of a burden with the deaths of Alarr's fiancée and Ingrid emblazoned on my soul?

Despite his many cuts and bruises, despite his obvious tiredness, Ceanna saw the pleading hunger in his eyes. She handed him Sandulf's sword. 'I doubt I could swing it anyway if it came to it.' She rapidly outlined the scheme she and Sandulf had devised. 'You can get it to him when I reveal myself. All eyes will be on me.'

Danr gave the sword a few practice swings. 'It is well balanced. I prefer my own sword, but this will do until I can retrieve it.'

'Sandulf is going to need that.'

Danr made an overly innocent face. It was easy to see how women fell for his charm. 'You said he had a dagger. And things can happen very quickly in operations like this.'

'Sandulf and I agreed the plan. Follow it.' She added 'please' as an afterthought.

His eyes danced even more. 'I'll see what can be done.'

'My lady, the sun rises,' Bertana shouted from the door.

Ceanna ground her teeth. Arguing with Danr was pointless. She lifted her hood and concealed her features. 'The time has come.'

'If you slit his throat,' Lady Mhairi cried out as the assassin pulled Sandulf's head back and he could see the horrifyingly familiar scar, a double star with a cross as well as a newer scar overlying the old one on Lugh's ugly face, 'they will search for the murderer.'

'They will, but not very hard.' The rough hands slipped about Sandulf's neck, cutting off his oxygen.

'Giric, the King's Regent, is already hunting the assassin who murdered Aed. The last thing we need is the King's guard sticking its collective nose in our business, Brother. Patience. Your thirst for blood will be quenched. I agree with my lady, we wait and allow the crowd to tear him limb from limb.'

The hands about Sandulf's neck loosened. He gulped in life-giving air. 'I will wait for now.'

'What is going on here? Stepmother, why is this man tied up?'

Sandulf's heart stopped. Why could Ceanna never

stick to an agreed plan? She had put herself in danger without any back-up. The townspeople were still to gather in any significant number.

'Lady Ceanna! By all the—' He started again in a different tone. 'It is excellent to see my bride alive and well.'

'I understand you've arrested this man for my murder, Stepmother.' Ceanna pointed towards where he stood. 'Release him. As you can see, I am very much alive.'

Sandulf's eyes narrowed. Where was his sword? How could she have forgotten it? She seemed to think mere words would alter this. He fought against the ropes, but one knot was more stubbornly tied than the rest.

'Brother. I can take her before anyone notices,' Lugh said in a low voice. 'Blame it on the Northman, trying to escape. The villagers will lap it up. I can preach a sermon on it.'

'Do it.'

Sandulf twisted his wrist to the right, to the left and slid his hand out. He grabbed the dagger from his boot, pivoted, but saw he was too far away for an accurate throw. Lugh was nearly upon Ceanna. Then he saw him, his battered but unbowed brother standing in front of her, with a drawn sword, their family's battle cry emerging from his throat.

Lugh belatedly tried to change course, but his momentum carried him forward. But with one motion, Danr connected with the robed assassin.

There was a gurgle and Lugh fell to the ground at Ceanna's feet. Danr made a little flourish with his hand and bowed towards Sandulf. Always the showman was Danr, Brandt used to say.

Sandulf clenched his dagger until his knuckles ached.

'Brother, you were supposed to be resting from your ordeal.'

'I believe I've saved your life, Sandulf. Do not throw it away so easily next time.'

'Guards, seize them!' Lady Mhairi shouted. 'These heathens have attacked and killed a monk!'

Nobody moved. All shocked eyes seemed to be on Ceanna.

'What are you waiting for? That man, that heathen, slew a monk in cold blood,' Feradach shouted.

The guards and the now-gathering crowd remained still.

Ceanna raised her arms. 'For the sake of the love and affection you have given me and my family, I beseech you, stay your hands. These men have saved my life. There has been a plot against me and my father. My stepmother and Feradach, the captain of the guards, seek my death.'

The crowd began to mumble. A lone woman's voice called, 'God bless Lady Ceanna! Hooray that you are alive!'

The cry was taken up, growing louder and louder until the roar shook the buildings. Ceanna's mouth dropped open and she stood still for a heartbeat.

She retrieved the sword Lugh had been carrying and held it above her head. Her smile became genuine as the crowd responded with even greater cheers.

Sandulf watched Feradach and Lady Mhairi. The crowd would prevent them from escaping, but they remained dangerous.

'Lady Ceanna is touched in the head, like her father,' Lady Mhairi proclaimed. 'There has been no plot.

Merely a misunderstanding. The holy priest was going to embrace her. Ceanna, look at what you have done.'

'I overheard the plot that you, your lover and this supposedly holy man were concoting,' Sandulf said. 'Even men secured to posts have ears.'

'And you are?'

'Sandulf Sigurdsson, husband to Lady Ceanna of Dun Ollaigh.'

The woman's mouth fell open. 'You can't be.'

'We married at St Fillans with my aunt's blessing,' Ceanna proclaimed loudly.

'Mother Abbe gave her blessing?'

'Yes, and it cannot be undone,' Sandulf said. He judged the distance between the woman and the captain of the guard. Even now Danr was slowly moving towards him, getting himself in position.

'Where are the royal children, Stepmother?' Ceanna asked and Lady Mhairi's head swivelled towards her. 'The sons of the late King Aed that the false monk promised he would take to Éireann. I presume they are somewhere in Dun Ollaigh.'

Her stepmother took a step backwards and stumbled. 'You said it was Ceanna, Feradach. You said it was her before the coffin was nailed shut. We buried her.'

'It was all her idea!' Feradach said, looking about him wildly. 'Lady Mhairi and my brother. Concocted in St Fillans. Nothing to do with me. I can't stand her and her whining ways. Dried-up stick of a woman. Guards, arrest her!'

'You liar! I will stop your lying mouth.'

Lady Mhairi rushed forward and wrenched the dagger from Sandulf's hand. Before he could react, she plunged it into Feradach's throat. He gurgled and fell forward.

The crowd looked on in stunned silence. Urist, who had stood quietly during all this, rapidly looked about him and fell to his knees while he loudly proclaimed his loyalty. That he had recognised Sandulf and had not given him away.

Ceanna ran over to Sandulf's side and threw her arms about his neck. 'My husband.'

The crowd roared their approval.

'It would appear they have missed you,' Sandulf murmured, watching the crowd and Ceanna's reaction to it. They loved her and it would seem she revelled in it. The knowledge struck him like a knife. How could he ask her to give this up? His duty was to his family and hers to these people.

He had worked for years to avenge the murder of Ingrid and her unborn child. His brothers would need him at their side. And Ceanna wouldn't need him at all.

The thought made his chest ache. He wanted her to need him—to love him with her whole heart and not just say the words because he had put himself in danger. He wanted to prove that he was worthy of her love.

With an effort he pushed the thought away. He focused on the present objective, rather than worrying about battles to come.

'I think you had best come back to Dun Ollaigh, Stepmother,' Ceanna said in a very quiet voice, holding out her hand to her as the cheering died away. 'We have much to do.'

Her stepmother's eyes were wide and darted everywhere, never resting on anyone or anything, a contrast to the earlier gaze Sandulf had endured from the woman. 'I need to see to your father, Ceanna. It has been most unconscionable that you have been gone for so long.

You worried him to the point of near death. I actually feared your funeral would be the death of him. He did insist on going. And he will have to be told gently that you are, in fact, alive.'

'You buried another woman's corpse.'

'That man, Urist, he led me a merry dance with a closed coffin. Feradach told me his brother had lost control back at the clearing when you wouldn't answer him. I feared him, truly I did, and his brother was worse. I couldn't look. He said your head was totally crushed.'

'That is not what you said to Feradach,' Sandulf said. 'I believe you wanted the shock of the funeral to kill your husband, Lady Mhairi. You knew that body wasn't Ceanna's and played along. Urist, to his small credit, refused to tell you where Ceanna was when Feradach threatened the life of his son.'

'Indeed.' Ceanna's voice dripped ice.

'You have always been far too headstrong, Ceanna. All I have ever wanted for you was the best.' Her stepmother gave a little simpering smile. 'No doubt you told these men a pile of untruths and embellished stories, but you and I know the full truth, don't we? I have never been your enemy, Ceanna. Search your heart. You know that to be true.'

Ceanna signalled to two of the townspeople who grabbed her stepmother's arms. 'My stepmother needs to return to Dun Ollaigh with me. My father should have the opportunity to hear what has happened here.'

A small smile which Sandulf distrusted appeared on her stepmother's lips. 'I'd be grateful.'

Ceanna rapidly organised the villagers, all of whom obeyed her words without questioning. She was in her element, here, moving with assurance and command

'Your stepmother is probably the most dangerous of the lot. Do you trust her guards?' Sandulf murmured as he stooped to regain his dagger.

'I agree with you.' Ceanna handed him Lugh's sword and wiped her hands on her gown. Her eyes were bright with unshed tears. 'I need to find my father. He needs to know I live while time remains for us. He deserves the truth, but my stepmother is right, it will have to be gently done.'

'We will all go.' Sandulf put his hand on her shoulder. She briefly rested her head on his chest as if she was drawing strength from him, but then seemed to remember something, stood up straight and began speaking to various well-wishers.

'My Lady, I wanted to say I was sorry, sorrier than you will ever know. And I didn't betray you. I told them a Northman kidnapped you and I expected you were dead in the forest. But I couldn't be sure seeing as how my head ached so bad.' Urist, shame-faced, stepped in front of them. For a change, he was speaking Gaelic.

'I overheard them saying they'd held a sword to your son's throat and threatened his life, but your story never varied,' Sandulf said. 'Thank you for keeping quiet and protecting Lady Ceanna in your own way.'

Urist stood up a bit straighter. 'I was right to get that body, but I was wrong about who was going to attack us. I thought this here Northman would, except now they say he is your husband and that means he will be my lord soon. But that Feradach was thoroughly bad.'

'I hope my father lives for some time yet. And I am grateful...'

'And I didn't betray your man neither. I could have

done, but I didn't. My loyalty, my lady, does belong to you.'

'Your delay assisted us both times,' Sandulf said in Pictish and held out his hand. 'Shall we put the past behind us?'

'Why didn't you tell me you spoke my language? You are one of the good ones.'

'Remember that,' Ceanna said, fixing Urist with her gaze. She did not fully trust the man, but what he had done had certainly helped them. 'My husband *is* one of the good ones and I want no more trouble from you.'

Urist went running off, shouting about how Lady Ceanna's new husband was a good Northman.

Sandulf controlled his features. He was under few illusions that the people who lived here would accept him if not for Ceanna. In time, he hoped... He dragged his mind away. The future stretched out uncertainly before him.

'Your lady is far more of an important personage than I first realised. You've done well, Brother,' Danr said in an undertone. 'I assumed she was some woman you picked up on your travels. Pretty enough in her own way, but...'

Some woman. Like one of his faceless women? Sandulf pitied his older half-brother. He didn't understand the difference. Ceanna had ruined him for other women. He now totally understood Brandt's overwhelming anger at Ingrid's death. He hated to think how he'd behave if such a tragedy had befallen Ceanna. But what he felt for Ceanna was far too new and overwhelming to be confessed to his brother.

'I realise what you are saying,' he said when he trusted

himself to speak. 'You made a mistake. Ceanna is far more than some woman. She is my wife, my Skadi.'

'A force to be reckoned with.'

'That she is.' Sandulf watched how she stopped to talk to people and allowed herself to be enveloped in a variety of hugs as she started towards the fortress.

He had thought it would be a relief to be able to give Ceanna's protection over to someone else, but a huge hole opened in his insides. He wasn't ready to give it up yet. He wanted to be her hero, the one who gave her everything her heart desired, and it frightened him. He had nearly caused her death today. It was his brother's actions which had saved her, not his. He needed to remember that he did not deserve her yet.

Chapter Fourteen

Ceanna tried to concentrate on the little things which needed to be done, rather than the enormity of what had happened. Sandulf had narrowly escaped with his life. Her body still shook from the memory of that man's hands about Sandulf's throat. And then the sight of the naked sword heading towards her. Danr had been correct when he predicted that she would require his help.

Easier not to think about what could have happened by ordering the townspeople to bury the bodies and bind her stepmother. Little things. When she could do no more, she started towards Dun Ollaigh with Sandulf and his brother. Her stepmother, flanked by Bertana's husband and another man, followed along behind.

'Do you think the guards will be loyal to you or to your stepmother?' Sandulf asked as they neared the gate. His words were oddly formal as if he was still embarrassed about her earlier outburst where she'd offered him her heart and he'd refused it.

'I will deal with it whatever happens.' Ceanna balled her fists and concentrated on putting one foot firmly in front of the other. Even saying the words out loud made her feel more confident. She hadn't time to waste on dreams or wishes. She had to concentrate on what she could accomplish. 'The people of Dun Ollaigh deserve better than what they currently have. I alone can rectify that.'

She kept her head up. She was done with begging anyone for love. Her heart ached for him, but his did not ache for her. She could not force him to think she was indispensable.

'You alone?'

'I am developing a plan as we speak.'

'You and your plans.'

Ceanna stopped abruptly. Sandulf had to see that she could make a difference here. Coming back had taught her that she'd been mistaken—she was far from alone. The townspeople trusted her to help them. And they had helped her once they realised what had been happening. They loved her, even if he had no true feelings for her. 'This one worked, didn't it?'

He gave a smile which made her insides melt. She stiffened her spine. He didn't need her love and he didn't want it.

'Danr, staying hidden until the last heartbeat, was a master stroke.'

Danr laughed. 'Sandulf, you are married to a woman without a romantic bone in her body and who is more like your Aunt Kolga than Ingrid. Do you remember how you swore you'd never marry anyone like her? You were always going to marry Ingrid's lookalike.'

The laughter died from Sandulf's eyes. 'My wife is nothing like my aunt.'

'I didn't mean any offence.' Danr held up his hands. 'It is Kolga who was the one who was always thinking ahead and making plans for Maerr, according to my late mother. A practical person rather than a dreamer.'

Ceanna hated the stab of envy which sliced through her. Danr was right—she was practical. But she wanted Sandulf to think she was like Ingrid—worthy of love. 'I'll take that as a compliment. Practicality gets results.'

Sandulf lowered his brow. 'We will speak, Danr, but know that I and my practical *wife* had everything in hand without your interference.'

'My interference, as you term it, saved both your lives, oh, baby brother of mine.'

Ceanna cleared her throat and they both turned in surprise to look at her. 'You two can argue to your heart's content later, but we must attend to the task at hand— securing Dun Ollaigh and ensuring my father recovers. I suspect my stepmother was doing something to make him weak. My aunt said that my stepmother and Brother Mattios nursed Father Callum, the priest who died unexpectedly. Something about that story sounded all too familiar.'

'What did I say? Practical to her fingertips,' Danr said. 'Once I'd worried that you would find someone with other desirable attributes and not a single thought in her head.'

The way he said it with a slight curl of his lip made a knot of unease grow in Ceanna's stomach. She wanted to be the sort of woman Sandulf chose willingly to spend the rest of his life with.

Now that they had dispatched both Feradach and his brother, there was no reason for Sandulf to continue to protect her until she reached a place of safety. And she had.

'My father will be in his chamber, I believe.'

Sandulf squeezed her hand. 'Are you nervous about encountering your father?'

She pasted on a smile, grateful for the excuse. The last thing Sandulf needed was her mooning after him in front of his brother. 'It is harder than I thought it might be.'

The colours in his eyes deepened. 'Undoubtedly you already have plans for every eventuality.'

Ceanna concentrated on the great door at Dun Ollaigh. 'Something like that.'

'All this belongs to you?' Danr asked.

'After my father dies, it will be my responsibility along with my husband's. But I hope that day is far in the future.'

Danr thumped Sandulf on the back. 'You always did have a knack of smelling sweet even when you fell into a pile of dung.'

The look Sandulf gave Danr spoke volumes. 'My wife's home is not a pile of dung, Danr.'

'A figure of speech. I am sure your wife understands—I am pleased for your good fortune.'

Sandulf gave a grunt and banged on the door for it to open.

The guards looked at Ceanna open-mouthed. Ceanna greeted them by name and they quickly recovered their poise.

'I believe you should let me in to see my father.'

'Is it truly you, my lady?' one of the older guards asked. 'We'd heard rumours, but Feradach said before he left that we were to keep everyone out save him and Lady Mhairi.'

'Feradach always did like twisting the truth and he is no longer able to issue orders.' Ceanna rapidly explained the situation before gesturing towards her stepmother. 'I believe my lady stepmother needs to rest after her ordeal.'

'That sounds like a good idea,' the guard said.

Her stepmother was taken to her chamber. She went meekly and without a fuss. She shot a dagger look at Sandulf, but it was so quick that Ceanna thought she must have imagined it.

'Will you take me to my father? He must be informed of Feradach's demise and my resurrection, as it were.' She gave a weak laugh, but her stomach was in knots. One or two let out ragged cheers while they watched Sandulf and Danr with careful eyes. Feradach had been feared rather than admired. But Ceanna immediately saw that they were no more certain about a Northman potentially being in charge.

'Daughter! My daughter! You have returned,' her father said in a reedy voice from where he lay in his chamber. The maid curtsied and left the room when they entered. Her father's hand plucked at the coverlet. 'They said you were dead and took me to your funeral. Mhairi said that I'd only be upset if I saw your body. But when I laid my head on that coffin, I knew in my heart you were alive and would return to take your rightful place as the Lady of Dun Ollaigh. I don't know where the thought came from, but I have clung to it with all the strength in my body that I would live to see you again and be able to ask your pardon for marrying a woman like your stepmother.'

Ceanna went immediately to him and covered his hand and his fingers tightened about hers. The last time she had touched him he could barely curl his fingers.

This time the response was far stronger. 'I returned, Father, with my husband. We have rescued you.'

She gestured towards where Sandulf stood, watching with wary eyes. If anything, he seemed further away than ever, as if somehow he was looking for an excuse to go.

Something of her father's old fierceness returned. 'You are married to a Northman? How can this be? A man from the North as my daughter's choice? That does beat everything!'

'With my aunt's blessing.' Ceanna kept tight hold of his hand and rapidly told the tale. She silently prayed that he would refrain from making any horrible remarks about men from the North.

Her father muttered, 'If he is truly your choice, I will be content.'

'We uncovered a plot against Dun Ollaigh and your life,' Sandulf said in a quiet voice. 'Your captain of the guards plotted with your wife to seize control. It's possible the plan was hatched before you even married her.'

Her father closed his eyes and was silent for a long time. Ceanna wondered if he had fallen asleep or if it was just all too much for him to take in. 'I overheard them talking a few days ago when they thought I was asleep. I half-hoped I had dreamt it, but I knew in my heart I've been a foolish, selfish man who allowed a viper to enter my home and poison my family. I thought I'd lost my beloved child. I'm not dreaming you are here, am I? You are here, Daughter, aren't you? I wanted to beg your forgiveness. To say how much I love you.'

His hand tightened about hers again.

Ceanna blinked away tears. Her father believed her. 'I'm real, I'm alive and I'm here. And you are going to get better. I met a healer on my travels—Mother Mildreth. She will come and look after you, I am certain of it, particularly because I believe she is the estranged sister of the tavern keeper's wife. I will send a messenger tonight.'

Her father collapsed back against the pillows and gave a tremulous smile. 'I have barely been able to eat since you were supposedly killed and my mind seems less fuzzy as a result.'

'I believe you were being poisoned. I also believe my stepmother poisoned a priest at St Fillans. My aunt…'

'Abbe always wanted to shape the world the way she wanted it. Mhairi was her project. I was a lonely fool.' He closed his eyes. 'Sit with me. Please.'

After they had discussed a few things and her father had drifted off, Ceanna remembered about her other task and summoned the maidservants back into the chamber.

'Feradach's brother, the false monk, had two children in his care. Has anyone seen them?' Ceanna asked.

'They are safe in Dun Ollaigh,' one of the maidservants said. 'One of them keeps crying and asking to return to court. Brother Mattios—'

'Go and get the children, please, and bring them to the hall.'

'You are back to stay,' her father murmured as he awoke. 'We will have a feast to celebrate your marriage. I assume Northmen feast the same as us.'

Ceanna noticed Sandulf's face become thunderous. 'No need for a feast, Father,' she said awkwardly. 'Sandulf and I have much to do. Much to put right.'

'Dun Ollaigh needs you, Ceanna. When you were gone, everything went wrong. It will all be right now that you are home and have your husband by your side.'

Ceanna brushed her lips against his forehead. 'Try to rest.'

The maidservant rushed back in. 'My lady! Your step-mother!'

Ceanna put her finger to her lips and motioned towards where her father lay. The woman nodded and followed Ceanna and Sandulf out of the chamber.

'What is the problem with my stepmother? Has she tried to escape?'

'The Lady Mhairi is dead!'

Ceanna staggered backwards. It was only Sandulf's reassuring bulk which kept her from falling. 'How?'

'Lady Mhairi kept the herbs for preparing your father's medicine in her chamber. When I went in to ask about the children's exact whereabouts, I found her with a goblet by her side and her box of herbs open and empty. Dead.' The maid's words ended with a little gasp.

Ceanna put an arm about the maid. Her stepmother had taken the easy way out. She would not have to answer for her crimes or face awkward questions about what she knew. Ceanna knew she should feel sad for the woman who had been married to her father, but all she could feel was a sense of relief. 'It is good you came to me.'

'His lordship?'

'His lordship will be informed when he wakes,' Sandulf said before she could think up a suitable response. She gave him a grateful look. 'He needs to rest. He has had enough shocks for today.'

The maid curtsied while another rushed in to say that the royal boys were eating apples in the kitchen orchard. Ceanna issued orders that they were to finish their food and then be brought before her, and that messengers needed to be dispatched to find Mother Mildreth and to inform her aunt of what had happened.

'Are you all right?' Sandulf asked in the sudden quiet. 'You had barely any sleep last night and now you are dealing with all of this.'

Ceanna looped a strand of hair about her ear. 'Me? I'm completely fine. I thrive on activity.'

Sandulf pulled her into the circle of his arms. With a shudder, she burrowed against his chest and allowed herself to draw strength for a long heartbeat. His arms fell away. 'It's not an admission of defeat to admit you need help, Ceanna.'

She stood there, trembling, then she pushed away.

'I have recovered,' she said with pinched white lips. 'We need to get those boys safely away from this kingdom. They need to go to Éireann where they were supposed to go in the first place. I have to put things right, Sandulf, before the King's Regent finds out what has happened.'

Sandulf's heart thudded. He had known he'd cared about her, but seeing her like this made his heart turn over. These people needed Ceanna. They depended on her. She was vital to them and their future and they knew it. They were not going to let her forget it any time soon.

And what was he? Who was he vital to? Not even his brothers trusted him to complete his task. And he wanted to be needed. He was tired of being alone. He knew he should never have refused her love, however it was offered. But saying anything now when there was still so much to do and to sort out would be a mistake.

'The first thing you are going to do is eat,' he said instead. 'I insist on it, as your husband.'

She patted his cheek. 'In good time. Then we will plan what happens next.'

He started to protest but stopped. She still needed him. It was something.

'Are you going to tell me why you are acting like this?' Danr asked the next morning when Sandulf was left alone with him in Dun Ollaigh's great hall while Ceanna went to see about the sons of Aed. Danr appeared refreshed after a good night's sleep and was finishing off what looked to be a large breakfast. However, Sandulf noticed that he had not attempted to flirt with any of the maidservants in the entire time he had been at Dun Olliagh.

'Like what?'

'Like a bear with a sore head. You are far worse than our father for being grumpy. And you are avoiding speaking with me. Your lack of curiously as to why I am here astonishes me.'

Sandulf gritted his teeth. He could hardly explain about his earlier mistake with Ceanna to his brother. How he felt like she was slipping away from him. How he was trying to ease the burden on her. How he didn't know what do to next. 'Why did you come? I explained to Rurik that I was more than capable of despatching Lugh on my own.'

'From where I was sitting, you required my assistance. Your flanks were exposed and you were in danger of being overrun.'

Sandulf slammed his fist on the table, making the tankards jump. 'You managed to get yourself taken prisoner.'

Danr shrugged. 'Whose fault was that? And there

is that black look again. Father could not have scowled better if he'd tried.'

Sandulf pinched the bridge of his nose. 'Why are you here, then?'

Danr withdrew a golden arrowhead with a line of silver running down its centre from a pouch. 'I managed to keep this safe despite everything. Annis discovered it in her father-in-law's things. Both Rurik and I agreed you needed to see it.'

Sandulf took the golden arrow and dangled it from his fingers. He struggled to keep from retching. Even after all this time he had wanted the other two pendants he'd discovered to be a mistake, trophies stolen during the raid, rather than…a payment. Or that his mother had indeed sent Rangr on to his uncle's ship to look after him. 'Alarr's birth pendant. The one my mother claimed to have lost before Brandt married Ingrid. Where did Annis find it?'

'In her father-in-law's belongings after he died.'

'Do the others know?'

Danr shrugged. 'Brandt is with Alarr. They may do. Why?'

Sandulf took his necklace off and held it out. 'I have the other two—Brandt's and mine.'

'Your mother sent you off with them? In case you needed it?' Danr gulped. 'Brandt was angry that day, but I know he wanted you to stay. Once his anger had gone, all would have been well.'

Sandulf rolled his eyes. Brandt's words still echoed down the years, but they had stopped hurting. Sandulf mentally searched for the hard knot of anger that had been part of him for so long, but discovered it, too, had dissolved.

Sandulf explained about how he'd discovered both pendants. And about the Valkyrie which Lugh had secreted away. 'I keep wondering whether my mother was involved? Or did she just want someone to look after me?'

'When did you last see Hilda wearing them?'

Sandulf closed his eyes, trying to think. 'Certainly last Jul, as Father made a big noise about her wearing them and they had a fight. I remember because Mother called him a drunken bully. All this leads me to believe that my mother has questions to answer.'

'Yes, she does. Her silence on the subject is telling.'

'I will have to visit her before I take Ingrid's golden Valkyrie and Lugh's sword to Brandt.'

'You are not doing that on your own, Brother. You are Hilda's baby boy. She will only lie to you and you will believe her because you want to. You are her son. Me?' Danr tapped his chest. 'I know her methods, how she twists words and feelings to suit her, how she plays with people's lives to advance her own agenda. I have the measure of the woman and I alone will get the truth from her.'

Sandulf stared at the three pendants. Everything Danr said was correct. He would believe his mother's words because he wanted to. Even now, he wanted to believe that she'd sent someone to watch over him because she loved him, rather than an assassin to finish him off. 'Then we go together.'

'I'd be honoured.'

'You're doing what? Visiting your mother?' Ceanna looked up from the muddled household accounts in confusion. She thought he'd understood that she needed his help, that she wanted him by her side, but now, at the first opportunity, he wanted to leave. He'd told the truth about not wanting her love and he'd kept his oath: he had stayed with her until she reached a place of safety. The page of figures swam before her eyes. She blinked rapidly. 'Why? We have other responsibilities—those children need to get to safety before anyone finds out they are here. They're both a danger to us and also in danger themselves from the Regent. They need to be with their aunt in Éireann. You agreed, Sandulf.'

'It won't take long, Ceanna. Danr says that my mother left Maerr for the Isle of Skíð with Joarr. I didn't even know my mother had feelings for him in that way. Apparently, they married almost before the ash in my father's pyre was cold.'

'And we need to take that Valkyrie to your brother,' Ceanna continued. 'He needs to have it. He needs to know you fulfilled your promise—the man who murdered your brother's wife is dead. Surely that is more important than meeting your mother and her new husband!'

Sandulf stared up at the carved ceiling and attempted to control his sense of frustration.

'Sandulf?'

'I will do it when the time suits me!'

She let out a little noise somewhere between a sigh and a tsk and put her hands over her mouth. Remorse washed through him. He started to gather her to him, but she flinched. He stopped and ran his hand through his hair.

'It's my brothers, not you, who put me in this foul temper.' The explanation sounded feeble. 'Shouting at you was never my intention.'

'But you did.'

'I did and I beg your forgiveness.'

She nodded stiffly. 'What has Danr told you? You owe me that much. Why is it so important? Why must it be done immediately?'

Sandulf explained about his mother's pendants and how they had all three been found in the possession of assassins. She listened in stony silence.

'Your mother needs to be consulted. She is the only one who can clear this up.'

'Exactly. It is why I need to go with Danr. Danr says that he can get the truth from her.'

Ceanna nodded. 'Allow Danr to do it on his own. He can extend an invitation to your mother to visit Dun Ollaigh. Why would she not want to visit her youngest son and meet his new wife?'

'But...' He ran his hand through his hair again; trying to explain was beyond him. He didn't want her to think him a coward for not facing the possibility of his mother's cruel betrayal. He wanted her to continue to see him as her hero and, when it came down to it, he wasn't sure he was ready to face Brandt. He still didn't feel... man enough to be welcomed into the fold.

'But what?' She crossed her arms. 'You have done what you set out to do. Lugh is dead.'

'Not by my hand. I promised to see him dead.'

Ceanna shook her head. 'Men! As if it matters who killed him. You are alive and Lugh and his brother have been stopped. Your hand ensured the death of three other men involved in the plot if you and your brothers are right about those pendants. Be grateful to Danr for saving your life. I am.'

Sandulf swallowed twice. It was more complicated than that. He had wanted to be able to look Brandt in the eye and say he'd been the one. Brandt would have had no choice but to forgive him. It would have shown that he was finally forgiven and that he was worthy of trying for her love. 'I am grateful to Danr.'

'Then tell him.' She looked at him squarely. 'He blames himself for not being at the ceremony or in the longhouse that day of the massacre. You're not the only one who feels guilty. Let him do this on his own.'

He stared at her in astonishment. He knew Rurik carried burdens about not being there, but he hadn't considered Danr might feel guilty as well. 'He confessed that to you?'

'It is why he had your sword.'

'But I was there and I failed to stop it. Brandt entrusted me with Ingrid's safety and I froze when I should have rushed towards the attackers. I tried to look after Ingrid and I failed.' He took a deep breath. 'I'm not a hero, Ceanna. I can never be one. Stop trying to make me into one.'

Her face closed tight. He knew he'd hurt her in a way he had not intended to, but he'd spoken the truth. He still wasn't worthy yet. But, by all of Odin's ravens, what would it take? The assassin was dead and he'd kept his own wife safe. But he still didn't feel worthy of her love, of Brandt's forgiveness.

'I didn't ask you to be a hero.' She jabbed a finger at his chest. 'I can manage perfectly fine without someone protecting me. A hero smoothing my way and keeping me in an impenetrable tower as my destiny? Stop insulting me. Stop trying to control me. It's the last thing I want.'

Her words lacerated his soul. Somehow, he'd managed to throw away something very precious, something so precious he hadn't realised he had it until it was gone. Maybe he wasn't worthy of her love, but he'd had it anyway. His chest ached as if his heart had been wrenched away. What had he done?

'Then we are settled on this.'

'Yes, we are. I will take the children to Éireann tomorrow. I will keep the promise we gave to my aunt. You may accompany me or not, as you choose. Go with Danr, if you want. Show him that you do not trust his judgement. Show him that you consider him unworthy for the task.'

She started to walk away.

He knew if he let her go, he'd lose any hope of winning her back. He had made a grave error back at the square, but he had to hope them travelling together again would restore something of their friendship. 'I will go with you. I want to go with you. I made an oath to your aunt as well. Danr is capable of handling things on his own for a little while before I join him, or he reports back here.'

She turned back towards him. Her eyes blazed with fury. 'After we deliver the children, you and I will go and see your brother. No excuses, Sandulf. No waiting for Danr to report back with what he learns from your mother. Your eldest brother needs Ingrid's Valkyrie. He needs to know the man who killed his wife is dead. Doesn't he deserve peace?'

Sandulf rubbed the back of his neck. Seeking out his mother to find out the truth wouldn't have been an excuse to avoid Brandt and their unfinished business exactly, but Ceanna was right—she and those young boys

needed him as their protector on the journey to Éireann.
'What if he turns his back on me?'
'Then you will have done your duty.'

Chapter Fifteen

Ceanna looked at the prosperous settlement in front of them, which they had reached several days after depositing the sons of King Aed with their aunt. Sandulf had insisted that task had to be accomplished first.

He had barely touched her since they started this journey—since they had had the fight about Sandulf's plan to travel with Danr to question his mother. She meant what she said that day about not wanting a hero.

The ease that they had enjoyed on the journey to Dun Ollaigh had vanished. Rather than treating her like a friend, or a wife, Sandulf had started to treat her as though she was made of precious glass.

He could barely stand to look at her and she knew what that meant. She knew what was coming. He was going to find a way to tell her that he was abandoning her. He didn't want to share the responsibility of looking after Dun Ollaigh. He didn't want to be her husband.

She knew she wanted more from her marriage than a name or a lukewarm partner. She also knew that she was in no danger of being pregnant.

'All we have to do is deliver Ingrid's Valkyrie,' she

said. 'It should be a quick crossing for me.' At Sandulf's look, she said quickly. 'I can't ask Mother Mildreth to stay longer than necessary.'

Her heart pounded. She longed for him to reach out to her and understand what she was asking. She knew he wasn't the hero of her childhood fantasies, but she loved him with her whole heart. But he had refused her love when she had offered it and she was not going to make that mistake again.

'I understand.'

'Then we had best get about it. The sooner it is done, the sooner our lives can begin.'

He bowed correctly over her hand. 'As my lady requests.'

Her heart broke little by little. She knew that by forcing him to go to see Brandt, he would be welcomed back into the fold with open arms and she was going to lose him for ever. But she loved him too much to keep him.

Sandulf's stomach was knotted tight as he entered his brother Alarr's new hall. They had arrived during the main meal, but had been ushered in.

To Sandulf's surprise, his reason for being there was not questioned. He wasn't even sure that the guardsman took down his name properly. He and Ceanna were simply ushered into the main hall with men standing at either side.

Sandulf glanced at Ceanna, who gave him a nod and squeezed his hand before stepping away.

I believe in you, she mouthed.

He nodded back. He was grateful that she was there to witness this and had not left to return to Dun Ollaigh.

He walked over to where Brandt and Alarr sat. Both

had aged considerably since he had last seen them. Brandt's expression had settled into harsh and forbidding lines. He seemed like a far harder version of their father. However, both faces instantly cleared when they saw him.

'Sandulf?'

He knelt in front of Brandt and laid Lugh's sword at his feet. 'The sword of the man who killed your wife, Brother,' he said in the language of his childhood.

A flicker of something crossed Brandt's face. 'I told you there was no need.'

A sense of anger welled up in Sandulf. Despite Rurik and Danr's assurances, still his eldest brother dismissed him as if he was nothing. 'There was every need.'

Brandt raised a brow. 'We shall have to disagree on this.'

'Listen to Sandulf. He has been through much to achieve this for you. He has come to make amends, not ignite old rivalries.' Ceanna held up her hands to silence his brothers. Her entire frame quivered as she spoke in badly accented Norse. A lump rose in Sandulf's throat; she was truly his Skadi, even if a coldness had sprung up between them on the journey. And he knew who bore the blame.

Alarr raised his eyebrows. 'And you are?'

'Sandulf's wife, Lady Ceanna, the mistress of Dun Ollaigh. Hear him out or this will truly be the last time you encounter your brother.'

His brothers glanced at each other, both their mouths dropped open and their eyes widened. Sandulf normally did not think of them as looking alike, but their shocked expressions were identical.

Alarr's wife, Lady Breanne, rose and shooed everyone else out.

'Sandulf, you are always so quick to take the bait,' Alarr said when the family was alone. 'I see you are well matched with this woman. She may be small, but she is ferocious and determined to protect you. And she can speak our language, after a fashion.'

'Someone has to be,' Ceanna said in Gaelic, lifting her chin. 'I've heard what his brothers are like.'

'Ah, Sandulf, I've missed you for the entertainment,' Alarr said. 'Come, Brother, let us not quarrel. My wife sets a good table.'

Sandulf grabbed Ceanna's hand. She squeezed, but let go. This time she stayed by his side rather than retreating. It gave him hope that their troubles could be solved. 'I agree, Brother, it appears we both have been fortunate in our choice of wives.'

'We can see that.' Brandt's features hardened, reminding Sandulf of his father just before his temper exploded. 'Continue, Sandulf. Don't keep us all in suspense.'

'In addition to the sword, I have retrieved this for you, Brandt.' Sandulf held out the carved wooden box they had discovered in the abbey. 'It belonged to Ingrid.'

A muscle twitched in Brandt's cheek. 'My wife never owned a box like this.'

'Open it, please, before you reject it out of hand,' Ceanna said. 'Much blood has been spilt to get you this.'

Brandt lifted the lid. The colour drained from his face.

'Ingrid's morning gift?' The lines on his face became harsher. 'She despised it, you know, and kept it hidden away in a secure place. I haven't thought about it in years. Thank you for returning it, but it wasn't worth one drop of the blood that was shed for it.'

'Father insisted she wore it to the wedding feast as you were away. Danr said that she had been looking for it just after you left, but she obviously found it as it is there. The assassin Lugh always took one thing from his victims.'

'And this is what he stole from my Ingrid.' Brandt started to pick up the figurine, but his fingers stilled on the cloth. 'Did you know this was in here?'

'What?'

He held up a Thor's hammer pendant on a broken chain. The gold gleamed in the light and bounced off the walls of the hall.

'Neither of us noticed it at the Abbey at Nrurin when the box was last opened. It must have been wrapped in cloth or wedged at the side of the box and come loose during our travels,' Ceanna said. 'Is it important? Is that worth the bloodshed?'

Brandt clutched the pendant so tightly his knuckles went white. 'It belonged to my late wife. She claimed she always wore it over her heart, but when I couldn't find it after she died I thought...'

'Her final words make sense, then.' Sandulf went over to where Brandt sat and placed a hand on Brandt's arm. His brother did not shy away.

Sandulf concentrated on making sure Ingrid's last words were correct. 'She could only say one or two words between gasps. Love. Whole. Over heart. Always. She died with your name on her lips, though, so I believe she meant them for you.'

Brandt looked up at Sandulf. His eyes swam with unshed tears. 'She had time to speak? I didn't know. I never considered.'

Sandulf stepped away from him. The wrong he'd done

his brother that day in keeping Ingrid's words from him was far worse than he'd ever considered. 'One of my deepest regrets about that day is that I could not tell you those words before I departed. I allowed you to think she had died without saying anything and she tried so hard to speak, Brandt. The knowledge has haunted my sleep. Forgive me. Neither of you deserved that.'

He waited as Brandt continued to sit there, his fingers gripped tight about Ingrid's pendant and prepared himself for the explosion.

'I went down to the harbour, but your ship had gone.' Brandt's low voice was unrecognisable from the heavy emotion. 'I wanted to make amends for losing my temper. I wanted to tell you that I was angrier at my failure to be there with her, ensuring her safety, than I was angry at you. I wanted you to stay, but you had left without a backward glance according to Kolga. Will you forgive me, Brother? Because I forgave you a long time ago.'

'I forgive you.' Sandulf tried for a smile. 'Our aunt always had a way with words.'

A naked vulnerability showed on Brandt's face. Sandulf knew he'd never seen his brother like this before. 'Would you have stayed, if I had arrived in time to speak those words? I lost my wife that day. I had no wish to lose my youngest brother, too.'

Sandulf pressed his thumbs against his temples. Would he have stayed? How to answer that? How could he begin to explain what was going through his heart? He glanced at Ceanna's determined face and knew what he had to say.

'It was always my choice to go, Brandt, not your command. Perhaps the boy I was then would have stayed.' He lifted his chin and stared directly at his brothers. 'Yes,

I like to think he would have. I always wanted your admiration back then.'

'And now?'

'The man I am is pleased that you did not reach the ship in time. I like who I have become because of the trials I have endured. I learned about survival and persistence. I learned about resilience. I learned about true friendship. But most of all I learned that you never leave your brothers behind, no matter how far you travel, for they are always with in you in your heart. I was not alone. The lessons that all my brothers, but particularly my eldest brother, bestowed on me guided me and ensured I completed this quest.'

'Then you will stay to assist in what is to come? I have no wish to lose my brother again. We have much to discuss, not the least of which is where Danr has hidden himself.'

Ceanna gave a slight gasp and covered her mouth with her hand. All the way here, she'd been dreading this—the confirmation of what she knew in her heart. Sandulf needed to be with his brothers and plot out what to do when Danr returned with the information he'd gleaned from Hilda. But she couldn't stay. Being in this hall reminded her of her duties back in Dun Ollaigh. Someone had to be there, ensuring practical things were done. Her father still wasn't back to full health and he needed her help.

Her insides felt very hollow. She was delighted that Sandulf had been able to return to his family. He had always been clear on what he longed for. He had never asked for her love or her heart even though he had both.

'Sandulf,' she said to the rushes. 'I should…well…

I am no longer needed here. You are back with your family.'

Sandulf caught her hand and dragged her against his body. She pushed him away slightly and he let go as his brothers looked on in interest. 'We need to speak.'

'Yes, later. You have much to discuss with your brothers. What we have to say to each other can wait.' She silently winced. It sounded mealy-mouthed when she wanted to scream at him, but she couldn't make him choose. He would carry her heart with him wherever he went and she'd hope for his safe return.

Sandulf lowered his brow. 'Now, my dearest wife. My darling Skadi. My Ceanna. And we speak alone.'

Her heart soared and she knew that she could not deny him anything when he looked at her like that and had such warmth in his voice.

'Take all the time you need, Brother. We will be here.' Masculine laughter trailed out after them.

Alarr gave a nod to Lady Breanne, who ushered them into a small chamber. 'You should be able to speak without interruptions here.'

'Whatever is the matter?' Ceanna asked when they were alone. Sandulf was watching her with an intense gaze which unnerved her.

He reached out and twined a lock of her hair about his little finger. 'Do you know how beautiful you are?'

'Has all this gone to your head?' She shook her own head, but inside she glowed. Sandulf thought her beautiful, which was saying something when she saw Alarr's wife.

'No, I am seeing straight for the first time. When I said Ingrid's words to Brandt, I finally understood what she meant. I saw her face again as she said it and how she struggled to let him know her love in the last moments of her life.'

'Even after all this time, I am sure they mattered to him.' Her voice caught in her throat. Hearing his words made her want to weep. It was going to be harder than ever to leave him, but she knew in her heart she had to return to her responsibilities at Dun Ollaigh. 'Her shade will be at peace and your sleep should be easier.' She tried for a laugh, which came out as a hiccup. 'Or maybe you enjoy being haunted?'

He cupped her face between his palms. 'Must you always make a joke and try to deflect me from something serious? Why can't you think more of yourself?'

'It is easier than believing in things I shouldn't.'

'What, like lasting passionate love between a man and a woman?'

Ceanna gave a slight nod as her throat closed. 'A sweet fantasy, I have always thought.'

He laced his fingers through hers. 'Then I will have to believe in it twice. For the both of us.'

He lowered his mouth.

'There is no need. I am willing to believe if you are,' she whispered against his lips.

He lifted her chin, so she was forced to look into his deep gaze. 'I love you, Ceanna, with all my soul and every fibre of my being. I have liked you since I first saw you in the tavern when you stood up to the owner and I have loved you since you fell asleep in my arms. My heart knew that I always wanted to wake up watching you, but I had to be worthy of your love. But then when I said Ingrid's words to Brandt and thought about her struggle to say them, I knew that waiting until my final breath before I said something was wrong. I may never be worthy of your love, but you need to know you have mine.'

'I love you as well. I meant it when I said it that day in the square when you took Danr's place,' she gasped out before he could say more. 'It happened when I wasn't looking for it. I know you will carry my heart with you wherever you go.'

He drew his brows together. 'Where am I going?'

'Your brothers may need your help and I can't stay. My father needs me, but more importantly the people of Dun Ollaigh need me.'

'Your commitment to your responsibility is one of the many things I love about you.'

'I thought you found it infuriating. I forced you to do so many things, to make so many oaths.'

'I can think both things at the same time.' He gathered her into his arms. 'Skadi, you are very wrong about where I am needed. My brothers might want me to stay, but they don't require my help. Brandt was right long ago—they can solve this without my interference.'

'Interference?'

Sandulf gave a half-smile. 'I was a very annoying nuisance when I was a boy and desperately wanted to be included in everything they did.'

'What are you saying?'

'I need you at my side and in my bed. I know that means Dun Ollaigh, rather than being with my brothers, but it is where I want to be, if you'll have me.'

'I thought…'

'I said things I regret because I was afraid to come here. If I hadn't, I would always have wondered if I could keep my oaths, if I could be trusted. If I could truly be the husband you require and deserve. I want to believe I can be, with your love to give me hope.'

'You are already the man I want to spend the rest of my life with. I tried to stop loving you after you rejected me, but I failed miserably.'

'I'm pleased you failed. That day I pushed you away, it was because I was afraid. I want your love. I have always wanted it. It keeps me breathing.' Sandulf traced a gentle line down her cheek. 'Ceanna, understand this: I may carry my brothers in my heart, but all of it belongs to you, my whole heart. And I'm no longer afraid to tell you how I feel.'

Ceanna stared at him in astonishment. He wanted to be with her. He loved her. Truly loved her. 'I thought all heroes were figments of my fevered imaginations, but I was wrong. You are my hero. I have been dreading us parting. You carry my heart with you. I tried to become indispensable to you when we were at Nrurim so you would keep me with you, but I realised I had to be me, as I am, with all my faults and flaws.'

'Indispensable, vital, crucial and essential is what you are simply by being you.' He laughed. 'You were magnificent with my brothers. I've never known them to quieten so easily.'

'Let's listen to what they have to say. Our help from Dun Ollaigh is there if they require it. Always.'

'And afterwards, we cross the sea to our home, our people and our lives.' He put his hand on her belly. 'And one day, our children.'

'Agreed.' She gave her mouth up to his.

'Sit and explain yourself,' Alarr said, gesturing to a pair of stools and Lady Breanne poured two cups of ale.

Sandulf rapidly explained about the voyage out to Constantinople, the attempt on his life on board ship and how he'd survived. Then he explained about hunting the assassins after he'd overheard a conversation in Constantinople and how he'd recognised who they were. And how he'd finally tracked Lugh down to Nrurim.

Ceanna took up the tale and explained how Danr had been rescued, how he'd saved her life and how he'd volunteered to find out the truth about the pendants they'd recovered from the assassins. Sandulf was grateful neither of his brothers objected to his passing that duty on to their half-brother.

'A good choice,' Brandt commented. 'Our mother knows how to bend us to her will. Danr is the most likely to be able to discern the truth from it. Is it too much to hope for that you saw our father's murderer's face that day?'

Sandulf shook his head. 'Only the back of a shadowy figure.'

'Then the search goes on. Honour will be restored, if not our land.'

The brothers lifted their ale and Sandulf swore an oath to the sons of Sigurd and to restoring family honour with his brothers. Somehow, this time, it felt different, because he was swearing it with his brothers.

'Will you stay with us while we wait for Danr's safe return?' Lady Breanne asked in her lilting voice after the oath swearing. 'It has been a long time since the brothers were together in friendship and harmony.'

The last little ache in Sandulf's heart eased. His brothers were proud of him. He did matter to them, but he had another life, one where he was more than vital. He held out his hand to Ceanna, who came over. She squeezed it and he knew it was her way of saying that she'd support him in whichever decision he made.

'I will always be there for you, my brothers, when you need me, but I must return to Dun Ollaigh with my bride. I made a pledge to help its people and I will. I want to dedicate my life to them and my bride.'

* * * * *

*Read on for a teaser of
the next instalment of the
Sons of Sigurd series*

Redeeming Her Viking Warrior
by Jenni Fletcher

AD 877—Isle of Skíð, modern-day Scotland

The woman appeared out of nowhere. One moment Danr Sigurdsson was alone, his body cradled amid the tangled roots of an oak tree, the next she was looming above him, the spear in her hand pointing straight at his throat.

He stared up at her, absently wondering who she was and where she'd come from, then gave up the effort and closed his eyes. His head and chest were throbbing. So, too, was his pulse, so hard and fast it felt as though his heart were trying to force its way through his ribcage. Considering how much blood he'd lost over the past few hours, he was surprised it could still summon the strength to beat at all, but at least the pain in his arm was fading to numbness now.

If he kept still, he could almost forget the angry red gouge where the blade had caught him, slicing through skin and muscle and tendon. If he didn't move at all, scarcely allowing himself to breathe, in fact, he could forget almost everything.

The rustle of leaves overhead had already faded to a dull murmur and the light behind his eyelids was dimming, narrowing around the edges like a tunnel collapsing in on itself, enveloping him in darkness.

Something prodded his neck and he prised his eyelids open again. It was the woman, the blunt edge of her spear nudging his skin. What did she want? Was she threatening him? If she was, then she didn't need to. At that moment he couldn't have put up a fight with a kitten.

The very air felt heavy, pinning him to the ground as if there were a fallen tree lying across his chest. He was going to die whether she impaled him or not and he wasn't going to protest either way. Perhaps it was best that she went ahead and put him out of his misery quickly. He would have failed his brothers—*again*—but at least it would have been while trying to fulfil his oath.

He curled the fingers of his good arm around the hilt of his sword, Bitterblade, determined to die with it in his hand like a warrior, even if he couldn't lift it, but the woman didn't move as much as a muscle. As far as he could tell, she didn't even blink.

He felt a flicker of unease, wondering if she were some figment of his imagination or perhaps an apparition. She looked like one, her narrow, expressionless face streaked with grey smudges while her hair tumbled in such wild, half-braided, half-loose disarray that it resembled a cloak of golden hay around her shoulders.

She was a lot like a spear herself, he thought, sleek and slender with a flat chest and shoulders the same width as her hips, though he hated himself for noticing. Apparently it was true what Rurik had always said, that Danr would still be looking at women on his deathbed...

Well, he was on it now, so perhaps it was only fitting.

A woman had brought him into the world, albeit reluctantly, and now a woman was going to take him out of it. It would be a fitting revenge for all the ones he'd known and discarded in between.

He waited, feeling increasingly uneasy beneath her silent scrutiny. Even from where he lay on the ground he could see that her eyes were pale and striking, like oyster pearls, mirroring the sky behind her head, an iridescent grey speckled with flakes of silver that looked a lot like... *Snow?*

Somehow he dragged a laugh up out of his chest. This was truly the end, then. He hadn't even realised that it was cold enough for snow yet, though now he thought about it he could see whispery coils of air emerging from his mouth. From *hers*, too, which at least proved she was a real flesh-and-blood woman, no matter how spectral she seemed.

Snow was filling the air all around them, covering his broken and bloodied body in a gauzy white layer. After everything that he and his brothers had gone through, after they'd travelled so far and fought so many enemies from Maerr to Éireann to Constantinople to Alba, now he was going to die here in a forest all on his own and be buried in snow. His body would probably lie where it was all winter, encased in ice, refusing to rot away until spring. Maybe Hilda would be the one to find him eventually and know that she'd won.

He gave a grunt of disgust and then froze, the hairs on the back of his neck rising at the sound of an answering growl. With an effort he lifted his head, his already pounding heartbeat redoubling in speed at the sight of a wolf—no, *wolves*—stalking through the undergrowth

towards him, their teeth bared in twin snarls, no doubt
drawn by the scent of his blood.

Quickly he shifted his gaze back to the woman, trying to convey a warning with his eyes since his throat
was too dry to speak, but she appeared not to notice, her
expression unreadable as the wolves came to stand on
either side of her like a pair of dark sentinels.

Maybe she really was an apparition after all, Danr
thought with a shudder, an unforgiving ice maiden like
the ones his mother had told him and Rurik stories about
as boys, a supernatural force able to control the animals
of the forest as well as the elements. If she was, then he
was entirely at her mercy. She could do whatever she
wanted and there was nothing he could do to stop her.

He swallowed, waiting for her to decide his fate. At
least a spear would be quick, whereas being torn apart
by wolves… Surely not even *he* deserved that?

Did he?

He dropped his head back to the ground and closed
his eyes for a few seconds, feeling the kiss of cold flakes
on his lids and lashes, but when he opened them again
she was gone and the wolves were nowhere to be seen.
All he could see was snow.

*If you enjoyed this story, be sure to read the first
two books in the Sons of Sigurd miniseries*

Stolen by the Viking
by Michelle Willingham
Falling for Her Viking Captive
by Harper St. George

*Don't miss the next stories in the
Sons of Sigurd miniseries, coming soon!*

Redeeming Her Viking Warrior
by Jenni Fletcher
Tempted by Her Viking Enemy
by Terri Brisbin